MY MOTHER:
DEMONOLOGY

WORKS BY KATHY ACKER
PUBLISHED BY GROVE PRESS

Blood and Guts in High School
Don Quixote
Empire of the Senseless
Great Expectations
In Memoriam to Identity
Literal Madness
My Mother: Demonology
Portrait of an Eye
Pussy, King of the Pirates

MY MOTHER: DEMONOLOGY

KATHY ACKER

GROVE PRESS   NEW YORK

Originally published in hardcover in 1993 by Pantheon books, a division of Random House, Inc.

Published simultaneously in Canada
Printed in the United States of America

Grateful acknowledgment is made to the following for permission to reprint previously published material:

Harcourt Brace & Company: Excerpt from "The Fire Sermon" in "The Waste Land" from *Collected Poems 1909–1962* by T. S. Eliot. Copyright © 1936 by Harcourt Brace & Company. Copyright © 1964, 1963 by T. S. Eliot. Reprinted by permission of the publisher.

R. Piper & Co. Verlag: Excerpts in German from *Leider auf der Flucht* by Ingeborg Bachmann. Copyright © 1978 by R. Piper & Co. Verlag, Munich. Reprinted by permission.

Library of Congress Cataloging-in-Publication Data

Acker, Kathy, 1948–1999
    My mother: demonology / Kathy Acker
    ISBN 0-8021-3403-3
    I. Title.
PS3551.C44M9   1994   813'.54—dc20   94-21534

Design by Judy Christensen

Grove Press
841 Broadway
New York, NY 10003

00 01 02 03   10 9 8 7 6 5 4 3 2

This book is dedicated to Uma.

After Hatuey, a fifteenth-century Indian insurrectionist, had been fixed to the stake, his Spanish captors extended him the choice of converting to Christianity and ascending to Heaven or going unrepentantly to Hell. Gathering that his executioners expected to go to Heaven, Hatuey chose the other.

CONTENTS

MY MOTHER:
DEMONOLOGY

My mother began to love at the same moment in her life that she began to search for who she was. This was the moment she met my father. Since my mother felt that she had to be alone in order to find out who she was and might be, she kept abandoning and returning to love.

My mother spoke:

1

INTO THAT BELLY OF HELL WHOSE NAME IS THE UNITED STATES

ONE

MY MOTHER

I'm in love with red. I dream in red.

My nightmares are based on red. Red's the color of passion, of joy. Red's the color of all the journeys which are interior, the color of the hidden flesh, of the depths and recesses of the unconscious. Above all, red is the color of rage and violence.

I was six years old. Every night immediately after supper, which I usually was allowed to take with my parents, I would say, "Good night." To reach my room, I'd have to walk down a long dark corridor that was lined with doors on either side. I was terrified. Each door half-opened to unexpected violence.

Morality and moral judgments protect us only from fear.

In my dreams, it was I who simultaneously murdered and was murdered.

Moral ambiguity's the color of horror.

I was born on October 6, 1945, in Brooklyn, New York. My parents were rich, but not of the purest upper class. I'm talking about my father. At age six, I suddenly took off for unknown regions, the regions of dreams and secret desires. Most of my life, but not all, I've been dissolute. According to nineteenth-century cliché, dissoluteness and debauchery are connected to art.

I wrote: *The child's eyes pierce the night. I'm a sleepwalker trying to clear away the shadows, but when sound asleep, kneel in front of their crucifix and Virgin.*

Holy images covered every wall of my parents' house.

Their house had the immobility of a nightmare.

The first color I knew was that of horror.

Almost everything that I know and can know about my pre-adult life lies not in memories but in these writings.

Religion:

Days and nights all there was was a sordid and fearful childhood. Morality wore the habit of religion. Mortal sin or the Saint of Sunday and the Ashes of Wednesday kept on judging me. Thus condemnation and repression crushed me even before I was born. Childhood was stolen from children.

Never enough can be said, muttered and snarled, when one has been born into anger. THEIR criminal hands took hold of my fate. HER umbilical cord strangled me dropping out of her. All I desired was everything.

Listen to the children. All children come red out of the womb because their mothers know God.

The night's replete with their cries: unceasing flagellated howls that are broken by the sound of a window slammed shut. Harsh and drooling screams die inside lips that are muzzled. We who're about to be suffocated throw our murmurs and screeches, our names, into a hole; that hole is

8

Searching, I traveled to Berlin. There I lived with a doctor named Wartburg whose apartment I wouldn't leave. I never saw anyone but him. I had wanted to give myself to another and now I was beginning to. Wartburg put me in a dog collar; while I was on all fours, he held me by a leash and beat me with a dog whip. He was elegant and refined and looked like Jean Genet.

At that time, *nobody was able to look for me, find me, join me.*

What dominated me totally was my need to give myself entirely and absolutely directly to my lover. I knew that I belonged to the community of artists or freaks not because the anger in me was unbearable but because my overpowering wish to give myself away wasn't socially acceptable. As yet I hadn't asked if there was someone named *me.*

At this time I first read de Sade. Perusing *The One Hundred Twenty Days of Sodom* exulted and horrified me; horror because I recognized my self, or desire.

Living with Wartburg ended; I had no money nor friends in Berlin. All I wanted was to be entirely alone. I had strong political convictions, so I took off for Russia. There I couldn't speak any language.

Loneliness, and my kind of life, in Russia physically deteriorated me to such a point that I almost died.

From that time onward I have always felt anxiety based on this situation: I need to give myself away to a lover and simultaneously I need to be always alone. Such loneliness can be a form of death. My brother found me in Russia and brought me back to New York.

I first attempted to dissipate my anxiety by deciding to fuck and be fucked only when there could be no personal involvement. I traveled on trains, like a sailor, and made love with men I encountered on those trains.

My attempt failed. Friends said about me, "She's on her way to dying young." But I wanted, more than most people, to live, because just being alive wasn't enough for me. Wildness or

15

curiosity about my own body was showing itself as beauty. My brother placed as much importance on sexuality as I did. When I met Bourénine at one of the orgies my brother gave, I was ready to try again to give myself to another, to someone who was more intelligent than me and a committed radical.

Anxiety turned into a physical disease. Bourénine said that he wanted to save me from myself, my wildness, my weakness. He made me feel safe enough to try to give myself to him.

I became so physically weak that I stood near death. When Bourénine believed that I might die, he began to love me. I began to hate him, yet I worshiped him because I thought he protected me. My gratitude has always been as strong as my curiosity, as is mostly true in those who are wild.

Even then I knew that most men saw me as a woman who fucked every man in sight. Since Bourénine wanted to be my father, he didn't want me to make my own decisions. I saw myself as split between two desperations: to be loved by a man and to be alone so I could begin to be. When I met B, he was married. I didn't mind because I didn't really want to deal with an other. Since B immediately saw me as I saw myself, I saw in B a friend and one who wouldn't try, since he was married, to stop me from becoming a person, rather than wild.

From the first moment that B and I spoke together in the Brasserie Lipp, there was a mutual confidence between us.

I had pushed my life to an edge, having to give myself away absolutely to a lover and simultaneously needing to find "myself." Now I had to push my life more.

Bourénine's inability to deal with what was happening to me turned him violent and aggressive. During this period, B and I met several times and discussed only political issues. As soon as I began speaking personally to him, we commenced spending as much time alone with each other as we could.

Wildness changed into friendship.

16

I had already written: *No religion: this is the one event that will never change. No religion is my only stability and security.*

Mother insisted that I see her priest, to such a degree that I had to.

Let me describe this Director of Human Morality. (One of the Directors of Human Morality.) While his hands were sneaking everywhere, all he could see in my words was his own fear.

Right after I saw him, I wrote down in my secret notebook: "Religion is a screen behind which the religious shields himself from suffering, death, and life. The religious decide everything prior to the fact; religion's a moral system because by means of religion the religious assure themselves that they're right.

"From now on I'm going to decide for myself and live according to my decisions—decisions out of desire. I'll always look . . . like a sailor who carries his huge cock in his hand. . . . I'll travel and travel by reading. I won't read in order to become more intelligent, but so that I can see as clearly as possible that there's too much lying and hypocrisy in this world. I knew from the first moment I was that I hated them, the hypocrites."

As soon as I had written this down, I knew that I was dreadfully and magnificently alone.

I am now seventeen years old.

All around me are termites, familial households without their imaginations. They would never rise an iota above their daily tasks, daily obligations, daily distractions. Everyone who's around me has lost the sense that life's always pushing itself over an edge while everything is being risked.

So now there's going to be a war! Hey! Finally something exciting's going to happen! The United States's coming back to life! The government of the United States is realizing that someone's angry about something or other and's descending to offer its people a target for their bilious bitterness. O emotionless sentimental and sedentary people, because your government's a democracy and responsible to you, it is giving you a whole race to detest, a nation on which to spit, a religion to damn, everything

17

you've ever wanted. You're incontestably superior to men who wear dresses. Again you will become important in the eyes of the world.

You Americans need to be right. This war will not only be a pathway to future glory: once war's begun, you'll feel secure because you'll no longer have to understand anything else. You will again know what good and evil are.

Tomorrow you're going to give your sons joyfully to the desert, maybe daughters if you're feminist enough, because you're emotionless and, in war, you can be so emotionless, you don't have to exist. Therefore war allows people to surpass themselves. The English know this full well. As soon as you have tanks and dead people all around you, you'll be able to feel alive, once more powerful, magnanimous, and generous to all the world.

All that your grandparents and parents, educators and society showed you, the triumphal road, the right way, the path of true virtue—the RIGHT, the GOOD—is only Liberty mutilated and Freedom shredded into scraps of flesh. The raped body. A man's a child who walks down the right road—a street thoroughly carved out and signposted—because all he can see is the word danger.

TWO

Letters from My Mother to My Father

(The days of begging, the days of theft. No nation that began for the sake of escape and by fire can be all bad. Even if democracy is a myth. Myths make actuality, that's what myths do. Me, I've always been on fire for the sake of fire.

(Listen. They thought they could have their freedom through something called democracy, but they forgot about knowledge, and no one's ever had freedom, anyways. So now it's all falling apart, this economy, a so-called culture and a society, so-called, and anyway, there's never been anything except loneliness, the days of begging, the days of theft.

(This is what the books tell about American history: you can travel and wherever you'll go, there'll be no one but you. Listen, American history says: the sky's blue and every shade of purple and then so bright that your eyes have to be red in order to see it.

(A sun declines in front of you. The sunless air'll make your fingers grow red, and there spots will swell. Every possible color in the world'll sit in this sky until evening black spreads over the air or your pupils, and you will never be able to know which.

(JOIN THE U.S. ARMY

(GET KILLED

(Solitary, mad, deprived of community, depraved and proud of all your depravity, you dream, no longer of a lover, but solely of sex the way a rat desires garbage.

(Stronger than dreams will be your inability to forget what you don't know.

(Specifics: northern California. Myths say settled by white bums and white prostitutes desperate for gold. Who, as soon as they had found the yellow, tried to eradicate all nonwhites. And kept on trying. Born out of attempted murder, loneliness, and wildness. The yellows who survived formed their own gangs. The cities born out of riffraff who, unlike those back East, knew no culture.

(Said that they could never be poor.

(What we're dealing with here is a race of degenerates. A mongrel people that doesn't know how to do anything but hate itself. No wonder they love God so much, because God doesn't exist. We're dealing with a people manifestly incapable of Manifest Destiny.

(Thieves or imbeciles. Take your choice, or chance. Sooner or later some people'll govern these lands, but not until all their inhabitants have died.

(In other words: ungovernable.)

LETTER

Dear B,

Our friendship has no stability. Our meetings are taking place only by chance. Well, maybe that's how things—reality is.

All my emotions, fantasies, imaginings, desires are reality because I must have a life that matters, that is emotional.

I don't want to speak anymore about anything that's serious. I just want to speak.

I'm writing you and I'm going to keep on writing you so that all the fantasies that we have about each other, through which we keep perceiving each other, will die. After that we'll be so naked with each other that I will be your flesh. You mine.

I don't need to tell you any of this because you already know. But you're still running away from me and I hate it when you do this.

This is what I want to say: When I saw you in the early evening, sometime around seven-thirty, your friend, whoever was with you, looked right through me. Just as if I was still a child wearing the ring that I always wanted, that renders its bearer invisible. I'm not your child.

If I could be invisible and go everywhere, I would. To outlandish lands and where there are great people.

While your friend was staring through me, you stood up and walked past me without noticing me. I remember the first time we met alone: we talked together for hours, almost until the sun rose, then, despite my shyly asking you to stay, you left my brother's apartment.

None of all I've just said matters. That's the point.

All that matters to me now, has mattered to me, to the point that it's painful, is that we tell each other everything. Since I fear rejection more than anything else, I must have trust. Then I won't be able to leave your life and you won't be able to leave mine. Despite the fact that—I'm not going to waste my time trying to explain this to you or convince you that this is true— your world is cozy. Me—I'm nothing. I promise you that I won't blame you for your smugness. You need that kind of crap: images of richness, maybe because you weren't born that way, so you can live confidently in this world. I need to be invisible and without language, animal.

If you want to contact me, you'll have to find me.

If you really know me, you can do this.

I started writing you because I believed that if we told each other everything, there could be only trust between us. Then we wouldn't be able to hurt each other so much that we destroyed each other's lives.

I just told you that I despise your bourgeoisie and your wealthy friends.

Maybe it isn't possible for two people to be together without barriers in a state of unredeemable violence.

(I think that Mother was still with Bourénine, but I don't know for sure.)

LETTER

Dear B,

The more I try to tell you everything, the more I have to find myself. The more I try to describe myself, the more I find a hole. So the more I keep saying, the less I say, and the more there is to say. I'm confusing everything between us.

I'm not being clear here.

I don't want to tell you anything.

The only thing that's possible between us is a car accident. A car accident's now the only thing that can deliver me from the anguish that's you.

I'm dumb, wild, and I don't want anyone coming too near me. But the more emotion comes out, the more I want you.

I've been writing down every type of fatal accident I can imagine. Whenever I do this I feel calm, and as if I'm orgasming. I know I have to follow death until its end. That road passes through putrefaction and disintegration.

Whenever I'm traveling that road, I'm calm.

When I'm lying in your arms, I'm calm.

At the same time I have to battle you; there's something in me that has to oppose you in even the most trivial of matters.

I still tell you everything, as if I'm more than naked with you. I hate you. My mind's moving round and round, in tighter and tighter spirals. It's going to end up in a prison, a void, destroying itself. I always try to defeat myself.

Until the present I've thrown away my past. As soon as something's been over, I've gotten rid of it; I've acted as if that relationship never happened. I never had memories that I wanted.

Now I believe that, though I'm still doing everything possible to defeat myself, our friendship, to misunderstand you, and to view everything in the worst possible light, you're going to always be with me. I believe you're not going to leave me. I believe without understanding this that you see exactly what I am and that you're guiding me.

At the same time I've been observing that our friendship's changing me: I no longer know who I am and I'm beginning to see what I am. So when you're observing me and know me and are guiding me, you're perceiving I-don't-know-who-anymore. This combination of your eye and I-don't-know-who-anymore is a work of art made by both of us, and it's untitled.

Now I'm rational.

I know you hate me when I'm rational because, as you've told me, you don't like it when there are rules. You don't like rules.

Here are my most recent thoughts: When I met you, I was drowning because I wasn't going to let another person be close to me. (This frigidity is named "wildness.") I asked you, rather than anyone else, for help because I knew that you're an emotional paralytic. Perverse, as usual, I hollered, "Help!" so that you'd beat me over the head so I'd finally drown or fall off a crumbling cliff. What I really wanted to do. You're just what I want, B: a better death method.

I decided to tell you everything because by telling you everything I'd make you kill me faster. I always want to test everything to the point of death. Beyond.

(Children and dogs squatted in the dirt.

("This looks like the high road to Hell," one kid said.

("From Hell."

(It was a desolate land, a populace that had nothing except government criminals, and now it was going to war. Since no one knew where the country they were fighting was, no one thought anything was real.

(What the weapons might be in this war of the imagination-made-actual no one knew. Half-buried skeletons of cows, horses with mouths dried open, cats' and goats' legs.

(IN THEIR OWN LANDS THE ARABS TEAR OUT EACH OTHER'S EYEBALLS AND RAPE THEIR OWN CHILDREN. IF ONE AMERICAN SOLDIER GOES INTO BATTLE, BECAUSE RIGHT MAKES MIGHT, HE HAS TO WIN.
                              —some American government official

(When a man on his deathbed had told the child that he had killed many men, the child was envious.

(Through the rest of his childhood, the child bore the idol of a perfection that he could never attain. All he could be was a mercenary.

(Every son is heir to the death of his father: every son needs this death to experience a preliminary death, and every son must have his father die so that he can live.

(What about his father's life? When a child inherits the father's life, he inherits his place in the prison of morality and can never break out.

(In other words: we are the children without inheritance.

(He was fucked over as a child. When he grew up, he looked for a trade. Searched. Since he always wore black, people thought him a preacher. But he had never witnessed anything that had to do with God.

(The country went to war as it always did, in some other country.

(He watched men being killed in many ways and women left for dead and forgotten.

(Then he glimpsed ships. He observed vultures as large as any tree but too high up to be seen in detail. He was too lost to want to do anything but soar.

(One day he came upon a woman who told fortunes. He thought, As if there's a fortune to be told.

(Asked her about the fortune of the lost. "What's going to happen to me?"

(She gibbered at the night.

(Asked again, "In a society of murderers, how can children be educated to something else?"

(The beautiful woman answered that they should be raised with the wild dogs.

(He replied that life wasn't a laughing matter.

(The woman asked, "How's it possible to be lost? How can anything that exists be lost?

("The cards have been lost in the night. Pull out these cards."

(She turned his cards over: "Your problem is desire. You've tried unsuccessfully to resolve, dissolve desire through work. As a result of this repression, either you must go to war, or you are at war. The cards are unclear on this temporal point. You're now moving through the negative part of that dialectic; there'll be synthesis when your centralized power has died.")

25

LETTER

Dear B,

At this moment because I'm perverse I'm telling myself: Without you I'm lost. I'm letting myself realize what I don't usually let myself. And as soon as I see that I need you, I imagine your absence. Again and again I'm picturing you rejecting me. This is the moment I love.

(I never had a father. This isn't correct because, science says, every animal has a father. I never knew my father, which fact, for me, is the same as not having a father.

(I'm writing about my father, whom I never knew.)

LETTER

Dear B,

I doubt everything.

You're asking me two questions: Do I think that you don't love me because I doubt your love? Do I think you'll never trust me because I doubt?

No.

When I doubt to the point that emptiness sits under my skin and someone or something feels nausea, I begin to be. Everything that used to irritate and still rasps me is now wonderful and desirable.

Of course there are times when I can't bear this relationship with doubt. When I hate that which gives me the most pleasure.

I don't want everything to be complex; I don't want to live in closed rooms like some academic. I want everything between us and everything to be simple. That is, real. Like flesh. Not hypocritical.

But in the past, when I tried to kill off hypocrisy, I destroyed possibilities for love.

26

I will not descend into the night, for that romanticism is a disease.

(My dream: We're kissing, but I feel nothing. He takes my clothes off me, then picks me naked up off the floor. Carries me into somewhere. In there he cradles me as if I'm a child. I grab what I feel to be safety. At that moment he starts systematically hurting me. After hurting me for a long time, he holds me and the world opens up.)

(Mother moved into her brother's apartment.)

LETTER

I said that I wanted us to be so naked with each other that the violence of my passion was amputating me for you.

Listen. I am not a victim.

I don't know what the end of all this can be.

At the moment, neither of us is in danger.

(Mother didn't want to live with my father.)

CONTINUATION OF LETTER

I want to be clearer about what I just said:

You don't believe that you own me. What you think, precisely, is that you've put me in slavery and I'll always be your slave. You now control, limit, imprison, bar, categorize, and define my existence.

I'm hot.

As soon as you saw that I got pleasure from yielding to you, you turned away from me. Then I really laid myself at your feet.

You stated that you were denying me because you needed to be private.

27

But what's real to you isn't real to me. I'm not you.

Precisely: my truth is that for me your presence in my life is absence.

I'll say this another way: You believe that everything that's outside you ("reality") is a reflection of your perceptions, thoughts, ideas, etc. In other words, that you can see, feel, hear, understand the world. Other people. I don't believe that. I believe that I'm so apart from the world, from other people, that I have to explain everything to every single person to such an extent in order to communicate at all that, for me, communication's almost impossible. Day by day, my actuality has become more and more hollow and is now breaking apart like a body decomposing under my own eyes.

You've destroyed every possibility of religion for me and I want you to help me.

(The United States, begun on less than zero, on dislike, negation, and fire, had inflated itself into an empire. Now it has returned to less than zero. My mother realized this. The Christ of her mother had taught her that she had no right to exist; love had taught her otherwise. Fuck all of that, my mother thought. She wrote love letters to my father, knowing that they didn't matter.

(Mother said, "Nothing matters when there is nothing.")

LETTER

Dear B,

I've told you that I never want to live with you. (I can't live with you because you're married.) Now something more: I have to be alone.

This isn't rejection.

I'm going to go away from you so that I can find something

28

new, maybe a "me." Then we'll be able to be completely naked with each other and perceive each other as each of us actually is.

Whatever it takes so this can happen.

I know you think that my desire to be alone is just one more instance of how I run away from everything. That I've tried to run away to the extent that I no longer wanted to have a self. (If there is a self.)

This is what I think: In the face of death,

(There's no more education, no more culture—if culture depends on a commonly understood history—and perhaps no more middle class in the United States. There's War.)

when all is real,

(In the face of this very real American death, there is only the will to live.)

I will be able (to have a self) to say something: "I've seen him. I can say his real name. I know that nothing, including this, matters."

In other words: there's nothing.

Because there's nothing, I don't have to be trained, as females are, to want to stop existing.

But: your desire for me when I see you halts my breath. Want torches my mouth into contortions. No longer a mouth. You're mad.

If only in public I could throw myself on top of your feet and kiss them so everyone would know. But I can't have anything to do with you publicly.

I'm frightened that my ability to go all the way with you, to give myself to you in ownership and at the same time know that everything between us has to be a lie in the face of your marriage

29

will destroy me: my honesty, my integrity. For by railing and revolting against bourgeois hypocrisy, I became me.

It's because of you that I now sleep and want to eat. Since I'll not deny my own body, I now know that I can and will lie ignobly, superbly, triumphantly.

(Mother thought that there must be romance other than romance. According to Elisabeth Roudinesco in her study of Lacan, around 1924 a conjuncture of early Feminism, a new wave of Freudianism, and Surrealism gave rise to a new representation of the female: nocturnal, dangerous, fragile and powerful. The rebellious, criminal, insane, or gay woman is no longer perceived as a slave to her symptoms. Instead, "in the negative idealization of crime [she] discovers the means to struggle against a society [that disgusts].")

LETTER

Dear B,

You want me to live a lie and you admire me for my honesty. Repeatedly you've said that you respect my intelligence more than that of any woman you've ever met, and you treat me convulsively and continually like less than a dog. Female variety.

I still believe that you know everything about me, yet I don't think that you understand anything that has to do with me.

The only conclusion to all this is that reality has reversed itself. The reversement, which is a window, has set me on fire.

My conclusion isn't sweet. You call it "a penchant for the night." But I no longer have a penchant for the night.

At this moment I'm halfway between life and death. And death and life.

I'm now trying to write down something called *truth*. Which isn't *my truth* because I'm not an enclosed or self-sufficient being.

My conclusion: You're no longer behind everything that happens. You, sexual love. Since you're no longer at the bottom of everything, where I know I can always find you, no one can mean anything to me anymore.

I hate our wildness. The only life each of us has is when we're together. Just as I had to escape my family, now I have to get away from you, from the mad rhythm named *us,* from our nights, from horror.

A FARSI LESSON

آن پستان شیرین است.

(*An pestan shirin ast.* That breast is sweet.)

نَخَیر، این پستان تُرش است.

(*Naxeir, in pestan torsh ast.* No, this breast is sour.)

کُجا میرَوه م؟

(*Koja miravem?* Where are we going?)

آیا ناویهای مُرده ناویهای سفر توی مُرگ اند؟

(*Aya navihaye safar tuye marg and?* Are sailors journeying into death?)

دَحر، پستان مُردرست وَ شَب سُرد است.

(*Naxeir, pestan mordest va shab sard ast.* No, the breast is dead and the night is cold.)

اینجا آوازهای پستانان اَند.

(*Inja avazhaye pestanan and.* Hear the breasts' voices.)

32

THREE

CLIT CITY

dedicated to Dario Argento, of course

I GO BACK TO SCHOOL

All I thought about was B. Sometimes I felt that I couldn't live without him; other times I wanted him out of my life so much I wanted him to be dead.

I knew that I hurt, but I didn't as yet know why. I couldn't understand what was causing pain.

I told myself: Just stop feeling pain, you're not a baby. And I did. And all I thought about was B.

I thought: When I was a kid, my parents had sent me to one of the best (most expensive) of the private schools in New York City. There, no one, not one of the teachers, had ever mentioned pain. In the history books, in the poetry we read, no one ever tried to tell me what causes pain.

In the school that I attended I learned, seemingly by chance, that pain, if anything, is a bad smell.

And I tried to run away from the pain named *childhood* like you flush a huge shit down the toilet. I've been running ever since.

Loving B was like running away.

"Holy farts whatastink," I had said when I finally got out of school. "Don't academic people ever believe they have bodies and take a bath?"

Today a hippie informed me that the English always stink cause they take baths, not showers, and in the tub, all the scum on their bodies moves to the top of the bathwater, so they get out of their bath by rising up through their own scum, which sticks to them. I don't trust hippies.

At the same time, according to all the American media, a war had just broken out between the United States and several of the Arab nations. The media was presenting this war as my old school had presented the problem of pain. I decided to go back to school. A school that this time could teach me about pain.

The finest university in the Western Hemisphere was located in Basel because the Swiss are very clean and therefore more sensitive than most humans to bodily odors. *University* plus *smell* equals *body*. The same hippie who had objected to the English manner of bathing, or the English body, had also instructed me that starvation is the first step toward the attainment of Nirvana. Just as I wonder how a bodiless person can go anywhere, so at that time I thought that I could not feel pain without a body. Dead people don't know pain.

The University of Basel specialized in the field of dance. There had been no male students there for years.

When I looked through the glass doors of the one room that constituted the Basel airport, rain was falling in buckets. It smelled like poverty, like streets that have been turned into public pissholes, and I wondered why. What was the economic and political situation in this country of armaments, this country

34

which has never—as Germany perhaps now must do—faced and buried its undead?

Murder is a dream because lack is the center of both.

There were businessmen all around me so I started insulting them with their I-know-how-to-travel-with-only-a-briefcase looks on their faces though what (who) I really wanted was a taxi driver. No one could understand anything I was saying, anyhow.

I guess now you know all there is to know about me. That I don't like businessmen.

"Listen," I whispered to one of the female variety, "if you think that your vaginal smell is better than a rosebush's, you're kidding yourself."

The woman didn't answer, but then I saw a taxi driver. Though he wasn't wearing a sign that said *taxi driver,* I knew that's what he was.

"Hey," I said, "I've been looking for you for a long time."

The taxi driver, fat, with thick black hair, was looking off into the rain. I knew he was looking anywhere but at me. He probably expected his women to keep their mouths shut and curtsy afterwards.

In situations of desperation, I believe in getting whom I want. "You," I announced to him after I had walked up and tapped him. "I have to go somewhere. Besides that, you smell terrific."

I was getting somewhere. Somewhere is better than nowhere when it comes to romance.

"So let's go." I tried to drag him away by the crook of his arm. I'm pretty strong because B used to lift weights.

The taxi driver became angry and pulled the other way. He didn't like being shoved around by an arm.

I sighed. For in a foreign land it's hard to understand what people mean by what they do.

"I need you," I added.

I rarely want anyone, but whenever I do, I'll do anything to

35

get him. I haven't yet learned what I wouldn't do. Like a bitch in heat I followed that man who might or might not want me into the rain. It was still pouring. He opened one of his doors. I opened another. We were both wet. My heart pounded so fast, I leapt into the cab. "Taxi."

He understood what I meant.

I saw the driver pull a few of my cunt hairs out of the surrounding flesh. I questioned why he was doing what he was doing, but before he could answer, I quickly asked whether sadness had invaded his heart.

He replied that he was now watching his sperm shoot up into my heart.

We began to enter the forbidden realms. "My, what a nice, soft skin you've got," I remarked. One of the Swiss's hands placed a cigarette in his mouth and the other one lit it. Two draws. Then the hand that had placed it in the mouth took the cigarette, moved it in a straight line back and forth, a half-inch away from my breasts.

I told him that what he was doing was interesting.

Felt, but didn't see him put the lit end against my neck. While I was still astounded both of his hands lifted my head so that my lips slid over his cock.

I had forgotten to tell him my destination. Not that it mattered, for he couldn't speak English; the Swiss in Basel speak German.

German had been my parents' language.

I wrote the school's address down on a piece of paper.

Saying something in German, the taxi driver started the car.

I'm always excited when I'm traveling in a foreign land because I've lost my sense of direction.

It was still raining.

As if rising out of this rain, a building colored red, colored differently from the other edifices, appeared. It looked as if it were constructed of brick. Frescoed animals, maybe angels maybe

36

devils, stood out from its upper surfaces. The rain obscured which.

I sensed that this was the school. The driver stopped the car in front of the building's stone steps.

At this time I began to experience that great cycle of historical dreams which now replaced the dreams of my childhood and into which the city of my infancy and adolescence now threw itself.

Instead of asking whether this really was the school, I said, "You've got a crummy taxi."

"Don't be such a snob."

Since he did speak English, he was a liar. "Snob, the shit in my asshole. I'm the one who has to walk into this shitty rain."

It was raining harder than before. I could have checked on the weather before I had started on my journey, but maps never give that kind of information. Maps are dreams: both describe desire, where you want to go, but never the reality of the destination.

It was still raining.

Here's a story I wrote about my relationship with B before I returned to school:

"TWO GIRLS"

It's night. A man and a woman walk past each other on a street. Simultaneously both of them turn around and look at each other.

This one look is enough for agreement. The man informs the woman as to where and when she's to come; she begs for an earlier time.

As soon as she appears in the square where he told her to come, he doesn't tell her to go fuck herself. Instead he swears that from now on she will be his mother, daughter, and bitch, and that the moment she sees him, she will spread her legs and keep them open as wide as she can.

She repeats, "From this moment on, I'll be able to be who I am." Then she became terrified, muttered, "Thassa lotta bunk." She slapped his face and ran down the streets.

Apart from him, she thought to herself, "I'm an idiot. Most of the men whom I've had I haven't wanted. (Does that have anything to do with this present situation of lack?) Now when I come across a man I want, I run away.

"I'm going to do whatever I have to do with myself to be with him."

She crawled back to this man just like I will if B makes any indication that he wants me again.

Face-to-face with the man, all that she can see is his cock, whether or not he's clothed. Knows that he knows that she's drooling at him (or his cock or one of his hands stroking his cock through his clothes). So that's why one of his hands is moving his cock still through the pants material, now to the left, now to the right.

The second she dares to touch this cock, through the pants, he whacks her so brutally that she hits the pavement.

The sailors fuck whores because they're not whores.

Orders, "Don't get up." And he spits on her. "The dogshit right there becomes you."

Whenever he said that she was beautiful, he meant it.

The moment she raised her head up to him and recognized he was James Dean, she knew that this was the man whom she had always wanted. For the first time in her life she was being allowed—by no one—to give herself to a man.

If you can't be it, fuck it.

She knew that he was reading her heart when he then stated, "Since you're a whore, you have no rights; you have no right to want." Stepped on her. When bored of this action, ordered her to roll over a newspaper, part of whose headline said BAN ABORTION, into the shit that was gurgling out of the black and brown gratings.

"Sonofabitch!" she exclaimed, feeling that this was the appropriate description of the situation.

"Cut it out, kid. You're not dead yet."

He kicked her because one always kicks a good man when he's down.

Aware that she had finally done one of the most unexpected things in this world—found a good man—remembering that Lazarus had been raised from the dead, she tucked her arms into her waist then rolled and rolled until she got to the gutter.

She thought: I'm not supposed to be doing this. It's like watching myself in a dream go to the bathroom on a chair in public so that everyone can see what I'm doing. Jesus. I have never been so mortified. That Turk standing right there must think I'm a nymphomaniac. I wonder whether what's-his-name (she didn't know the man's name) will ask him to stick his dick into my asshole.

She thought about the pain, then played being a dead animal.

The man asked her if she was talking again.

When she came to, she found herself lying in a shit pool that wasn't going anywhere. Her hair, though she couldn't quite see it, looked as if it had turned into rat hair; lipstick was smudged; and her pupils rolled around and around. Everything was yellow. But these eyes were anything but dead: they were irredeemably hungry.

The streets of Berlin used to be cesspools of vice.

Part of the cunt's mind thought, I want to get out of here. *I want to get out of here* means *I want to be innocent.* The saints Verax and Lilac heard her female prayers.

While she had been a dead animal, the man had laid his lips upon her in such a way that their breaths flowed together without any pressure, the pressure of lips, and remained there for eternity. The more she had desired her father, the more he was going to reject her, yet he was never going to allow her to remove her gaze from his cock.

In this manner they reached the ruins.

Here's the church.

"Come while you're coming," he told her at the portals.

I would like to talk to the birds, but it's not yet time. Last spring I saw storks. They were still gray and thin, like the dead branches on which they were building their nests. Later they would pick up their sad wings and with the old noise of disjointedness, seize their flight.

So the man bound her wrists with knots of linen, that she might be able to enter the church.

Inside the church.

Two young girls, Verax and Skunk, are tranquilly shitting into the holy-water basins and then, as much as they can separate the two processes, pissing into the ciboria.

Girls don't go to the bathroom in the same way that boys do.

Understanding this, Verax uses a communion napkin soaked in the holy water to wipe off her ass. (She's not interested in being clean, but rather in smelling a certain way. A rose.)

For soon Verax will be forced to return to her normal life, where every hour is joy and hatred.

For there will be no more boredom.

Dragging the sacred suppository around in her asshole while walking on top of the altar, Skunk now spurts it forth with bits of shit, so that the altar breaks into pieces beneath her.

At last it is clear that the Church reels in its own shit and that every text is a text of desire.

MURDER

I had found the school for which I had been looking.

Found in that pouring rain.

To the taxi driver, I said, "Wait for me."

The blue and red rain soaked me.

When one of the red double doors opened, a gray head appeared and asked, "Do you want something?"

I replied that they were expecting me.

In no uncertain terms she told me to go away.

No matter how long I knocked, the door wouldn't open again.

The rain fell down more heavily than it had before. According to my memory.

Inside the taxi, where it was warm, though I couldn't see through the rain, I watched the other red door open and a girl who looked like me race past it. I couldn't see clearly.

When I tried to see more definitively, I saw only rain and the colors of gunmetal.

I have always wanted my dreams to be like that of childhood or of Radley Metzger's film of the book *Therese and Isabelle*.

A woman returns to her school.

A private school like mine.

I had wandered away from the others to the lavatories. The sound of Baudelaire still in my ears. An odor hung inside the cubicle. . . . A tenderness defined my hairs. I leaned over the bowl.

My best friend came into the toilet.

"Kiss me on the mouth."

"No. It's too soon."

I hadn't wanted to go to school in the first place. My mother made me do it so she could be alone with her new husband. I told her to her face, while he was standing with her, that he had married her only for her money. They both denied that.

So I was forced to attend boarding school.

Memories do not obey the law of linear time.

Through the bars I saw the headmistress, her hair in the mandatory bun, enter and welcome me to the institution. Then she escorted me to my room and told me that I would come to love my new home, a bare mattress, as a monk loves his cell. "These doorways," she said, "are as inviolable as the walls of a fortress."

I am interested only in lapses.

Memory: My mother tells me that she loves me.

Memory: When I wake up in boarding school, a girl who

41

looks okay offers to help me unpack. A teacher hears her swear and punishes her.

I've always had a thing for wild girls.

Memory: The school was built out of love. The trees were so beautiful, especially their tops, where the leaves were.

Memory: I was bicycling with my best friend, the girl who helped me unpack, down the lane and a young man in a car wanted to pass us. We wouldn't let him because we wanted to be bad. In the end, he passed. The two lines of trees on either side of us seemed to extend forever.

I said, "Riding makes me free."

Isabelle said, "I have only my mother."

That's all I've got.

Memory: I ask Isabelle about boyfriends and she becomes irritable. Angry. I don't understand anything. When I ask her what's happening, she can't talk to me.

Memory: I no longer sleep in my mother's bedroom.

Memory: I can't go to sleep so I walk to the library. The real or interesting library lies in a room that is like large drawers above this library. But I descend series of spiraling stairs until I reach bottom. Here is the magic room, a ·library, which the witch inhabits.

In the next memory I see girls sobbing. It's night and Isabelle tells me that she wishes we could be alone together. It was usual for us to spend the night in our best girlfriend's bed in that dorm full of single cots because, for us, there was no difference between sex and no sex.

The next morning there was no Isabelle. She had gone to her mother's for the weekend. I had nothing to do so I went into town. There the man whom Isabelle and I had seen in the car asked me for a date.

I stayed there with him. The closer sexually I let him get to me, though I was scared, the more bored I became. Between sex and friendship there seemed to be an impassable gulf that was increasing.

We lay on the dirt in a graveyard. He said that now I had to fuck with him and I wanted to and I didn't want to so I ran away from him.

Returned to my miasma of indecisions.

I didn't understand why all the girls (except for Isabelle) talked about the boyfriends or superstars they were in love with, but I couldn't.

All the schoolgirls passed me by.

My mother's new husband was saying, "You know what they say about finishing school for girls?"

No one said anything.

"When they come out, they're finished as girls."

"But that happens everywhere." Finished as girls. My mother was in her dressing room.

I had come home for the weekend. I ignored the pervert. I wanted to tell my mother I loved her so I informed her I now had a best friend named Isabelle. For the moment the creep shut up. My mother replied by informing me that she and *her husband* were rejecting me again by taking their summer in Algeria, like all the rich Parisians, and I would remain in school so that my presence wouldn't ever bother them.

Back in school, I masturbated in my cot while I thought about my parents.

Being able to come, I decided while touching myself, necessitates being able to relax and enter another world. To come is to dream. I don't know how it is for males. But I just can't come when I need to protect myself from my parents, and this is the time when I need to most.

Must.

Another memory: I had now become one of the top students in the school, not because I was scared of the teachers, but because the world of learning had nothing to do with my parents'. I (Isabelle) returned to the school from one of her mother's weekends. Her waist had become tiny and her breasts were as huge as pillows.

All of us used to ask her how she could sleep on those fluffy things. She tried to explain that they don't hurt.

Miss St. Pierre, the literature teacher, was a lesbian because she stuffed her bra with pads and their tips stuck upward like WASPs' noses.

After she came back, Isabelle and I arranged to meet alone in the church.

"I missed you."

"I missed you."

I dug her neck into my teeth. Then I nailed her hands against the floor. Her pincers tore at me. I followed everything inside me. From now on her legs would always be spread open. I stormed her openings as if she was a beleaguered fortress.

"Tell me."

"I love you."

"Again."

"I love you."

"Again."

"I love you."

Another memory: Night after night when it was dark I crawled into I's bed. We held hands and told each other our stories of childhood.

"The school," she said, "was burning down."

No. Our cunts.

I don't remember. Don't describe what can't be remembered. What will never be seen. What's between the legs, I and I. She was discovering the little organ that the cock imitates. My limitations are too painful. I transformed into the sex of a dog, red and unbearable to my own eyes.

It has come.

(For this reason women don't need Christ.)

Our comings can't end.

Then I peered out from beneath the sheets at an overflow of nipples.

I began once more where I had left off. A kitten rubbing and rubbing its own fur which reeks overflows into total sex. I know that night will soon be leaving us. I want to run away because this sex cannot stop, but we can't run away because we have to be at school.

We both knew that soon it would be morning and that morning, not the orgasm, was our end.

We both knew that soon it would end and that the end would be, not orgasm, but morning.

I told me to go and to be careful, for one of the other students might be awake.

The next day the girls mocked us because they knew what we had been doing in the chapel.

Girls'll do anything, especially something nasty, in order to destroy what they think isn't normal. I remember that Wendy Janover became the class creep when she announced that the United States was a racist society. We began our torture by ostracizing her for a week.

All my childhood I thought about running away.

Sex goes on and on. One day, desperate to be alone, I and I went to a brothel we had heard about, but we didn't like it there. Everyone was laughing at us, so we couldn't have sex.

I did learn that anyone will do anything for money and that man-eating plants die from food poisoning.

That night, both of us horny as hell, we fucked inside the forest that was right outside the school. In our fantasies, the murderers were hiding. I made my way inside as I climbed outside. Our corpses decayed. Now the night, no humans, watched us. My clit turned into a crawling sea monster, hers likewise, until we were nothing but sea monsters leaving trails of slime.

Whoever was "I" became traces of dust.

As her fingers withdrew, pleasure turned into something else, for nothing in this world can disappear.

"We'll never reject and abandon each other."

"Never."

A few mornings later, when I looked for I, she was no longer there. Her drawers had been emptied of all their belongings. I's mother had taken her away to foreign, unknown lands.

And I learned absence, which is the same as death.

I sob. I stand over myself and watch myself sob. My lips are very thick.

The guard told the woman that it was time to close up the school. Her visit was over.

The guards closed the gates.

Memory isn't able to return the rememberer to reality.

The girl I had watched dart past the red door ran down lightless streets until she reached the apartment building in which the most popular (bitchy) student in the school resided.

The bathroom of this apartment was the pink that a young girl's dress should be.

One of its windowpanes, blowing open, showed the blackness that lay beyond. The student, Thais, whose hair was as black as the outside, closed the window as quickly as possible because she was scared. The pane slammed against her finger.

She felt safe.

Being Catholic, she crossed herself.

When, to test her safety, Francesca looked through the glass a second time, she saw gigantic cat's eyes looking at her and touched the bottom of the cross, her cunt.

Then an arm moved through the open window so that she

could be strangled. Another hand, cased in a black leather glove, sliced her neck with a knife.

Perhaps in response to the lack of sight, the heart poured out its blood.

There's no memory of the words "I love you," but there is of the hymen being broken.

Francesca's body hung from a long Tampax string attached to the bathroom ceiling, all the way down to the luxurious tiled vestibule below. Her blood streamed out of every part of her and made all of the apartment smell like bleeding cunt.

A jagged piece of glass had cut her hymen, or identity, into two parts.

A DREAM OF YOUNG GIRLS

That night I didn't know that a girl's murder was taking place. I dreamt that I had been invited to a party. Even in dream, going to a party is a rarity for me. I protested to the inviter that I didn't have the proper clothes. The inviters, my friends, told me that I could wear whatever I liked to this party, that no one cares what anyone wears anymore.

The next morning when I woke up, I felt lost, so I decided to go to the party.

In the bathroom, or in one of the bathrooms in the house in which the party was being held, a heavy-set man in his forties or fifties who was with his wife in this bathroom clearly indicated that he wanted to fuck me in the bathtub.

"I don't know whether it's right since you're not my husband." But I really wanted to. (In the dream I remembered that B has a wife.) "And this isn't my house."

Both of us were on fire for each other.

After we had fucked, paint lay splashed over bathtub, walls, and floor tiles.

47

No matter how hard I cleaned, I couldn't make the paint go away.

I kept trying because this wasn't my house.

The bed in the room outside this bathroom, which must be a bedroom because a bed occupies most of its space, was covered with makeup. Each bit of makeup—mascara, eyeliner, lipstick, etc.—came in a tiny paint tube. Fucking always erases my eyeliner. But every time I put on some makeup, as soon as I laid it down, that paint tube began squishing out its contents. I decided that either the room or I was too hot.

Paint was covering everything. That must mean that I destroy either myself or the world whenever I fuck. Especially, destruct rich people's houses.

Lots of mazes lay outside this bedroom.

The beginning of the actual party was taking place in the largest room I had as yet seen. Dark, wood-paneled ceilings and walls striped by olive velvet curtains that swept to the floor. For several minutes I watched a living still life of soberly dressed old people sitting like dolls in armchairs so huge they made these people into children.

I strolled past the portraits of American death to the room's end, then past the party's hostess, whom I recognized as the editor of Poison Press.

An almost-as-large long room lay perpendicularly off the first room. As I entered this room, I saw first a long table laid out with delicate, expensive appetizers. Right behind me, my hostess shrilled, "Why's she here?" because she recognized me as an enemy-of-the-literary-world-according-to-the-literati.

I ran out of the adjoining rooms because I was being condemned as an outcast and, perhaps, because I am.

I was caught in the maze, or in a maze.

Tried to escape by figuring out where I was, by finding out who I was, but I couldn't because I was in a maze. (Amazed.)

Then I saw an exit. Walked through the door. Once I was in

48

that room, I realized it was a closet. It was all gray and the doors were locked. I knew that finally they had captured me.

Even in dream, my deepest fear is being enclosed, trapped, or lobotomized.

The next day, the sun was shining clearly, and, in an oversized, elegant doorman's suit and cap, I stood in front of the house where the party had taken place. I was the doorman and my will was gone.

The house plus winding street in front of it covered in snow was a scene out of Paris.

The confusions and terrifying dream of the night had passed. I trotted up the four steps to the red doors and knocked.

"Where have you been? We expected you last night," another nag said.

I was introduced to Mrs. Selby, a handsome woman in her late thirties or early forties. A bun imprisoned black hair. She was the acting directress of the school, I was informed, for the actual directress was absent.

Police were walking everywhere over gleaming black-and-white tiles. Mrs. Selby explained to me: last night when I should have been at the school, a student who had just been expelled was murdered.

Then she began talking to a cop.

The athletic gym teacher informed me that since the room that I had reserved at the school was not yet ready for me, I would be staying in the apartment where the ex-student had been killed.

I didn't want to live in the room of a murder victim.

She assured me that the arrangement was temporary. She herself would introduce me to the student who owned this apartment, the wealthiest and most popular girl in the school.

"You should consider yourself very lucky."

Since this was one of the finest women's universities in the world, there were almost no men on its premises.

49

The teeth of one of the few remaining men, the janitor, formed the most visible part of his face. Deep rot had turned each one a different color. Besides that, dog hairs were jutting out of every other inch of facial flesh.

Besides the janitor, a few other deviants lay in the cracks.

Before going to my new apartment, I visited the locker room. Some of my classmates, sprawling all over the benches and floor, were discussing the one they had recently ostracized. Her insecurity and vulnerability were exciting their derision. If she wanted to ever be spoken to again, one girl said, she would have to learn how to fight.

My new landlady, a natural blonde, didn't give a shit. The little jailbird wasn't worth her attention. She deigned to talk to very few girls, and only to ones with intelligence.

Here and there a few boys' names cropped up. They weren't worth much—boys—and they were always handsome and rich.

All of the girls, I learned, arrogant or not, overworked their studies and their bodies.

I asked why the murdered girl had been expelled.

Later, when I lay in her bed, I wondered whether she had been the one whom I had seen in the pouring rain.

Then I tried to imagine murder. The more I tried to understand, the closer I came to the place where murder is that which isn't conceivable.

Only emotion conceives in sensual forms that which isn't conceivable.

I remembered that the girl at the red door had uttered certain words. Verbal forms. Whenever I want to remember definite names or verbal forms, my memory fails.

I was dreaming about sexuality or, more precisely, about something just prior to sexuality. Later I would realize that I am dreaming about young girls . . .

I ENTER THE SCHOOL'S BODY

The girls said, "You understand that it's only with the highest form of feeling (whatever that is) and not because we hate you that we're going to take our ease in your homes and mansions, your innermost sanctuaries, we're going to sleep in your beds (you want us to anyway) on your unbloodstained mattresses on the sheets on which you fuck your wives. We want to feed on your flesh. We want—we're going to reproduce only girls by ourselves in the midst of your leftover cock hair, in your armpits, in whatever beards you have. We're going to sniff your emissions and must while we're penetrating (with our fingers) your ears, nostrils, and eye sockets. To ensure that you'll never again know sleep. Then we'll shit on you because you as politicians taught us what shit is; in the future, we'll never conceal anything about ourselves (unlike you) because our only purpose here is the marking of history, your history. As if we haven't. Because you said that we hadn't."

One girl said, "Every time I walk into my room, I think about how you locked me up for years in that shack with a zinc roof. There you sentenced me to spend my earliest and formative years, milking the boys to whom you introduced me. 'Hi, Cherry. This is my son, Harold. I know you'll know what to do.' I said, 'O daddy. You're the one who knows what to do.' 'No,' you said. Then, to your son, 'Son. It's real easy. Just let it happen. I know you'll make me proud and not turn out to be a diseased faggot to whom I can no longer say hello.' "

Another student said, "Daddy: I want to kiss the undersides of your eyelids because they're the tenderest things I know. I won't kiss them: one of my little nipples'll lick them: the odor of *poisson* or *poison*, however it's spelled (smelled), or the scent of the drops that come out of the flesh under your arms will bring me back to normality. After all the bad things that I've done in my life, I know that I will have to convince you that I am sincere in seeking your friendship, but, please understand, that more than anything I need you as my business partner because I don't know how to do business because in my arms everything is allowed, nothing's forbidden, and pleasure turns me into a goddess, though only for a second or two."

In the first class that I took, a class about theory, the teacher told us about the works of the novelist Juan Goytisolo. "Goytisolo uses plagiarisms (other texts) in several ways: sometimes his characters read, discuss, or see other texts. Sometimes two simultaneous texts compose the narrative. Sometimes Goytisolo changes someone else's text in an attempt to contaminate and subvert something or other. Count Julian, I mean Goytisolo, subverts, invades, seduces, and infects all that's abhorrent to him by transforming the subject into an empirical self, a text among texts, a self that becomes a sign in its attempt at finding meaning and value. All that is left is sex alone and its naked violence."

I looked down between my legs and saw blood. I decided that I must be having one of those periods that are so heavy they could be natural miscarriages.

I felt how I think I should feel in a dream when I watch myself pissing while sitting, not on a toilet, but on a chair in the middle of a busy street.

". . . the hidden reason for your moral, artistic, social, religious, sexual deviation. From Goytisolo's *Juan the Landless*."

The teacher was staring at me. "What's the hidden reason?"

When I was five years old, I knew that Mother wanted me to be a red or dead child, because whenever I'd take a shower, she'd enter the bathroom and throw a pitcher of ice-cold water at my steaming body, in the hope that I'd move suddenly and slip on a soap bar.

When I was a kid, I must have desired reality to be a lie; now I hate hypocrisy, or morality, more than anything else.

World War II was the time of romance: the American soldiers

52

and sailors married whomever they could on their leaves so that they wouldn't die alone. My mother got married during World War II and then went to see a doctor because she had a stomach-ache. The doctor told her that her only cure was to become pregnant. My mother's new husband was rich. Three months into her pregnancy, my mother's husband walked away from her and never came back, only because, *my mother was always sure to inform me,* she was gravid with me.

"Why didn't you get an abortion?"

"Because I was too scared."

The day after he pulled me, red, out of her vagina, the doctor informed my mother that she had appendicitis.

After this, my memory turned black.

"What is the hidden reason?" she asked me.

I didn't know what happened.

I came to in a small and dark red room. A few women and one man were standing around me. Later I found out he was the doctor. Handed me a glass full of liquid the color of the room's walls, which I was to drink. I would imbibe the same medicine three times a day in order to build my red corpuscles. The medicine was red, he said, because females menstruate.

Mrs. Selby, who was standing behind me, butch as they come, informed me that I'd live in this room until I was strong enough to leave.

I no longer had to sleep in a murdered girl's apartment.

MAGGOTS

That night I had no idea how sick I was. That night, my first night in school, I dreamt about religion. This dream is based on a Buñuel film:

One scorpion of every possible color was perching on a rock in order to get a suntan. These were the years, as in World War II, when criminals were still romantic. A criminal rose way up above the scorpions and rocks. When he looked down, he saw a gaggle of Christian missionaries.

As fast as he could, the Steven Tyler look-alike raced back to the joint in which he was doing something like living so that he could tell the other hoodlums that the Christians had arrived.

Christians don't come.

Hermes, or the Steven Tyler look-alike, had become the bad guys' messenger because they had been starving for so long they could no longer move. In spite of poverty, they crawled out of their slum just so that they could locate the Christians and murder them.

Afterwards, many many Christians, who were now known as "martyrs," entered these lands: a Christian totalitarian state rose up.

When I woke up, maggots were crawling out of my cunt. At first I thought that Mother must have over–toilet-trained me. The maggots were coming out of my cunt because maggots come from meat.

In my first school I had been taught that through rationality humans can know and control otherness, our histories and environments.

In one of my dreams, the maggot, huge, translucent, and slimy, was my father.

Here is my theory of dreams: Maggots are dicks because they rise up, then writhe and turn funny colors. Worms rise out of red meat. (Worm- or dick-heads are the same things as nipples.)

Whereas houses are cunts. In the dream, the house is a maze. All sorts of rooms, all of which are magical, lie off of the halls.

The outside lies beyond the maze.

One result of this theory is the knowledge that all reality is alive.

It wasn't just my cunt. When I walked out of my red room, white dicks were falling out of the hall's ceiling, which wasn't alive. The tiny animals sat in my hair and curled around on my shoulders.

I used to believe that the walls of old buildings were composed of cockroaches. I was learning differently.

The European educational system is superior to the American.

The students who resided at the school had run out of their bedrooms into the hall. "It's raining dicks," a girl cried. Another one was looking as hard as she could between her legs.

In this chaos, Mrs. Selby appeared and told us that maggots don't come out of cunts. She explained that maggots can be born only in dead flesh.

This fact has been made clear in a Farsi poem:

دَستهای این بَچّه کثیف اَست.

(The child's hands are dirty.)

آیا رِضا از حُسَین کوچکتَر اَست؟

(Is Reza smaller than Hosein?)

نَخَیر. بُزُرگتَر اَست.

(No. He is bigger.)

"Though this nation is no longer economically dependent on the United States, we're still importing the majority of our red meat from American farmers," Dame Selby continued. "The American farmers have developed a new method of impregnating cows, thanks to their Moral Majority: by fucking them with giant fake dildos filled with the sperm taken from bulls. Often the bulls had died of cancer. Both bulls and cows are fed on their dead.

"One result of this method of unnatural fertilization is named 'mushy brain disease.' "

"Has mushy brain disease anything to do with the proliferation of maggots?"

It turned out that the answer was yes. The maggots were

coming, not from our cunts, but from cans of red meat that had been stored in lockers in the holes in the ceiling.

Though we had learned that our cunts and vaginas aren't the sources of disease, we had no idea how to get rid of maggots.

We had been fed on the meat.

THE ERADICATION OF MAGGOTS

Whereas most men want their women to smell (be) clean, Louis XIV of France delighted in as rotten as possible a stench way down in those parts.

I don't know whether we were feminists. We did establish political positions in our class by picking best friends. Those who didn't have anyone stood in danger of being ostracized for more than a week.

By the end of the first day, I almost had a best friend, Beatrice, who was blond and the school-champion tennis player.

I was with Beatrice in that maggot-filled hall. Selby told us that we would spend the rest of the night in the refectory, the only room free of worms, while the rest of the school was being decontaminated.

Two by two the students filed into the dining hall—as I remember, the largest room in the school—which was located in the basement and connected to the rest of the establishment by a wide red ramp.

Beatrice said, "This refectory used to be a stable."

Now rows of cots stood in the center of the room. A wall of hanging sheets that had been soaked in red liquid surrounded the beds. I wondered whether most students had gotten their first period without knowing what was happening to them.

In those days I don't know if we had sex with each other because I didn't know that women had sex with each other.

I knew I had had sex with B and now I was here. I began telling Beatrice.

56

"Shh," she whispered.

Someone—Selby?—turned off the lights and I crawled into Beatrice's bed.

"Shh. Do you hear the snoring?"

I listened. I didn't hear anything. "Girls can snore," I replied. "Is that what you want me to listen to?"

"You're not listening."

In that dark there was only black. I listened. I couldn't hear anything. In the bathtub, my grandmother's breasts had looked like huge potatoes floating on the water. They were the largest things on her body.

I told Beatrice what I was hearing.

"It's the headmistress."

"The snoring?"

"The snoring."

"That's Selby snoring?"

"But Selby isn't the real head."

I wondered why I couldn't smell the blood that had stained the sheets. In this school nothing made sense. Why had I run away from B, just because my relations with him were complicated? Why had I run away to this school?

Beatrice whispered something about the school's real head. I heard *red head*.

If maggots come from dead meat, how can maggots live in cunts?

That night I dreamt, in deep sleep, that I was riding around roads that were looped. As if two circles interconnecting.

Though I was riding a horse, the horse was like a motorcycle. At one point, it was as if bad weather: rain pounded into the gutter. One section of the upper circles are now dangerous to drive on.

Two dreams crossed, like these roads.

Below the center of the figure 8 road was a place where I could rest. There: a low stone building, Spanish style, but I can only

57

see its dark arched entrances, nothing of the insides. The center of the figure 8 road lay under the roof that projected out, into the outside, from the walls that formed the arches.

Here I dismounted or changed motorcycles.

A female novelist who used to be a friend of mine and another girl, both of whom were now my enemies, lived inside one black door of this house. I did whatever I could to avoid saying hello to them because I didn't know how to deal with this situation. And because I felt guilty about my confusion or dislike.

My guilt made me say, "Hello." As soon as I had said this, their plan to destroy me began: the gigantic, velvet, brown horse on which the novelist was sitting reared up over me. The horse jumped—now was a dachshund-like dog the same color as the horse perching in my arms. It or he or she shot venom into me.

A doctor who had witnessed the incident, and so knew the truth, managed to withdraw the poison from my body. Then he gave me fingernails that could shoot out like spears and inject poison.

And so I no longer lived in danger and was free to ride wherever I wanted because I could protect myself from the novelist.

ONE MURDER LEADS TO ANOTHER

For the witch will never tell us what she knows and what we can never know, said Rimbaud.

I know that I can't know anything, but I don't know what this knowledge is.

The next day, when I woke up, I learned what had really happened during the night.

Sun was flooding the outside and the insides of the school; there were no more maggots.

I felt that I was looking through new eyes: everyone I saw looked crazy. Every teacher I watched was picking her nose. It was then that I learned that the janitor, who doubled as the piano player for the dance classes and whose face had dog hairs growing out of it, was legally blind. His only eyes were a police dog.

During my first school day this hound had bit through the hand of one of the kids of one of the maids. In retaliation, Selby had thrown the human out of the school, saying, "The blind shall lead the blind."

This was only a prelude to the real story:

During the night of maggots, which was also the cleansing of maggots, the now jobless blind man stood in the center of the square of the Church of the Virgin. He was like a homeless person, not only with nowhere in the world to go, but also without idea or dream of direction. How can people dream when they can't sleep, woken up by storms, cops, whatever and whoever lies outside them? Without dreams, what is time? He had only his beast to follow.

Let your cunt come outside your body and crawl, like a snail, along the flesh. Slither down your legs until there are trails of blood over the skin. Blood has this unmistakable smell. Then the cunt will travel, a sailor, to foreign lands. Will rub itself like a dog, smell, and be fucked.

Here lies the life that I'm seeking: Saint Mary the Virgin of this church, Mary Magdalene, Saint Mary Margaret (whoever You are), and all the others—Saint Simon, Saint Simeon, Saint Joseph, Saint Pascal-Baylon, Saint Peter and Saint Paul, Saint Michael, all my guardian spooks and sisters and brothers in the quests, pray for me, a lost, poor sinner, that I will come into the Sacred Heart of Blessed Jesus, which is truly a cunt. An immense quivering, a bowlful of jelly that is always crying out for pleasure, for the reason Father was kicked out of paradise and Mom told she was only a hole. Your enormous lips are greedily parted and you secrete saliva like Pavlov's dog. Crying out for all of it, yes, and then wanting more, you wail.

At one point, the church bells must have been striking. The

blind man didn't understand why he had become scared. He knew but he didn't understand why he had become scared. When his dog smelled his fear, it jumped. When the bitch bit this time through the blind man's neck, the head was severed from the chest. Blood flowed out toward the Church of the Virgin.

PERIOD

As soon as I and the other students had learned about the janitor's demise, we talked only about death and murder.

Beatrice and I were lying in my bed back in the dark red room when I told her about my mother's dog, Pepper. He was black, white, and more vicious than my mother. Also, he was fat.

"Forget about Pepper"—like all girls, we spent our time giggling and for fun we stole—"there was my mother. She taught me that I should wrap up my carrot-juice Kotexes in lots and lots of toilet paper and then in newspaper so it . . . I . . . could never be seen again."

"Carrot juice?"

"I forgot to tell you."

"I've got something to tell you," Beatrice mentioned.

"One day when I walked into my parents' apartment, my mother started screaming at me. In their apartment, one hall ran perpendicular into the other. I saw a line of newspaper wads and then a single stream of toilet paper leading from one hall into the next. I followed that line until I reached an orange, actually a dark red-brown and white pad partially chewed up, which lay like a bone under the dining room table. Pepper, fat and growling, was on the other side of the pad.

"Now Pepper had three favorite foods:

"First. My father used to eat only beef, lamb chops, lobster if he had to, raw onion rings, and, after this, coffee ice cream.

According to him, all other foods, especially vegetables, were 'nigger food.' "

"I've got something to tell you," Beatrice mentioned.

"Every night either my brother or I would guard the beef or lamb that was placed on the dining-room table so that Pepper wouldn't digest it before we could."

"I've got something to tell you," Beatrice mentioned.

"Dog stories are important.

"Second. The runner-up in this Miss America—like contest, 'Pepper's Dog Food,' was the chocolate wrappers that he could find in my mother's toilet bowl. Toilet water minus wrappers would do.

"Third, for Pepper, best though last, was used Kotexes. Especially mine."

"Will you listen to me?"

I tried listening. In the blackness I didn't hear anything. "Now I'll tell you about my Kotexes."

"Listen."

Since I didn't know what or whom I was supposed to be listening for, I couldn't hear anything.

"There are footsteps."

I heard the footsteps. It was a raccoon walking across my ceiling as if my ceiling was a floor. In the blackness.

"It's the teachers. Every night they walk on that floor to the same place."

I have this recurrent cycle of dreams in which I walk to a magic place which is, formally, a snail's center.

Outside the dream, snails leave slime trails.

"They walk to where the headmistress is breathing."

"Selby doesn't live at this school."

"Selby isn't the real head."

What Beatrice said resembled another cycle of my dreams. The cycle of being in the magic house and sometimes being

61

chased by murderers. I remembered the murders. I remembered that I had heard the student who had been murdered utter certain words as she was running out of the school. Utter them to someone who was behind the red door.

I told Beatrice that I knew what these words were, though I didn't yet. "It's like the body."

"Words are like the body?"

I tried to explain. "I can't find out who I am. I know nothing about my body. Whenever there's a chance of knowing, for any of us, the government, Bush if you like, reacts to knowledge about the female body by censoring."

"Bush as in *bush*?"

"Bush on bush, Bush as in *blush*."

"The word has made flesh."

"I'm going back to the past.

"The first time I got my period, I was standing in the porcelain bathtub in my bathroom. I saw drops of red-orange liquid, my memory says 'orange,' inside one of my thighs. My mother happened to walk into the bathroom and told me that this wet stuff was carrot juice.

" 'Once a month,' she said, 'from now on, carrot juice is going to fall from between your legs.'

"I became confused.

" 'Because you're a woman.'

"Since the carrot juice was unbearable, or unmentionable, whenever it came out of me, I would have to walk around the house and everywhere else with a thick cotton pad between my legs. Whenever I went to the bathroom or if the pad became all orange on its own, I would bury it in wrappings of toilet paper, then in rolls of newspaper, then place the whole bundle down into the hidden recesses of the garbage can so that no one would ever see it, me, again. I was now unmentionable.

"This is how periods led to a dog."

Beatrice had fallen asleep.

PREPARATION FOR THE UNMENTIONABLE BASED ON A PUN

I have arrived at a crossroads.

On a motorcycle. Now I have a choice: I can ride to the right, straight ahead, or to the left.

I turned left, down a single-lane road, slightly uphill. A narrow brick bridge lay just ahead of me. But I didn't want to go there.

I turned around and rode back the way I had come.

Back where I had started out, only a few feet farther down the entrance road. Now I was in an area that was a sunken square basin. Behind me, from where I had come, I saw a ramp whose shape was a squashed Z. To go back to where I had been, I would have to ride through this Z. My problem was that I didn't know if my bike could handle the Z's corner turns.

Something in my character made me decide I'd chance it.

I was still in the basin. To my left, at the very beginning of the road that moved across the bridge, an accident had taken place. Two men. One had hit the ground. It was now necessary to pay some kind of toll to ride the Z.

The toll booth was sitting in the center of the lowest and nearest Z line.

In order to pay the toll, I would have to perch on a black bicycle seat that was balanced on top of green, insect-like metal legs. This whatever-it-was formed a cross between a bicycle and a motorcycle. I sat on it, on some loose typing-size paper. The toll consisted of a few sheaves of this size paper, which I would toss at the booth when I passed by.

I was still in the center of the basin.

Suddenly I remembered, or became conscious, consciousness was like memory, that I didn't know where my motorcycle was. Panicked, I thought that someone must have stolen it while I had been climbing up onto the bicycle seat. I perceived a man in front of me at an edge of the square, sitting on my cycle, and then I perceived a gorgeous Spanish woman, made-up and dressed in dark red and black, on her bike. She punched the creep out and laid him on the ground so that I could have my cycle.

When I walked over to her to thank her, she flashed a smile.

Then, the tough beauty and I formed a pact.

The next day I asked Selby if she or anyone had learned anything about either the student's or the piano player's death.

She simply told me that I shouldn't bother myself, that the police take care of such matters.

I was so angry that she wouldn't deal with my fear and so scared of her authority that I became confused and told her what I never should have told her. I told her that I knew something.

"What could *you* know?"

The bitch was noticing me. "The night I came to this school, I saw the girl who was murdered."

"How do you know this? You've never seen her."

"I saw a girl racing away from the red doors. I heard what she was saying." For the first time, I knew what those words were.

At the same time I remembered that, as a child, I would sit in the bathtub for hours because I was a fish. I don't know why.

As if she hadn't been listening, Selby answered that my words didn't concern her. Murder is only the business of the authorities. By *authority,* she meant *cop.*

I was standing inside a building. I was starving. I'm always hungry. I wanted to cook this big potato. In order to cook it, I would have to run a nail through its center into the wood-paneled wall.

Though I didn't believe that this is how a potato is cooked, anyway I did it and saw a fire in the hole in the wall around the big nail, so I knew this was how to cook this potato. The only problem with such a method of cooking is that the building

with a gigantic gardener's shears. After each fingernail was short-ened, he thrust a butterfly pin under what was left of the nail. All the murderers got together, which is difficult for murderers to do, and dressed the kid up in too many clothes, clothes that were too large for him, clothes that stifled him, clothes that buried him, murderers know nothing about fashion: they combed his hair and then they poured Superglue over everything. After they had drenched him in glue, as if you can put Superglue into buckets, the student was instructed to hug and lick their old stinky faces. The murderers slapped whipped threw around a little scratched made bleed stuck knives into drugged up tor-tured beat the kid madly, foolishly until dawn. Just as he was about to die, they saved him, promised him that they weren't going to touch him anymore. Then they bathed all his wounds in rose water. Now the murderers informed him of the rules: they're going to hire him out to the school's visitors who'll caress all the ridges of his new scars."

The dormitory had been carved out of those grand rooms once polluted by aristocrats and rich people.

Beatrice had disappeared from my world.

I was in Prague. Caught among buildings that were dark: a square of buildings. The poet of these buildings, Pierre, and I, lovers for many years, were fucking on a tattered red carpet in a hotel. I had to find my hotel.

Pierre pointed to an old, as if marbled, red column that rose above the city, so far that I couldn't see its top. He explained to me that this is his family's home: the column runs through the sky horizontally over the whole city.

I ascertained that Pierre's parents are wealthy. I had never known this before.

Pierre left me.

The dark square of buildings, named "The Dormitory," in which I was standing lies in the upper right quadrant of the city.

A long, narrow, black plank or street connected this square to its twin that occupied the city's upper left quarter. I had to reach the second square so that I wouldn't be murdered.

As I started walking the black plank, the sky above the black was yellow.

Now I was in the second square, standing in a hotel, which was Pierre's hotel. So it must belong to Pierre. Since I hadn't wanted to be in his hotel, I had to be lost.

I was lost in a foreign city, as I've been time and time again.

I forced myself to ask for the directions to the hotel in which I had made reservations.

Winding streets lay all around me, streets too narrow for vehicles. It was impossible for me to know how to proceed. On each side of each street, I saw empty raised garages, huge butchers' trucks, warehouses, factories without windows. There were no shops here, nor women.

When I looked at the map I carried on me, I saw that the street I had been looking for was approximately four streets south of Pierre's hotel.

I found myself standing back in the right-hand square. I had to walk a second time across the black plank, then to Pierre's hotel, in order to reach the hotel to which I wanted to go.

As I was leaving Pierre's hotel for the second time, I imagined that my destination lay at the end of a curving, cobblestoned street. Now I recognized that I had already stayed in this hotel and that this hotel was my place of safety in the midst of foreignness.

For the first time in the city, I knew where I was going: the unknown had become known while remaining unknown.

Suddenly I knew that I had reached the street I had been searching for, for I saw the arch, the entrance to the cobblestoned street that I had imagined. I walked through it. The winding cobblestoned path greeted my eyes.

Veered right.

At its end, up steps, was the place for which I had been looking. There was a grand, fake gold doorway. Though there was no sign, this was the place I desired.

Two women whom I didn't know and I waited in front of the register, which resembled a movie box. Slowly our group was showing up and checking into the hotel. One of the women, whom I now recognized, and she was a bitch, of course had to register before me. So I let her do exactly what she wanted since I'm a wimp.

Finally it was my turn to check in. Suddenly I had to decide whether to get one double or two singles because B, with whom I had just broken up, was going to arrive by the end of the day. I had to decide immediately whether or not I really wanted to break up with him.

Anxious, I told the girl, "Two singles."

All the other women had boyfriends.

Now I was standing in the upper-right quadrant of the hotel's second story. Red carpet covered the floor. This floor's topology mirrored the city's: to reach my room in the upper-left quadrant, I would have to walk across a narrow portion of carpet in the center's upper half, for a large descending staircase took up most of the central space.

B arrived; we fucked in my room. My anxiety turned, as to a lover, to another situation: that night B's rock 'n' roll band was going to give a performance in this hotel. All of us students were going to play in his piece.

Chairs, especially armchairs, filled the concert hall. Since I was late, I got the last seat, an aged pink armchair. The girl who was sitting opposite me didn't have a face. Then I didn't know what I was going to do because I don't know how to play an instrument or how to do anything.

I'm going to sing.

Beatrice must have become frightened by my dreams because she ran out of my room.

She no longer knew where she was.

Instead of leaving the school as the first student had done, she penetrated the areas she had never before been.

Outside the school, both the sky and the buildings were blue, even though it was night.

Beatrice ran into the blue room where she had never been before. The room was empty. She locked its door. She must have thought that she was safe, far from the outside and nestled in the inside.

When the doorknob started moving, she realized that she wasn't. The doorknob turned a few more times and the tip of a knife blade showed in the crack.

As the murderer came through the door, Beatrice broke through a window high up in the wall. She thought that she was escaping the danger that was inside, but she was only moving more inside.

She fell into a room that had no bottom, only interstices: rounds and curls of wires like razors. Monster Slinkies. The Slinkies tossed her body up and down, and when they had totally caught her, the knife that was the extension of the murderer pierced her flesh. The flesh around the entry line became a cunt.

Beatrice is the name of the woman whom Dante desired, who changed the poet's life, and whom he never fucked.*

NO DREAMS

In my dreams, the cunt was triangular: Father, Son, and Holy Ghost. All I knew were my dreams. I could no longer reach them.

The next morning when I asked some maid where Beatrice was, she replied that my friend had disappeared.

What did that mean?

* See "Beatrice's Story," p. 88.

"Disappeared. Beatrice is no longer here."

Nobody in the school, including the maid, knew what had happened to her.

Perhaps, said the French teacher, Beatrice has run away with her boyfriend.

I remembered that there was some boyfriend: two or three times, Beatrice had mentioned a name. I had no idea who he was or if he was real.

I tried to remember specifically what she had said about him. The only thing I could remember or that she had said concerned a job. He was a psychiatric consultant. I must have remembered that rather than made it up, for I didn't know what a psychiatric consultant was. Then I remembered the abbreviation *UN*.

In the phone book I found the local office and dialed. I blabbed something about being a writer for a woman's magazine, I think I said *Manner Vogue*. The man whom they gave me to talk to admitted that he knew Beatrice.

He said that he recognized her name.

I asked him if we could meet later that day.

Gallehault, a tall, dark, respectable man, told me that he had no idea where Beatrice was. We both agreed that this was unusual.

When the psychiatrist realized that the matter was serious, he started to reveal details about my friend that had been unknown to me.

She had come to him for help for certain psychological problems. Her father had suicided. Afterwards, she had, as she put it, entered a black hole. She recognized what had happened to her only when she began to climb out of that hole, ascend rocky ridges that seemed vertical.

Her descent, however, hadn't been caused by her father's suicide, Gallehault further explained, but by a masochism or desire to be nothing, black. Herein lay the greatest pleasure.

73

This desire could be a form of anger, anger so terrific it had been forced to turn on itself.

Anger against parents.

I said that I understood.

Precisely, her breakdown had occurred not because she desired to be nothing but when that desire had been repressed.

Gallehault had fallen in love with her. He quoted the poet, "Love that releases none, if loved, from love . . . led us toward a single death." During their meetings, he had begun to understand that phenomena or orders that seem to be psychological dysfunctions, even disorders, such as masochism, though on the surface obviously caused by childhood and other social disorders, actually arise from other sources. (Sorcerers.)

"From where?"

"Freud himself discussed this when he wrote, and I paraphrase, 'We suspect that instincts other than those of self-preservation operate in the ego. Sexual love'—displaced parental love—'presents us with a similar polarity—that between love and hate. We recognize the presence of a sadistic component in the sexual instinct. Isn't it possible to believe that this sadism is a death instinct that has been forced to move from the ego to the (always sexual) object?' "

Rather than for psychological, Gallehault, in love, began searching for . . . he didn't know what word to use here . . . not quite social or political . . . causes:

"I can only explain historically. By using history.

"You understand that this society is sick.

"In the year 1321, Philippe de Valois, Count of Anjou (and later King of France under the name of Philip VI), sent a letter to the current Pope, John XXII, in which he stated that on Friday after the Feast of Saint John the Baptist, the sun had appeared inflamed, as red as blood, and that during that night, the moon had been covered in spots, otherwise as black as sackcloth. Forty-five-mile-an-hour winds had raced through the land.

74

The next day, knowing that the world was about to end, the people had attacked the Jews because of their heinous and evil deeds against the Christians.

"As some Christians were searching the house of a certain Jew, Bananias, in a casket in a secret room they found a ram skin on which Hebrew characters had been inscribed. Its gold seal showed a gigantic Jew standing on a ladder and shitting on Jesus' face.

"This ram skin was a letter, the future French king continued, addressed to Amicedich, king of thirty-one kingdoms (all Jewish ones), to Zabin, Sultan of Azor, to his Magnificence Jodab of Abdon, and to Semeron, etc., etc. The gist of the letter was as follows:

" 'Know ye that we the Jews have bribed the lepers to poison, avec reptile blood and certain herbs, water so that all Christians will die. The lepers, weak or devoid of Jewish blood, have told the Christians about our plan. Know ye that we rejoice over the subsequent poisoning of the Christians and massacre of the lepers by the remaining Christians. Now it is time for all Jews, with the help of the Muslims, to take control of the French throne.'

"Pope John XXII's response to this Hebrew letter was to send the Christians out on Crusade. As for the Jews, he didn't exterminate them, because Jews are rich, but took their monies.

"Philip V himself received 150,000 livres tournois from the Jews and then burned a few. Jews.

"Two years later, the new king, Charles IV, threw all the Jews who were still in France out.

"More history:

"From 1435 to 1437, the German Dominican Johannes Nider worked on his *Formicarius*. He had collected the evidence for his tome with the help of the Castelan of Blankenburg in the Bernese Simmenthal, Judge Peter van Greyerz, and the Dominican Inquisitor of Evian and reformer of the convent of Lyons, both of whom had presided over witch trials.

"Nider stated that witches are women who cook, then eat, children, including their own, summon demons, shit on the Holy Cross as often as they can, and make potions or lotions out of the cooked children.

"Evidence of witches: in 1466, according to Alexander V's Bull, two Jewish men and two Jewish females placed a young girl on a heap of burning straw in a barred room in Chambéry in the presence of a monster and two toads.

"This historical development, from lepers to Jews to witches, is clear. It is the history, our history, of prejudice, sexism, and racism."

"Do you know more about witches?" I went to an all-girls' university.

"According to the Dominican Friar Ruggero da Casale, Inquisitor of Upper Lombardy, in 1384, Sibillia, wife of Lombardo de Fraguliati, and Pierina, wife of Pietro de Bripio, though the two women did not know each other, confessed to similar, if not the same, events.

"They told this story:

"Once a week, on a Thursday, they attended a school run by someone named Oriente. Oriente, the headmistress, was always treated with reverence: upon entering the school, every student curtsied and said, 'Be well, Madona Horiente.'

"Oriente gravely replied, *'Bene veniatis, filie mee.'*

"The school was a commune or an institution of learning for animals. Every type of animal that had climbed onto Noah's Ark, except for asses because they had stupidly borne Jesus' cross, went to this school. At times, hanged and decapitated humans also attended, but they were ashamed to raise their heads in the classrooms.

"The students learned to housekeep, cook, use herbs and spices, care for and cure the sick, locate stolen goods, and dissolve evil spells. They were given only one rule: never to mention the name of God the Father.

"Oriente herself could predict the future and restore life to dead beasts. But not to humans.

"It was a school for bestiality."

"They had a girls' school back then?" I inquired.

"I have not mentioned the school's underlying purpose. And of schools such as this one.

"The Greeks, and after them the Romans, called the moon Diana, goddess of menstrual blood. It was said that Diana travels at night, on the backs of beasts.

"Either through remembrance or more deeply, Oriente's teaching was connected to this Artemisian cult. The students periodically plunged into ecstasy and left their bodies in order to enter an invisible spirit or animal. They traveled on beasts.

"This journey is named *the journey through the land of the dead.*

"This," he concluded, "is why you must take care."

"Beatrice?"

"According to history, any school of all girls is a school of the dead.

"Remember that dream, that little death, demands, in order to exist, that mind leave the sleeping body.

"One more piece of historical, as opposed to psychological, evidence:

"In 1480, Contessia, having been condemned to the pillory, then to a three-year banishment for worship of the unnamed and multinamed 'mistress of the game,' during exile founded this school."

"Mine and Beatrice's?"

"In the beginning of the nineteenth century it was burned to the ground. You and Beatrice are living in the remnants, built up into a prominent dance university."

I still didn't know what had happened to Beatrice.

He promised to phone me if he learned anything.

None of this was true. I remembered *The Waste Land.*

77

A BAT AND I BECOME FRIENDS

I dreamt something about animals. A parrot and a monkey. A parrot and a monkey are in the kitchen; they're eating my food. Parrots love to eat hamburger. Soon all the tea is gone. "I'll make the tea," says the parrot.

All my friends had gone. I had to travel down a steel slide, down through a tunnel, in order to meet my friends at Grand Central Station as we had arranged.

We were discussing when we could meet at Grand Central. I was planning to return from the country around the eighteenth. But they were away from the twelfth through the sixth.

How could we meet? There was no way.

Though it wasn't possible for us to meet, Beatrice and I did, in her apartment.

In Beatrice's apartment, I was with the parrot. I asked the bird what kind of tea I should get at the grocery store.

Parrot replied that since I couldn't afford the . . . no name . . . unnameable one (mu), I should purchase damiana because damiana makes you sleep.

The next day at school, I felt as if I could no longer see.

During that day, no one heard from Beatrice.

When it was night again and I was alone in my bedroom, all the lights in the room suddenly went out. I was faced with a decision. I could either give up, try to hide my head, metaphorically, and let all the chaos that was threatening me, as if winds, do whatever it would. Which it probably does anyway. Or I could consciously enter the chaos and try to understand and be responsible for what was happening.

When I opened my eyes, my room was the color of my blood. Was I dreaming? The most beautiful things or phenomena I know are dreams. Recognition of the beauty of dreams made me decide that I wanted to comprehend what was happening, what was the relation between chaos and dream.

I opened the door to the outside. A bat that looked like my cunt hairs flew into my dark hair. Dark and smelly. Brushing my hands in front of my face, I ordered it to go away.

"No," said the rat.

"Go away, you fucking shitting skunk of a bumblebee. I don't know what you're doing in a girls' school."

The bat explained itself and we made friends. Then it announced that it was going to guide me through unknown regions. The shadows of night made my room resemble a dark wood.

"I need help," I admitted.

"Come," said the rat.

And so I came. In the hallway. Above my head I heard footsteps on the ceiling. "Those are the footsteps of the unknown," I told the rat.

"Only for the moment," said the bat.

My cunt hairs were itching, so I scratched them. "Where are you taking me?"

I found myself alone in a room in which I didn't want to be. My best friend, who had long, straight brown hair, was so dumb she had no brains. I had to get out of here.

I looked down at the bed on which she was sitting: messed-up white sheets; two large, wet stains, as if a man and a woman had both just orgasmed, but here there were no men. I suspected that I had made one of those stains.

Oh, dear.

There were cards all over the place, piles of, like Tarot cards when you place them in stacks to tell fortunes, only the pictures on the tops of the top cards were of unknown and commonplace objects.

I gathered up the cards and put them back into their case.

I thought, I have to get the fuck out of here.

I realized that I had murdered someone.

79

I knew that as long as I didn't confess to murder, no one would know. There was incredible and increasing pressure on me to confess, so I had to learn to dismiss my own thoughts and emotions so I could stay alive. If I was strong enough to do this, no one would ever catch me.

Though now a fish, I had not yet arrived at the source of dreams.

The bat was gone.

ABOUT CHINESE WOMEN

I walked up my first flight of stairs.

Like Beatrice, I had never visited this floor before.

There was a pantry. Inside this pantry were long, red halls. A fat Asian woman who was a maid was sitting on a wooden chair in front of the entrance.

It must have been her child whom the blind man's dog had bitten.

She was holding a huge, iron meat cleaver.

This was the realm of Chinese women.

In China, when a woman doesn't believe in God, she, like everyone else, validates her existence by believing in man. It all amounts to the same. The only way that she can escape this kind of structure (this society, this community, this language) is to make her own. But then she'd be outside society, or nonexistent.

I walked into the long, red halls. Here lots of maids were holding meat cleavers. Since they were all Chinese, I couldn't communicate with any of them.

There were times when I thought, I shouldn't be here.

I write in the dizziness that seizes that which is fed up with language and attempts to escape through it: the abyss named *fiction*. For I can only be concerned with the imaginary when I discuss reality or women.

80

The Chinese maids, as fat as pigs, regarded me the way one gazes at an object that is so other it can't be human.

I realized I was on the edge of existence.

Since I was no longer part of society, everything around me is malevolent to me. In this world, I'm only an object.

The kitchen that was within the red halls was a series of spotlessly clean plastic cabinets, gleaming tiles, and aluminum cookware and faucets. I couldn't see any food or food stains.

Having returned to the hallway outside the kitchen premises, I heard sounds of a storm nearing: tremendous gushes, an unexpected howl.

I ran from the oncoming tempest into a room where nature and art were indistinguishable from each other.

THE WORDS

Its walls were painted with nature.

Water lilies that were a white that was a real color floated on light gray and violet liquid whose center was a pond. Sometimes floated through weeds that curved upward until they were snakeheads. Until they were snakes.

I was the only human here.

Curtains of velvet as thick as whaleskins covered the windows or representations of skies. Stars peeped out of their folds of flesh.

Here was the Italian Renaissance as I had seen it depicted in paintings.

Leaves sat on drop-leaf tables and chair legs sprouted branches. Every tapestry was a curtain and every wall a door.

I had returned.

All the tapestries were, or presented, only mazes; there were two paintings; these paintings showed me my dreams.

The first painting was Chinese.

Dark, grassy hills and rocks of equal size descend, tumbling to a bottom that either can't be seen or doesn't exist.

81

When I'm with my boyfriend, who's Chinese, I turn into a bum like him.

The dark insides of a restaurant are constructed of four rooms, two directly above the other two. Like a chest of drawers sliced in half through its vertical. After the restaurant closes, my boyfriend and I make this our home for the night.

It became day. Sun flooded the wood floors of the restaurant, or dollhouse.

Though it was light, the guy and I were about to go to sleep, or to fuck. Then I saw a girl climbing out of the drawer-like loft that was the upper-left room. She was Chinese, and fat. Were she and my boyfriend lovers? Because the Chinese, being totally other than me, always fuck each other.

I didn't want to be with a guy (B) who slept around with other females, especially in front of my face.

I was no longer going to fuck with him here.

I lived somewhere, unlike him, and I asked him to come to my house on Friday.

B inquired if the Chinese girl could also come.

"No."

I decided that I would keep on fucking B, not in my house, but when I was homeless with him, because I have to be fucked.

This relationship would last as long as it lasted.

The second painting was contemporary American.

I'm wearing a pair of men's white briefs and my low-slung breasts are bouncing in the air, which looks cold, though I don't feel chilly. The beach on which I'm standing and the ocean in front of me are black. I can dimly see the beach.

I wanted to go swimming, but the ocean looked crowded with swimmers, black stick figures.

Then I saw that there were two lines of swimmers, streams of ants, from the beach to the deep, one line directly in front of me and one to my left. Since there were fewer swimmers in the line in front of me, I entered the ocean at that point.

Swimming is what I like to do best: the deeper the ocean, the greater my joy.

I decided to get out of the ocean and placed my motorcycle helmet on top of a black TV floating in the black water. Other helmets were sitting here. The TV might be a couch. As I was wading out of the ocean, the helmet might be a T-shirt.

As I walked away from the water, I thought, I shouldn't be bare-breasted (though I like not wearing clothes) and I should be cold (but I'm not), so I pulled a T-shirt over my chest. The T-shirt turned out to be white and sleeveless.

In order to cover up my skin, I then pulled at the T-shirt's bottom, which turned out to have a pink T-shirt hidden in it. Pink now covered my ass.

I was going back to school.

As I had had to walk away from the ocean, now I had to get out of the beauty of this room. In order to understand.

I began to look for a way out of the room other than the way I had entered, but it was as if I was in a maze.

There were two plaques above the two paintings:

The first said: IN A HAREM WOMEN DON'T EXIST.

The second read: IF FOLLY IS FEMALE, THE ESSENCE OF FEM-ININITY IS FOLLY. This plaque was signed *Erasmus*.

Away from the door through which I had come, and to the right, was a blue orchid. In the swampy regions of the cunt, Charon rowed and plied his boat as if the skiff was a finger reaching up. Nothing resembled these regions more than volcanic eruptions, and it takes a catastrophe or disaster to make a volcano erupt. In an abandon presaging only violence, I would finally be able to open up and enter the room of childhood. Now I understood how orgasms ravage the facial flesh—screwed into sobs, interrupted into fissures by howls.

I was looking, rather more desperately, for a way out of this incredible beauty so that I could get to the source of dream.

I remembered what I was looking for.

When the student opened the red door, she had said two words. I had known that the first word was *secret*. Secrete. Now I understood that the second was *pussy*.

Below the blue orchid were masses of black hairs.

When I pulled on these hairs, part of the wall opened. The space that was no longer wall was black.

I walked into blackness. Blackness may or may not have been outside.

CHILDHOOD

In that blackness there must have been a loss of consciousness.

I remember the night when I learned my mother had suicided, Christmas Eve, I didn't cry. For that night I rocked back and forth. I have no memory of the next month or two, except for the funeral. To experience my mother's death (which wasn't quite the experience of an other's death, but rather of my blood's death) was to experience that which couldn't be experienced. A loss of consciousness.

The blackness was a hall.

Toward the end of the hall I began to be able to see again. On the hall's walls was written the tale of Circe:

"When we entered the witch's abode, lions and bears and wolves ran out of her doorway toward me, Odysseus, and my men.

"The beasts, being friendly, licked both of my hands. I perceived that they wanted me to be one of them.

"Then, I entered the witch's room. She handed me a glass of red wine mixed with honey and certain drugs in order to render me slave to her will and desire.

"All of my men had already gulped down her wine and turned into swine, which is what they were. Since I knew she wanted to fatten us up for the kill, I refused to drink her.

"Afterward, when there were no more spells, we fell into love. For my marriage portion I asked that my pigs be changed back to humans.

"Also I said, 'You must dissolve this marriage whenever I want.'

"From then on, I was perfectly happy.

"Until I learned the foul bitch's sexual history.

"It was known that Circe crawled after every man she saw. Take the case of Picus, Saturn's son, who just happened to be beautiful and young. When he replied, 'I'm not interested,' she was so fucking angry, she carved away his cock and turned him into a bird.

"A woodpecker.

"Picus was so disgusted with being a woodpecker that he began pecking at himself and turned blood-red.

"Circe's cunt can summon up night, chaos, and death, which humans have named 'The Forces of Hell.' Blood stands like tears on the earth's flesh.

"As soon as I began to understand in what savagery, more wild than any ocean, she lies, I begged her to release me from our marriage just as she had promised.

"Her reply was 'Goodbye.

" 'Get the fuck out of here.

" 'As soon as you get the fuck out of here, sailor, you're going to enter the lands of death. There, you'll meet a blind man who can read the future. When his dog barks, don't fear.

" 'Everything that takes place in the room of death takes place by the grace of the Queen of Death.'

"When Circe turned silent, I cried because, above all, I didn't want to leave her.

"Every breath was a tear.

" 'So who's going to guide me into death, slut?'

"Slut said: 'No one. Only the dead can be dead.'

"Morning had come. I put on my clothes and left."

I was again in blackness.

I heard rather than saw.

"There's nothing else to do about it. We'll have to get rid of her."

I began to be able to see. On either side of the hall, doors half-opened to unexpected violence.

It was still dark, though no longer black. This lack seemed to be the same thing as sight. At the end of the hall, I saw three doors.

When I tried to crawl into the wood of the right-hand door that was shut, I heard my mother and adopted father whispering about me.

". . . don't know what to do about her."

"I don't know either, Claire." He always repeated what my mother said.

". . . [something bad]. She's evil."

I didn't have to hear my adopted father to know that he agreed.

"She should be institutionalized, or put away."

I didn't want to hear any more. The carpet beneath my feet was red.

When that door opened, I snuck behind it, as much as I could, into the still black wall, so I wouldn't be seen.

When I peered through the doorway crack, I saw Selby telling all the teachers, who were clustered around her, that they would have to kill me because I had been disruptive.

Now I saw everything clearly.

The teachers had cut up my friend Beatrice into little slices, especially her eyes, and these slivers were lying on the crimson carpet all around their high-heeled feet. The instructors had slaughtered her because they were witches.

Seeing my friend was the first time I ever saw a dead person. The flesh on the lower part of her face and all of her stomach had lines of neon green, orange, purple, and blue across the absolute white. All the flesh was puffed-up, swollen.

I ran back through the blackness the way I had come.

DON'T GET MAD, GET EVEN

It was at this moment that I decided I was going to devote my life to heavy metal. Just before I escaped into the room where art and nature were the same thing. Just as fake is the same as real.

The room looked as beautiful as before, but that no longer mattered. My grandmother's breasts were made out of china. This time I saw curtains at the end of the room of beauty.

Listen, I wanted to say to someone, we've come out of muck.

I wanted to attend the real Queen's Tea Party so I could smash everything.

The curtains were the soldier gray that's no color. I walked through the folds to a similar curtain. Curtains lay beyond curtains.

Janey's got a gun.

I heard breathing from what must be on the other side. And I know that there is no other side. My grandmother's breasts are made out of china.

Finally I walked through all the slush-colored curtains—there seemed to be no more blood here—into a slush-stained-by-piss-colored chamber.

The heavy breathing was growing louder. I asked the breathing to whom it belonged.

"You're the American girl and you're going to murder me." The voice sounded like my mother's mother.

Take me to the other side.

I tried to see Nana but I couldn't and she swung a huge knife at me, or a knife as big as a sword cut through the air in an attempt to cut through me.

I grabbed a knife which I saw on a lampstand and stabbed at the air. There was nothing else to stab. After I had thrust several times, I began to see an outline. I stabbed at that.

I must have been touching something because my grandmother turned into a mass of putrescent rot just like my mother had several days after she suicided.

But I don't need my mother's suicide to know putrescent rot when I see it. I have this society.

I stabbed. Because there was no more head, all of the teachers, who were above me, turned into putrescent rot.

Meanwhile I was running as fast as I could past all of the art and then all of the education rooms.

As I opened the red door that I had seen the girl open when I first came to this school, flames began to appear. And as I raced down the steps, and then the street, the school burned down.

"The place of lack or of desire is where the dream doesn't hold together."

(Beatrice's Story)

Beatrice spoke:

On the streets of the city in which I'm still living and don't want to escape, crack and other victims, often in packs, turn those who are other into victims. But the city is the only safety I know. Is familiarity safety? I have had nightmares and I hate them.

The more politically powerful Mayor ———— became, the more the city around him decayed.

* * *

When I said that I didn't like his photographs, my friend replied that his most famous picture was the one he had made of his girlfriend totally wrapped up in white bandages. Here only eyes and mouth remained unwrapped and had become black. I looked.

Many neighborhoods, lying next to and unrelated to each other, make up this city. The poorer each neighborhood, the more garbage, like shit, piles up in that neighborhood. The poorer the neighborhood, the less frequently garbage collectors, considered half-worker half-homeless, visit that neighborhood. Cops never visit those who are poor, unless they're dead.

In the city's late summer, when the concrete had been absorbing heat for months, cold air, coming from lost memories, sat on top of the heat and imprisoned it. The diseases had nowhere to run.

Influenced by the Nazi scientists whom the United States government had rescued at the end of World War II, the CIA in the 1960s had begun drug-testing in order to find a chemical that would induce total memory loss in those who had revealed political secrets under coercion and torture. Unfortunately, almost all chemicals that cause full memory loss also stop life. Some years after, a monkey escaped from one of the laboratories in a third-world nation and bit a civilian. The ensuing disease, which developed into the worst plague known in the twentieth century, spread from the third world, through what Mayor ———— and others considered the lower echelon of humans, blacks and homosexuals, to New York City, a conglomeration of third-world tribes in a first-world country. *Formerly* first-world country. The white New York society hated blacks (Puerto Ricans, Chicanos, Africans, American blacks, etc., without distinction) and homosexuals.

Mayor ———— was homosexual. He was terrified to give any

credence to rumors about the existence of the plague or to take any measures to halt its growth in the early days of its appearance, for he rightfully thought that if he admitted he was homosexual he would lose votes.

Father told me that the mayor hired female prostitutes for the purpose of kicking them down flights of stairs.

> Eyes, world-blind, in the fissure of dying: I come,
> callous growth in my heart.

The poet who wrote these lines was a Jew. Russians, then in 1941 German and Romanian forces, had occupied the town in which he had been born. The latter herded Jews into ghettos.

In 1942 they deported his parents to an internment camp. His father, there, died from typhus; his mother, murdered.

He escaped by traveling to Vienna. Then Paris. When he was forty-nine years old, by jumping into the Seine he killed himself.

Darker night.

HAVING LOST TRACK, THE GIRL PAUSES.

On the platform that he'd raise New York out of economic poverty, Mayor ——— won his first election. He fulfilled this promise by transforming the city's real estate. First he made a pact between the largest bank, the real estate moguls, and himself or the law. He or the law rezoned the poorer districts, areas formerly populated by small businesses and ethnic groups, so these two kinds had to leave. Then huge warehouse spaces turned into white artists' lofts; then rising rents forced out the few remaining Puerto Rican and black families. Where they went, no white cared. Simultaneously the bank, through white artists' organizations, was helping the artists gentrify their spaces. It was well known that Mayor ——— loved art. New York City was on its way to becoming the City of Art, not the City of

Refugees and Renegades. As soon as white artistic gentrification was established, the real estate moguls sold these spaces for fortunes. The white artists had to become more interested in profit than in art to hold on to the spaces they had gentrified and from which they had excluded the poor, not poverty. Never poverty.

Celan said: My flesh is named *night*. Than night as, if not more complex. Whether or not you touch me, my flesh'll feel desire to such an extent, it'll be named *desire*.

During Mayor ———'s first term, the white middle classes had believed that the mayor was assisting them by means of gentrification and artifying. Now soaring property prices were forcing these classes to become either rich or homeless. Vacation or vacate. Finally, though there never is *finally*, the rich and the homeless were the only groups, not classes, left in the city. In a way, history had proved Marx wrong. The leftover artists, by necessity rich, relied, nevertheless, totally on the controllers of money for patronage.

> Desire mirror steep wall. Down.
> —Celan

Steam heats the inhabitants and the city all through the dead winters. A trust fund had been established for the maintenance of the water pipes when they had first been built. In order to keep his early campaign promise, Mayor ——— used up all the trust fund monies. By the end of his third term, the pipes, fallopian tubes unfucked, unmaintained, wriggled, broke, burst open, upwards, rose up through all the materials above them. Sidewalks and streets, building floors and ceilings, air. Then spewed out, writhing and looking below them like asps about to attack, spat out asbestos over all beneath them. In the city, the snow turns to dog-piss in less than a day; since asbestos almost

91

never dies, the mayor had made the asbestos clean-up companies the most profitable in the city.

Two thirteen-year-olds, female, high on crack and low on johns, began patrolling Twelfth Street between Avenues A and First. Every time an old woman doddered up the pavement, they broke her fingers and grabbed her purse. Similar incidents commenced elsewhere. What were the poor to do where and when all the legitimate businesses were run by whites except have a drug business? Victims, not victimizers, become victimized; the nastier the tricks the poor learned to turn, the more the poor and the social exiles went under.

There are two kinds of men. The first, Mayor ————, when a young child, had watched his father abandon his mother. His mother then wanted him to be her husband. Now, the mayor wants to be daddy. As soon as he persuades a person he's daddy, he shits on him or her, then deserts the person. Mayor ———— does not really want to be daddy.

The father of the second kind of man had abandoned his wife just as the man was entering puberty. And this wife, unable to accept or recover from loss, tried to render her son unable to leave her. Now, the son loves to save people, especially women. As soon as a female accepts his offer to rescue her, he believes that she's putting a contract out on him and walks away. This man is an artist.

The mayor had overdeveloped his heart; the artist, his mind.

In order to keep continuing this story I'm walking into dream.

In just his first term, Mayor ———— had made New York into the City of Art. Though not for the sake of art. Then the common myth held by artists and others was that artists don't care about anyone or anything, which is why they make great art. Artists must be totally devoted to art.

The artist, who was my father, was considered one of the greatest, sometimes *the* greatest, of these artists.

Like many great men who compensate in one area for another, he was physically ugly, or deviant. Half of his face acted as a distorted mirror for the other. A knifelike slit ran diagonally through one eyebrow, then across the other cheek. Eyebrows and eyes more piercing than colored dominated the face. The rest resembled a Jackson Pollack painting.

These were now the first, the golden days of American culture, where and when girls grew up innocent. Even I, and I was born past those days of innocence, believed that a baby is made when a man and a woman, dancing together, and slowly, in formal attire, rub asses. Both my father's attitude toward sex and his sexual behavior were typical of artists at that time. Any girl (a woman who wasn't a girl wasn't worth existing) had to be fucked, over, because she was out to steal his money or his soul. If the chick managed to fight back successfully, the only possible indication of integrity, she might be worth respecting, though then she would probably be too damaged to fuck. Think of ———, and ———.

Since he was one of the greatest artists, he thought, and any female he had fucked or was fucking—it was all the same thing —must be out to fuck him, any female who entered his studio must be intending to steal a piece, unless she was rich enough to buy one or had been born almost brainless, which was all too possible. So as soon as Dad woke up to a cunt, he kicked her out of his house.

What had once been a city of renegades, of the poor who despised government, had turned into a city of artists. It was believed that an artist must be infinitely hungry and rapacious, physically and mentally, in order to be great. This artist will

93

spend almost all his sleeping and waking time thinking about his work: political issues will no longer matter; personal relationships will be regarded as aborted forms of prettiness or mannerism—above all, as hindrances to the pursuit of direct knowledge of the truth.

It was believed that for a great artist, and only for a great artist, sex is shit compared to pursuit of knowledge of the truth.

The only person, and female, whom Father cared about was me.

I adored Father because he adored me. Or: I adored him.

I think that children naturally love their parents and parents feel however they feel about their children.

A child loves, but how can a child obey a parent who has no honor? In this city of artists of rapacity, where rats scurry across planks though even the memories of pirates are dead, there's no honor.

I didn't have to be and I wasn't obedient to my father because I adored him so much I did whatever he wanted. My father was coming to the apex of his fame when I began to have my period. He told me that I was old enough to start providing for myself. Father said, A person makes himself through work. Even a woman. I couldn't conceive of fighting Father, though I knew that I didn't know how to do anything. Anything to make money.

Father became so immersed in painting that he forgot I was alive.

Out of the blue, Mayor ———, who was one of Father's patrons, said I could work for him. Not because he had need of anything I could do or because he wanted to have sex with me. Since he was in awe of Father because Father was an artist, he had to show that he, a politician, controlled my father.

Father, typical artist, despised politicians and flattered anyone who could buy his paintings. Not *despised*. Father wasn't *personally* concerned with the mayor's character because Father was

94

interested only in the pursuit of knowledge. Whereas the mayor was obsessed by power, especially by those he suspected might be more powerful than himself. But Father was arrogant. The more a patron helped him, the more he hated the son-of-a-bitch. Though Father was cold, his hatred or irritability could reach fever pitch. Then Father became paranoid. Paranoia turned anger even more ice-cold, ocean before a storm. What I'm saying is that Father was emotionless unless someone managed to penetrate through and touch him. I am going to tell you about the one time this happened.

Once penetrated, Father had to close up.

At this time, between the mayor and Father I didn't exist.

Father said, "For a moment consider that Freud's model of female sexuality, that a woman and her desire are defined by lack of a penis, is true. Then, in a society in which phenomenal relations are as men say they are, women must radically contest reality just in order to exist. According to Freud, a fetish for a woman is one means by which she can deny she's lacking a dick. A fetish is a disavowal."

The era of pirates had yielded to the era of artists and politicians. At the same time women began getting into more than fetishes.

Father was a great artist. The wife he took after my mother was an artist herself, sculptor and dancer, respected in her own right. After several years she decided she had to leave him, though not because he was continually fucking other women. She knew it would be impossible for her to leave him unless he first decided to leave her.

To accomplish this she fucked another man. Nameless, the pirates of yesteryear. Made certain that Father learned about this.

As soon as she had left our loft, he smashed most of her video equipment with a hatchet, then threw the rest out a window onto the street. She returned to the loft. He chased her down the building's back stairs, around the block, with the same hatchet.

Though sexuality moved strongly through him, Father wasn't interested in sex or in women, but in seeing. Paranoia, which occasionally appeared as sensitivity, enhanced his longing to see.

"An artist isn't and must not be a moralist. Within the realm of art, both the seer and his work occur outside of morality and social judgment."

Father loved to see women in the throes of sexual ecstasy so that he could draw them. "Whereas a man at the highest possibility of his development wants to see, a woman is infinitely sexually avaricious. She'll do anything, moving through physical and mental cons and disguises like a snake through his or her own coils—her tongue flickers, in order to get a man to sexually use her. To let her use him sexually. As they grow older, many European women, being among the most intelligent, learn to control appearances to such an extent that men don't see that the women aren't human."

I read a Japanese ghost tale. A man, because he was hot, married the Dragon King's daughter. They didn't have a single quarrel and never stopped fucking (being rich) until she informed him she was going to have his baby. She said, "You can't watch while I'm having this baby." He refused to do what she had told him to do. When he looked, he saw a snake whom he had believed was his lover, whose head had horns growing out of it, giving birth to a human baby. The female monster saw him looking at her and fled in shame.

(*Ghosts* equals *pirates*. The graves of sailors.)

("The dead woman fucked him again," Pedro Resaca muttered between his teeth.)

Father said, "Women don't smell human because they smell of cunt."

Father about sight: "If I could, I would replace all sight with all smell."

Due to his understanding of femaleness, Father desired me to have nothing to do with sexuality. He felt that he didn't even need to say this.

I felt that he was the Forbidder of all and kept me safe.

Father knew that whenever I left his precincts, sex surrounded me. It was dangerous for me to work, even for the mayor. (Father had forgotten this when he had become totally involved in painting.)

Though Mayor ———— was gay.

But because Mayor ———— was in awe of and looked down on my father and hated himself for this awe, he wanted, to fuck, me.

It was the era of democracy in which the state of art was the art of the state.

My fathers have taught me that if I let a man touch me, he'll touch me red.

Father, as soon as he emerged from painting and remembered, tried to stop me from entering the mayor's mansion. But the more he fought against his patron, the more the patron pulled at me. They hated each other. Mayor ———— commissioned my father, as the most well-respected artist of his time, to make a portrait of New York large enough to cover a wall of Gracie Mansion's main reception room.

Father was a businessman.

(The Dutch pirates had invaded, set up their world of shacks, of the outlaw city, of dens in which the body moved from disease to disease, of dens of iniquity of all sorts of vices or longings for the ways of the low, longings for deliriums. Where men cached their hushed pasts, hid their names and realms of names from the authorities. If not born into loneliness, hopefully about to slip into Newfoundland.)

Intended to start painting this by painting a street at night. A black street. But there you could see. The staircases and tenements like hands reaching. No out. A girl who is tipsy is beginning to walk down the street. Two teenage males, partly hidden by a piece of architecture's doorway, watch her. She looks up, sees one of them, shrugs her shoulders. It is the city of anarchy, not of anarchists. One of the boys behind her is reaching for her purse. He's a crack victim and she's not. When she turns around to hit him, his fist smashes the top of her head. Falls down. The male teenager is racing across an empty parking lot.

This is the era of artists and of businessmen.

Next to this section is a park. Blankets that are mainly holes sit on the black iron fence that encloses the concrete. The homeless live here. No civilization is the new civilization. A girl walks out of one of the gentrified tenements that surround the park and meets a homeless teenager. She takes him back home and they fuck. For several months he lives with her. During that time he cooks soup for the other homeless in the park. Then his girlfriend tells him that since she's going to move to another city, he'll have to leave within the week and be homeless again. He is boiling her cut-off head in a pot of liquid and vegetables so that he can feed the homeless in the park.

Father wasn't satisfied with these, not even sketches, because they weren't the horror of New York. He said, "I can't see anything until I'm it. Since in my normal life I'm too habituated to horror to see it, horror must occur outside my perceptual habits for me to see it:

"In order for me to paint horror, I have to see the horror in myself."

(Back, for those doomed to silence, unable to recount the fantasy that, though the only life, no one believes. Sensed, on the doorstep of preternatural senectitude—the senselessness of all adventure.)

Father taught me that the mind of thoughts is a snake in the whole of the self. It wants control: whenever it or he feels he can, he begins swelling, winding around himself until he's eating

98

himself. Therefore, if you allow this mind, or part of the mind, control, you can't paint. Father began painting New York by painting a portrait of the Brooklyn Bridge. The sounds of boats sailing under is brown like old menstrual blood sitting on cunt lips. A good number of Bedford-Stuyvesant inhabitants, skeletons in the distance, were walking across the bridge. They were going to join tribes of homeless and packs of crack victims for the purpose of breaking into the apartments of the rich and the homeowners (same as "the rich"). "Soon, New York City'll be in flames," Father said. "Most of the populations'll be smashed; the city'll be shredded."

Father said, "Prophecy is only opinion. If I want to paint New York, I have to paint horror. In order to paint horror, I have to see horror. Prophecy might come from sight: that's not my business as a painter. In order to see horror, I have to touch or fuck horror."

Father said, "It's necessary to know. For no reason at all. For art."

I'm innocent. Horror can't take away innocence. If a murderer murders me, it's not that I am no longer innocent; it's that I *and innocence* have died.

Father said, "A painting is simultaneously an object and mechanism. Paint, canvas, etc., compose the object. People can buy and sell the object. My purpose for my making, or the object's purpose, if objects can have purposes, is to make people see. In this case, since I've been commissioned to do a portrait of New York, see the horror in which they're living. See the horror that they cause and in which they reside. In terms of the process of sight, a painting is a mirror only if identity is, too."

Father said, "It might suffice, but I don't know for what, for a painting of horror to break down and through its viewers' perceptual habits so that they can see what their minds and hearts refuse to see and what is."

Father began again to paint by listing taboos. A taboo is

99

a rule or law whose breakage will cause a society's collapse. Father's two laws, or taboos, were the untouchability of vision and of me.

Father didn't want anyone to touch me, nor me to touch anyone.

Father said, "To paint horror, I must violate both vision and my own child."

In those days, Father thought that since a painting was partly an object, a painting was, or utilized, fiction. Father decided to make me the center of his portrait of New York. A crowd of males, including him, would stand around me. They'd set my cunt on fire.

The men surrounding me'd be either homeless or art patrons.

Father said, "I'm the only man who can take care of you." Perhaps *to take care of* meant *to paint*.

As soon as Father returned to painting, he forgot the world, about which he was usually only curious, and me. Except insofar as he made us fictive subjects.

The more my father abandoned me, the more I turned to the mayor. Who didn't want to fuck me, but wanted to control Father through me. So the mayor acted as if he wanted to fuck me.

His fictive desire made me want to run away, but I had nowhere to run. Not into emptiness.

Father said, "I see through the imagination."

Every day he tramped the streets of New York in search of material or specific desires. On Christmas Day, he penetrated the main cop morgue. No danger here. Corpses can't puke. The cops wanted to return home to their Christmas dinners. No other material or desires here except in the realm of death.

Father walked over to the St. Vincent's emergency ward where humans were dying rather than dead. A TB victim was sticking his tongue into the mouth of a former lover because he was still in love. Father wondered, Was it easier to be dead in a cop morgue or here? No material or desires here except in the realm of death.

Father said, "In order to see, I have to touch or be what I see. For this reason, seers are sailors. When seers become artists, they become pirates. This's about identity."

Father finally began painting his portrait of the city when, one night, between waking and sleeping, he saw my mother. She was sitting upright on top of his thighs. He looked up at her. Then she lifted her cunt over his cock and lay down on him. She moved herself up and down.

Father: "Are you telling me to come? Come where? Come to hell?"

When Father woke up, he drew pictures of my mother in orgasm. These formed the frame of his portrayal of New York.

I see through the imagination.

There's a point at which when I start to know a man well— this isn't true of women—I wonder whether there's something in him that's evil. Something that's pure and can't be touched. This quality of evil may be related to the quality of artistry, for an artist has the same characteristics.

The time when Father embarked on the second stage of his painting wasn't the dead of winter. But it was winter and there was more death around than usual. The era of art and business, or capitalism in its finality, is the era of anarchy. No one had the same language; the homeless couldn't communicate with the crack dealers. I began strolling among dying and dead bodies as if they were garbage.

The more businessman the artists became, the more common it was for artists to have assistants who made their art. ("Realized their ideas.") Father took an assistant.

Father said, "It's necessary to see (to know, to be) something in order to paint it. I've been commissioned to paint horror. Is horror torture? Can I paint horror by painting torture (or various forms of torture such as homelessness and crack dealing)?"

So, to see torture, Father strung his assistant up by his ankles. The assistant dangled by ropes from the ceiling of Father's art studio while Father's python played with his balls.

Father looked and looked at his assistant, whose face was red, and saw only his own curiosity.

He tightened the assistant's binds. When Father realized that he could go on tightening them due to rapidly increasing curiosity, he desisted.

Father said to his assistant, "You're in pain, so you know you're in pain. Whereas I'm not in pain, so I perceive neither pain nor happiness. How'm I going to see the pain and horror that I'm making you feel?"

Father decided that the answer to his question was more violence.

One day while I was masturbating, though I didn't yet know what I was doing, I heard screams. I saw the assistant, now right side up, bound as tightly as possible in chains, an unknown snake around his neck and about to bite. The assistant, though not in pain, was totally scared. Daddy, so entranced in his vision he had stopped drawing. When Daddy grabbed the snake's head between bite and about-to-bite in midair, I knew that he was incapable of hurting anyone.

And I loved him even more.

Father was growing more irritable and noncommunicative because he couldn't find the next step in his painting. Skulls and owls, death and life, inhabited one corner of his studio. Turned away from humans to animals. He would stare at the owls for days, at their curved beaks and claws. It was as if he were staring at impenetrability. At the limits.

A sailor on the ocean.

(Pirates knew that animals, kin to them, were also their natural enemies. As if civil war. Even if you hack animals to ribbons, pirates understood, if your sword hashes their flesh and rips their insides apart, in no time they recover their animal image and life. Not even if you thwack off an animal's head with one blow can you make, pirates said, the demons disappear, since animals not only possess the fabulous magic ability to know what others, including humans, feel, therefore think, but also are immortal and as all-powerful as the gods of their forebears.)

In a piece of literature, in accordance with her will and desire, a man takes off a woman's clothes. To make her more naked, he places a headdress of owl feathers, gray and black, over all of her head but her eyes and mouth. Trail down her back. Then he leads her out into the public.

Father said, "My problem's that I'm not listening to myself, my intuition. I must see horror. I said that to see must be to touch or become what is seen. But like most Americans, I keep pretending that horror is taking place outside America's shores."

Father said to me, "I love only to paint and you. To paint horror, I must violate both. In the center of my portrait, I'll paint the most horrible act possible being done to a fictive version of you. A fictive version of me will be part of the crowd around you, watcher and perpetrator. Vision, both in reference to the painter and to the viewer, will occur only for the purpose of murder."

What Father didn't say, but Father knew and he wanted to escape this, was that in order to paint a young girl's torture, he had to see it.

Like thoughts or a snake, coils tightened; Father became more unable to paint.

The deepest impotence of all made Father neglect, then avoid, me. I was used to what seemed to me egomania since he had entered into painting. This was something new. My hurt grew beyond my understanding. Into an appearance of irrationality, named *loneliness*. I didn't like it when bad things grew in me.

I knew that my boss didn't want me because he was gay and

wanted me only in order to touch my father. The more he showed he wanted, the more I had to show, and did show, that I didn't want him. The more he began to want to hurt me.

(In their darkest hours, pirates rumbled love songs:

> When the flesh shrivels,
> you're dying.
> When the flesh is shriveled,
> you're dead.
> When the flesh is red,
> love occurs.
> If I'm lying
> when I say "I love you,"
> the winds will kill my words.
> What disillusion:
> the winds are killing these words.)

About civilized poverty:

Someone with the stupid name of Iyemon, who's come down in this world, is forced by evil circumstances and an evil world to support his innocent wife and even more innocent child by constructing umbrellas in an umbrella factory. His brain deteriorates. He can't help it, but he resents his wife and child, who are forcing him to do mindless manual labor.

Next door to him lives a beautiful girl whose family has real money. To Iyemon she's everything that his wife isn't. And as soon as he fucks her, she can't live without him.

The beautiful girl and her family convince Iyemon to poison his wife. But Iyemon poisons his wife badly. Only her face mutilates and one of her eyes drops out red.

As is usual with women who are dependent on men, Iyemon's wife doesn't have any friends. Finally her hairdresser, to whom she's turned for friendship, reveals the truth to her: he shows her her face in a mirror. Hairdressers are very fond of women. The wife, who's been thinking she's going to see a new hairdo, a new person, looks at herself and screams. Oh. For some reason, she is a cross between the Phantom of the Opera and Miss America. Even though one of her eyes is no longer seeing because it's dropped out.

She realizes that it's her husband, a man, who's done this to her. Made her into Miss America.

"I understand what's going on in this world. I'll cut off his dick and mince it into red pieces. I'll give it—them—to the bums to eat so they won't go hungry."

The wife's become so angry that she's forgotten everything else. That she's one of the most mutilated people in the world.

When love dies, there's nothing and this world is only horror.

Perhaps love has not died. Perhaps there's never been human love.

Perhaps all that humans have ever meant by *love* is *control*. Iyemon believes above all that he is a man who doesn't hurt other human beings. So when he learns that his business partner knows about the poisoning, he murders the partner, whose name is Jesus.

Then Iyemon took Jesus' and his wife's bodies (his wife had finally died from the poison) and nailed them to the opposite sides of a door, which he discarded with the garbage in the East River.

Finally, Iyemon believed he had mended his ways and was ready for marriage. He loved the rich girl, Beauty, and she loved him, and this was the only happiness in life. Under the law and religion, they mutually pledged themselves to each other and, as he was lifting up her veil to seal her, he saw that he was really pledging himself to his mutilated wife. He saw an eyeball dangling red from its socket. She hates me, he thought. I don't hate women. I'm just the opposite. I guess I'll have to explain to her again why she's acting the way she is. I always get involved with these neurotic Jewish women. Instead of kissing her, he put his hands around her neck and strangled her. Then he saw he had murdered his bride instead of a dead woman. So he ran out of the hotel.

Just as he was running away, Beauty's grandfather tried to stop him. Iyemon thought that the old man was Jesus and killed him.

Iyemon started seeing his first dead wife's visage everywhere, just like some women keep seeing the face of the man they love. Love's obsession. He especially saw his dead wife's face, with the red eyeball hanging from a red thread of mucus, just as if human bodies in this world don't rot when they're dead, in streetlamps. When the lamps were bright, late at night, sometimes the rotten but not rotting face was on fire. At those times, holes emerged in its flesh. Simultaneously, water pipes burst through the streets' concrete. Through these holes. Through holes in the flesh, the faces of the dead stare at the living. Iyemon's mother said, "He murdered tons of people, and for that he can never atone." Then the beautiful mother stuck two fingers into her mouth and, instead of vomiting, stretched her mouth, as if it were rubber, out so far there was only emptiness.

The dead're screaming, "Through human guilt, we can see the living."

Iyemon screeches. But there's no help in this world except from the self, and all of us die.

What is it to see?

"Now I can see," said the young girl. Iyemon screeched and screeched. He ran into the river in which he had dropped the door. In the narrow streets that ran along this river, cats were eating dead fish. The cats were dying. Iyemon decided to go fishing. He threw a string into the liquid for something. His patience was rewarded. He pulled his-first-wife-and-his-business-partner-nailed-to-the-door out of the river.

106

If we forget history, public and private, we're lost.

In order to escape all his actions or the consequences of his actions, which were the same, Iyemon ran to the tip of Manhattan Island, where no humans could live. Here was the other side of nature, which the island's inhabitants think is nature.

A rat was eating a cockroach.

Iyemon decided this was his home. Iyemon decided that he had finally escaped from humans and all their ignorance and horror. Since there were to be no more humans, there would be neither love nor murder.

There was only part of an apartment building.

Perhaps there is an escape from horror through love, but there is no love.

As soon as Iyemon thought, I'm safe, his first wife's brother killed him.

Finally Father informed the mayor that in order to paint what he had been commissioned to paint, he had to have an innocent girl.

Mayor ———— said, "Girls come cheap."

Father said, "Not for my purposes."

When Mayor ———— asked Father what his purpose might be, Father replied that he wanted a crowd of men to set fire to a young girl. Including the mayor. That is, he wanted to see a crowd of men set fire to a young girl. Seeing isn't the same act as doing.

Mayor ———— asked, "Why don't you visit one of our prisons? Or walk into one of those slum apartments Puerto Ricans inhabit?"

(In the era in which men searched for and lived according to absolutes and women didn't exist—only their sexual organs— the pirates were renegades. When businessmen and artists came into power, in accordance with the necessities of late capitalism, men's desires for absolutes stopped. Became nostalgia and romance. The history of the century can be seen as defined by the struggle between a model of, or desire for, an absolute reality and a model, or recognition, of reality as indeterminate.)

Father said, "No. Normal life in this city isn't horrible enough for my purposes, because every New Yorker is so habituated to what's taking place in the streets, in the jails, in the burnt-out areas, that he or she no longer recognizes horror as horror."

Mayor ———— asked, "Why're you so concerned with horror?"

Father answered that he hated violence. He was both a liberal and a humanist, even though today both these concepts are treated with disdain. Because he was as he was, he saw that life in New York is violent and that violence is unacceptable. Father said, "Political violence, above all, isn't rational. When I portray violence, and this concerns how I portray violence, I want it to be clear as hell that violence is not understandable."

Father continued, "I'll give you an example of what sits outside our capacity to understand. About a year ago I saw a large apartment building flaming. The cars around the building exploding. In the imagination, there were charred human bodies inside the walls. Since I was living half a block away, I should have been scared. Instead I felt unlimited gratitude for being able to see so tremendous a sight."

Mayor ———— asked, "Does horror come from Nature?"

Father said, "The point is that when I saw those flames and thought that people were dying, I felt joy. Not horror. The horror has to do with me. In order to paint horror as horror actually is, or a portrait of New York, I need to show myself doing what's most horrible for me to do."

The mayor said, "Shit."

Father said, "I have to paint myself killing my own daughter."

The mayor said, "More horrible things're taking place in this city."

Father said, "The point is that if, as if I were writing a

108

magazine article for a targeted audience, I painted what I thought was horrible to other people, I would be putting a distance, ironical, between myself and horror, and then the horror in and of my painting wouldn't be so horrible. This is why I paint for myself, not for other people. To paint horror, I have to eradicate all distance between horror and me: I have to see/show my own horror, that I'm horrible."

The mayor said, "Do what you have to do. I want the painting."

Father reiterated, "To paint my daughter's murder, I have to see it. Since painting's partly fictional, I only need to see a young girl being murdered in order to see my daughter being murdered." Father asked, "Could you have a young girl killed? In the manner I've described?"

(The pirates knew, if not all of them consciously, that the civilizations and cultures that they were invading economically depended on the enslavement of other civilizations and cultures. Pirates took prisoners, didn't make slaves.)

Mayor ———— decided that the safest procedure would be to take a dead girl out of one of the city morgues. The girl or the dead person would be set on fire in a part of the city where there were only dead buildings. Almost no buildings. For the mayor wanted this painting, but he also had to preserve real estate values.

(On dreams and actions in pirates: Their rotten souls burn in their bowels. They only go for pleasure. For them alone, you see, naked bodies dance. Unseizable, soft, ethereal, shadowy: the gush of cunts in action. Running free. With a thousand silken fingers, the hands caress the pirates' cocks, maddened by sharp fingernails, red clouds, hurt then cradle, in the darkness of the holds. Sing lullabies mixed with passions' irrational moans, sing of the nipples' erect buds.)

Father said, "Also, I need to see a crowd of men standing around the girl. While she burns up, they do nothing to stop her from burning."

Mayor ———— said, "The fucking homeless're everywhere." The girl or the dead person would be sitting in an oversized black limo so that the homeless couldn't touch her. The politician added, "Men're easy to get."

Father said, "If men are easy to get, why's a good man so hard to find?"

STORYTELLING METHOD: THE ACT OF BODYBUILDING PRESUPPOSES THE ACT OF MOVING TOWARD THE BODY OR THAT WHICH IS SO MATERIAL THAT IT BECOMES IMMATERIAL.

This is a history of New York City.

The more my father turned to, into, his painting, away from me, the more I wondered whether he was evil. I wasn't dumb. By *dumb,* I mean *ignorant.* I knew that although my father thought he was a cowboy, his strength came only from his desire to see. It was this same power, resembling and perhaps kin to will, that made him turn so away from human morality that he no longer knew what that was. I was his sole link to ordinary emotion; in his painting he was finally choosing to turn away from me. That which exalted my father was destroying him.

Sexual desire was a simple hunger, and easily satisfied.

Unlike Father, Mayor ———— wanted to be powerful for no reason other than power and, like Father, thought he was. As is the case with most politicians, he confused appearance with reality, money with reality. This confusion was hollowing him.

* * *

110

I hadn't yet realized that no one can ever know another person.

Then I decided that I wasn't going to do anything or say anything unless I meant it. I hated the city during day and loved it most when night was deepest. When, since humans no longer appeared as they thought they should because this lack of light allowed anonymity, all who were still living played.

They put blindfolds around my eyes and wrapped what felt like bandages, only thicker, around the rest of me.

Now every neighborhood was black.

As previously discussed, a section of the city about which no one cared had been chosen. No one cared what happened. Cops never visit disaster and we're all cops. Future disaster.

Most of the section was a parking lot. At the peripheries, apartment and canine parts lay silent. The color of the lead air varied from gray to a gray that resembled black and overlay whatever constituted ground, as if the ground were an ocean if an ocean could rot.

The section had been written off before it had been born, as such sections're born.

There weren't many buildings anyway. In this section of rats and dead fisherman. Three inches above the wet, winds crawled on knees that no longer existed, like the whores they were imitating. Pirating.

No one lived here, for the poor live nowhere.

There were condoms, needles, small fires.

Do humans rot in the same ways animals rot?

(The pirates loved women who were sexual and dangerous. We live by the images of those we decide are heroes and gods. As the empire, whatever empire, had decayed, the manner of life irrevocably became exile. The prostitutes drove mad the pirates, caught, like insects in webs, in their own thwarted ambitions and longings for somewhere else. In the time of pirates, the prostitutes radiated with the knowing patrimony of priestesses whose religions are culturally valued. The pirates worshiped the whores in abandoned submission.)

They put me in a car. I didn't know why this was being done to me. Bound up, I could feel the plastic under my thighs. I didn't know where I was being taken, but since I was bound, I wasn't scared.

On the New York City streets, children play with used needles. Therefore, it's the dead who determine how the living act. Mother had taught me to avoid allowing a man to touch me correctly because, as soon as one man would begin to touch me correctly, I would begin to need.

Now I was being taken somewhere and I didn't know if it was against my will.

Father had said, "I see when imagination joins material."

METHOD: A MUSCLE'S BUILT WHEN AND ONLY WHEN ITS EXISTING FORM IS SLOWLY AND RADICALLY DE-STROYED. IT CAN BE BROKEN DOWN BY SLOWLY FORCING IT TO ACCOMPLISH MORE THAN IT'S ABLE. THEN, IF AND ONLY IF THE MUSCLE IS PROPERLY FED WITH NUTRIENTS AND SLEEP, IT'LL GROW BACK MORE BEAUTIFUL THAN BEFORE.

The blindfold was taken off my eyes. At first, I saw grayness, or I was hardly able to see. Then I started seeing light.

Differences in qualities of light became forms. I didn't see emptiness; I saw desertion. I saw no neon lights.

Then I saw, through the car window, black wire fencing.

Here was the beginning of the world.

112

The quality of its light defines New York City as the beginning of the world.

I didn't know if Father knew this.

In my heart and outside, the light was turning pale gray. I sat still, bound by thick bandages to the inside sides of the car. The only parts of me available for use were eyes and, partially, head.

Heard: "Going to set on fire."

On each side of me, forms. On each side of me, men who looked like the homeless who warm their hands over the fires in garbage cans.

Lit up Mayor ————'s face.

When seven years old, as had been told to do, perched on the laps of Father's patrons and asked them to buy his art.

A match fell, in an arc, through the beginning of the morning. Couldn't see around it. The flame disappeared.

Face appeared in, though it was probably against, the car window on my left. Face like Silly Putty, ridged. Must be homeless. I didn't want the face. Asked me for a match. No mouth. Went away.

As saw a second flame, heard, "A young slut who became diseased from doing that which was natural to her and unnatural to everyone else and who died from her disease is sitting in that limo." Mayor's voice: "I tied and bound the dead body for your appreciation." Was this to my father? "Throw the next match into the car."

Father (?) said, "Want to see this."

"If the car doesn't go up, throw gas over its cushions and try again."

"So there'll be enough light for me to draw."

Another voice. "Rip a hole in her. Her mouth. The three of us in her at once. Rip. Rip. Rip."

Voice. "But then since our dicks'd be touching, we'd be fags."

Mayor ————. "Now throw that match into the limo."

113

After hearing these voices, I asked myself what it could be that made me want to live.

Something physical. Something to do with the physical.

Somehow I knew that my father was looking, but still didn't know who I was.

Thought, Things must happen for a reason. I can't be sitting in this car solely for the stupid pleasure of stupid old men.

Mayor ———— said to my father, "If you're going to draw this, you'll need to see every detail of her face and body. Before and as she's burning up. Walk up to that limo right now."

Walked up to the limo. My father didn't see anything.

Though gagged, I said, "Set me free."

When Mayor ———— lit another match, my father saw me. A bum set fire to a pile of rubbish and dead dogs.

In the light, I saw my father looking at me. Father seeing every detail of my face as if he owned it, me, without wanting to possess it, me. Has every victim chosen victimization? Then I knew that I had, also, put myself in this limo for my father and that he was looking at me.

That which is beautiful is muscular, not diseased.

I could no longer run away. When my father recognized me, he didn't try to free me.

TOWARD A LITERATURE OF THE BODY.

The homeless gathered to watch the only spectacle in their part of town. At this time. One member stuck his head through the hole in the car where the window was almost down. He asked me whether when I grow up there'll be men whom I want to marry.

I couldn't answer.

The beggar asked, "Maybe you like women better?" Bums're sentimental. A flame's igniting of the cushion on which I was sitting stopped the sentiment.

I was scared. I cried and cried and cried and cried.

A small part of the fire ate the bandage on my right side. One of my arms and mouth were freed. I used the hand to gesture to the men around me. "My father's responsible for this."

"Yeah," a bum said as if at a football rally.

I said, "I'm not a criminal. I only look bad now. I'm good and I love my father."

Mayor ———— cut me off. "This girl's a hardened criminal and we're taking her back to where she belongs."

A bag lady asked, "What dirty words did your father use to turn you into a hardened criminal?"

"No," I protested. "Love doesn't work that way." The flames were beginning to rise.

"Did he ask you to do things that are sexually unacceptable?"

I said "Yes" so that the homeless would throw themselves like rats upon Mayor ———— and my father. I managed to free myself from the remaining bandages. The smoke obscured my exit.

Exit means *rose*.

During the following days, a public controversy ensued. One side wanted to give my father the death sentence for what he had done. The other side argued that, despite his and Mayor ————'s actions, his painting of New York City, the centerpiece of which was a portrait of his daughter in flames, was one of the masterpieces of art in the twentieth century, that century in which totalitarianism vied with humanism. Mayor ———— continued to hold the second view.

My father killed himself.

(Piracy seemed like an adventure dreamed in a night of passion, an illusion lasting exactly the time it took for a blind man to rub his only eye, an impossible sexual desire crumbling like a pillar of sand, blowing like winds. Legal punishments ranging from a simple fine to the more fearsome—torture, loss of property and of personal liberty—gradually succeeded in quenching even the pirates' illicit ghosts.)

My mother spoke:

From now on, whenever I dreamed, I called it *going back to the witch*.

I was now more alone than I had been before returning to school. In or due to this loneliness, B was more me than me. Since I could no longer see anything in this state, I decided that I had to destroy my obsession. Obsession. The only way to do this, destroy my deepest being, it seemed, would be to become a man.

The name of that man is Heathcliff:

FOUR

OBSESSION

MY FATHER

Cathy says,

For finally my father was coming back. As soon as the night turned as black as the cunts of witches, he walked through our door.

Once he had settled down inside, with his pint and slippers, the cat nodding drowsily against his shoulder, he told me that he hadn't brought back what he had promised me: my own whip. Instead he had come back with a nonwhite brat, outcast, orphan.

This devil's child, who was nameless, was a pale, skinny male. His hairs were blacker than a witch's vagina. When I smelled him, there was the reek of sheepdog that had never been taught anything.

I spent the night, sleepless, weeping into my pillow, and so did he.

I wasn't a good child. Or, the same thing, they (the males in

117

my family) told me that I wasn't a good child. I didn't know how to react to this identity, this reification, other than by throwing my badness, which my shyness always wants to keep hidden, into their faces.

But openly I loved the night. Whenever it was black, outside, I talked to those animals who sat around me and I knew they had languages and I began to learn their languages.

Then Father tried to make the gypsy brat into something less than outcast by giving him the name of a child who had already died. Day after day I watched the brat. Unlike me he wasn't bad because he was being told that he was bad; nameless, from as deep as his self, or sea, went, all he wanted to do was spit at the world. The human world that seemed nonhuman. I admired his ability; it didn't matter to him, as nothing mattered to him, that I did.

Even though he was only six years old, he would have stolen everything from this father's house, but there was nowhere to go with it.

Though I never spoke to him openly, I would have done the same thing.

My father loved his false son. Hindley, my father's real son, hated the new Heathcliff.

My father knew that I saw that all that I couldn't and wanted to do, Heathcliff did. "Why can't you be a good child, Cathy?"

"Why can't you be a good father, Father?"

OUTSIDE THE FAMILY

Soon after these questions had taken place, Cathy's father died. He would never return.

Both Heathcliff and Cathy grieved. Hindley didn't give a shit because his father had hated him.

Heathcliff and Cathy sobbed out each other's eyes, then ate each other's tongues.

Hindley (Hideous) inHerited the House, so Cathy and Heathcliff moved out into tracks beyond, and for them the human world went away. Their only adulthood, before begun, was gone. The world gone, there was only nature.

The days of grief, the days without shelter, announce to all old maids and to all those who are maimed and who maim that the actual churches are open.

Remained outside. Remained outside the family. Now Hindley became the father, for the true father is nowadays President Bush, so all the rest are orphans.

This was how Cathy began to want all that lay outside: nature and, most violent of all, the sun. Crags who wait under the sun.

Cathy announced, "I will not come." Heathcliff never announced anything. Heathcliff was naturally unapproachable.

IN THE BEGINNING, HEATHCLIFF DIDN'T MATTER TO ME

Cathy says,
"One day I will never come back and on that day I will keep coming back and coming back."

My nurse's name was Ellen.

"Hurry, Ellen, hurry.

"I know exactly where I want to go. I want to go to where a colony of moor game are settled, blue and purple feathers more aflame with green than any sun. I want to see whether they have made their nests yet. I want to see."

The sun.

My nurse replied that the birds didn't breed on this side of Penistone Crags.

"Oh yes, they do. I've been there."

"You're too young to travel."

"Only a little farther, I've got to go a little farther than I've ever been, climb to a certain hillock that I'll know, pass by a bank that I've smelled, leaves of certain rust, and one pile of shit, I know there are tracks, and by the time I get to the other side, without noticing it, I will have met the birds." Going to the other side and not dying. Whether or not I died.

My nurse didn't bother getting angry with me because she knew I was wild. Not wild enough. She just sighed as if she was swallowing her breath and whispered the only whisper of a socially good woman: "It's a pity that you're never going to be content."

I didn't hear anything. Not Heathcliff.

The next morning the first thing I heard was the outside. I woke up to the shrieking rain. The winds began to tear. Juice ran down the insides of my legs. Don't forget? How can I ever, even when dead? For I'm always holding an orphan's hand.

I'M PERVERSE

In order to complete his bushy family, Hideous found himself (somewhere) a child bride so that there would be a mommy and a daddy. Substitute mommy and daddy more than equal mommy and daddy.

The child bride, like most humans, was a substitute, too, because, being frail and weak and a good wife, she actively detested Heathcliff even more than her husband (did) and threw him out of the house every time Heathcliff returned to snatch some food.

At this moment, Cathy began to act as her parents wanted her to. Precisely: instead of being with Heathcliff, she stayed home. Then blamed her parents for making her and Heathcliff separate.

Was she, like me, scared of men?

So now she had reason to detest Hideous. Cliché: "Dear Heathcliff," she wrote, "I'm acting in such a way that the only relation we can have is that you'll reject me. Once you've fully rejected me, I'll be able to begin to love you."

By refusing to run away with Heathcliff, Cathy began to gain all she had longed for: to perversely enter into being with Heathcliff.

Or: *now that innocence was dead,* she and Heathcliff again began to be together through books. Living with her parents, Cathy was forced to go to school. Heathcliff was going nowhere outside. Cathy taught Heathcliff how to read; this teaching (creating hierarchy) poisoned her love, for identity is shit in the midst of childhood.

The kingdom of childhood is the kingdom of lust. Books, by replicating this or any phenomenon, cause perversity.

I'm not trying to destroy B, but to destroy how I continuously think about B, think about how our bodies burn together, by repeating these thoughts perversely.

THE UNSPEAKABLE

Cathy says,
Where the sun and the black sky are.

They now consider Heathcliff less than a person. "Heath," my new mother said, "if you must use the servants' bathroom, do not do so during working hours." But being nonhuman, Heathcliff doesn't need a bathroom.

I don't care about Heathcliff. Who will I pick to be? A person whose canopy is that velvet in which the stars lie. My family can kick the dogs, like Heathcliff, out of the house every day of the week.

I can't bear being without Heathcliff. Today Heathcliff and I ran into the fields, which are wild. We're never going to come back. I don't want my brain to hurt, and when my hand is stuck up my cunt, my fingers are all full of juices. I want to be in the wild forever and I want to be Heathcliff and I don't care about anything else. See. I'm breaking free.

When I've broken free, there'll be no more such thing as

loneliness, which torments me all the time. Alone, without loneliness: all there is around me is leaves and branches and winds
and fly-through-my-hairs and everything living and moving each
other and each vision, thing seen, is another living thing and
I'm never going back to being lonely where I now am.

I know what the society (my family) (here) is to which I'm
never going to return. The inside of the family is a maze whose
entrances and exits are lost to those caught in its entrails. The
family is foul; garbage lies in its streets. Street sign, NO HUMANS
EXIST HERE.

I can't be other than Heathcliff because to be other than
Heathcliff is to be human. Example: Hindley, who is only himself, beats up his servants or dogs, who are all the same to him.
His—this society is foul because it's based on hypocrisy: it
doesn't recognize violence or death. Hindley tells me that he
loves me and so, places me in his labyrinth. Hindley owns the
house, or labyrinths, which he's also inside; every street or portion of this maze is foul, not by hypocrisy, but by possession.

I must die for Heathcliff so that I'm no longer a human. Only
an outcast.

Today the witch went to see the sea because she had to hear
someone else's voice. There was a dead person. The only way to
raise the person from death is via the cunt. As it crashed waves
against the rocks, the ocean began tossing up tiny fish and then
swept, repeatedly, into the witch's crotch. The sun fell down
into the water.

And I have made my allegiances, although all allegiances are
hell.

I saw two seals.

*　*　*

The only way is to annihilate all that's been written. That can be done only through writing. Such destruction leaves all that is essential intact. Resembling the processes of time, such destruction allows only the traces of death to persist.

I'm a dead person.

Heathcliff says, "Down, dog, down."

STORY:
THE BEGINNING OF
THE WORLD

The servant, a FUNDAMENTALIST, complained to his master, that he, the master, and his wife never went to church to eat Jesus' flesh. In order to punish the servant for saying this, the master sent his own daughter to bed without supper.

Immediately Cathy rebelled by running away with Heathcliff, again, up into the moors. This time they stayed in the beginning of the world.

Time began here, outside, where there were no more humans. They wandered on the moors for days. They're only safe where everything's public.

On the other side of the moors, they found a house similar to theirs. Because Cathy's nature was perverse, or fucked-up, she wanted to be wild and to be part of society. In this total freedom, she said to her friend, "Let's find out what the inside of this house looks like."

They climbed down the crags, then peered into two of the windows. They gazed upon a rich boy and girl who were their age dismembering a puppy.

Heathcliff said, "They aren't nice people, those who live inside houses."

Cathy wanted to destroy the beginning of this sight, or world.

Heathcliff would do whatever Cathy wanted. Listen. "The name of that which is forbidden is *heaven*," Cathy said. "Do it to me now."

Heathcliff said he would do whatever Cathy wanted.

"Listen. I, Cathy, am dreaming that sex which is the witch's den. The den is located in the true house."

Rattles, colored wheels, amniotic rags, and an excessive number of teeth were stigmatizing all outcasts.

"I knew that there was a place where everything would take place. I started searching for that place.

"I was inside a house. Leaving some room, I began looking for tracks, a smell, these are the indications of the way to get to the room I want to reach. I dream, and I have always dreamt, of water.

"The *armier* Arnaud Gélis has said, for we do not need authorities but we do need information, that the dead, with whom he had the unfortunate habit of consorting, wanted all the men and women who were living to, also, be dead. Whether or not you admire this sort of thing. Doves, owls, weasels, snakes, lizards, hares, and all other animals who suck on the milk of cows, goats, women are the associates of witches. Behind milk lies blood; so, behind every witch, all the dead.

"Between two rooms, one is always walking to another room. I passed through a series of rooms.

"Finally I came to thin metal stairs that descended, downwards.

"According to our Inquisitors, who are only able to see the material world, the *Claviceps purpurea,* a fungus that grows out of rye, causes ergotism, whose symptoms are cramplike convulsions, epilepsy, and a loss of consciousness; ergot causes abortion and is antihemorrhagic. During such losses of human consciousness, visions can appear.

"I stood on the edge of the black metal stairs' first step.

"A mushroom that grows near fir trees and birches, *Amanita muscaria,* causes both ecstasy and lameness.

"I was standing in the middle of the flight of stairs.

"In China, the name for *Amanita muscaria* is 'toad mushroom.' Both toads and witches are crippled. In the fourteenth century, Billia la Castagna kept under her bed a large toad that she nurtured on bread, cheese, and meat so that she could make a potion out of its shit.

"I walked down metal staircase after metal staircase, descending. After long descents, I saw a floor that was stacks of wood shelves, even cabinets, all filled with books, between some of the shelves openings just large enough for a human to fit into, all around the spiraling stairs.

"Finally I descended to a huge room where there was red somewhere. This room, which was where I had wanted to arrive, was the library of the witch. I felt scared. I was at the bottom."

As they were looking into the house and making fun of the rich children, Heathcliff realized that it was time to leave. Starting to run, he pulled at Cathy's hand in such a way that she tripped.

A dog sat on and ripped her ankle while his purple, huge tongue half fell out of his lips, and these, pendant, dripped with bloody slaver.

Since Cathy was missing, Heathcliff told Cathy's family about what had just taken place.

HEATHCLIFF'S STORY OF
THE RICH HOUSE

The children are in their house doing their homework. These children consist of a young boy and a young girl.

The young girl was assigned a paper on Edgar Allan Poe. But she doesn't have enough time to complete her assignment.

In the classroom, the teacher talks. Teach is paying attention to many, almost all the other students and the girl can't manage to interrupt to say that she didn't have time to do her paper. She runs out of the school.

Being a good girl, she goes home, back to her room, and works on the Poe paper incessantly, cutting and cutting until only two sections are left. Each of these sections is a few paragraphs long.

Despite all these odds—as if Fate is sitting in judgment of her—the girl goes back to her school so she can present her Poe thesis. Now the institution is shut.

Seeing that she was thrust out of school against her will and desire, it is probable that the Devil rules this world.

The girl continued down the street, into the building next to the school. There she saw the spirit of Karen Finley. Seeing this spirit allowed her to take off all her clothes, which were now heavy, drenched in mud, icy from the outside mist.

The slut walked bare-ass through what was simultaneously a pub and a church.

Saw that none of the building's inhabitants, all of whom were male, gave a shit that she was naked. One of them even walked up to her and was very nice to her.

Later on in the pub, she decided to hide behind the entrance door so that she could slip a pair of shorts over her ass. But she couldn't find any.

"Shit. I didn't bring any shorts."

She had to put back on all the clothes that were still wet cold and dirty.

One of the men, all of whom were older than her, comments, "Nothing has changed. Nothing changes."

ME

Because I had told them about Cathy caught in the strange house, Hindley kicked me out for good. So I threw away the rest of my human trappings and I became an animal that didn't even clean itself. In order to toss their humanity into their faces.

Humans run away from their own shit, their ends, whereas I was now covered in mine: I had become twice a man.

When Cathy returned from strangeness, I loved her more than ever. She came back dressed like a lady, no longer like a wild thing. I didn't see her when she came in. She was silent about what had taken place in that strangeness. She told her father that she wanted to see me immediately.

But I was shit.

As soon as Cathy saw me, her heart leaped up *like the dog it is*. Even though romanticism pretends otherwise.

As if one can own shit, Hindley owned me, so he knew where I was and ordered me to enter the house and greet Cathy as a servant along with all the other servants. I am not.

I did as I had been told only in order to throw more shit into their faces. But, as soon as she saw me, Cathy threw her finery into a bathroom and climbed on me until her lips became my skin. Because it was thirsty, her pussy rubbed me. I knew that I will always hold her cunt in the palm of my hand.

Then she leaped back and informed me, I was only her servant and, worse, I smelled of piss. "Oh, Heathcliff, have you forgotten me?"

Since I was her servant, I couldn't speak.

Father said, "Since you're a servant, Heathcliff, you can shake hands with Cathy. Only once."

I mumbled that I wouldn't do anything. The lips of hell were opening and closing.

"You shouldn't be sulky because you smell of piss."

127

I was silent because I was a hound.

"Heathcliff. Now shake hands with me."

SOCIETY'S PROGRESS TO TOTALITARIANISM AROSE
AND KEEPS ARISING FROM ITS REFUSAL TO BE SHIT. I
touched her.

"Oh, Heathcliff, you are filthy dirty." Cathy was becoming
obsessed. *Obsessed* because she simultaneously wanted to touch me
and didn't. I knew every inch of her flesh, muscle, and liquids,
and I was hungry for her. "I didn't ask you to touch me."

Let the heavens open up, rain sperm.

Cathy said, "But I want to touch you." I knew, just as she
knew, that she would be unable to dream until the moment she
dreamed about me.

I knew that she knew that I knew this, so I decided, in order
to teach her, that I would become dirtier and dirtier until I was
so dirty that I would have nothing more to do with what her
family called *reality* and I would drag her down with me.

This is the way that Cathy says that obsession never rises from
and involves only one person: "Let all that matters be sex when
and where all is glowing."

I say: I don't need sex. I don't need a cock, my cock. Simply:
I am not going to and I am not living in hell.

As soon as I had announced my allegiance to filth to Cathy's
family, I got out of their house. I ran away to the crags and
moors and rocks that never belong to anybody.

Where it will always be raining, for the eyes will no longer
work.

For I, body, know who I am.

I will not deny the witches.

If Cathy was pure of cunt, she would follow the sperm out of
the cockless cock.

She stayed behind because she preferred to make her allegiance
to skin, her fancy clothes, trappings of society, rather than to

me, the gook inside the body. Because she was scared to shake hands with filth.

CATHY IN HER SOCIETY FINERY:

"But if I knew what men were really like, I would never want one. I say this so that I can be more desirable to men."

ME—PERVERTED

Heathcliff says,

But I cried all night because she was mine and she was hurting me. I cried, but I wasn't ever going to be demeaned. Naturally I wanted my skin to be other than dark and my hair to be straight, not so that I could live in a house, but so that she could look up to me enough to run away with me.

And then I'd sink my head into her stomach and my teeth would turn into her bones. I will not live without her—whatever I must do! I have sold myself to the devil! As do those who write.

The next day I woke up and then I heard a noise. When I peered through one of their infernal windows, I saw those two rich murderers, or children, walking into the black-and-white tiled hallway. Of course, I followed them inside.

As soon as he had passed the ceiling beams, the boy turned around and said to me that I should brush that horse's mane out of my face. I bucked, in the kitchen picked up a large pot of shimmering soup, ran back to the edge of the hallway, and threw the liquid into his visage.

I had seen Cathy standing in the hall and, then, the look on her face.

Here was the first time that I wanted to kill her. That night I dreamed that she died from giving birth to a baby. This was the first time I dreamed this.

According to Gilbert Lély, reciting some kind of Freudianism, one of the ways a sadist can prevent himself or herself from traveling from neurosis to psychosis is to sublimate his or her asocial instincts into art.

Freud.

After I had put the boiling liquid in the boy's face, Cathy loved me even more than before. I needed to believe that she loved me so that I could be alive.

I kept turning nasty because there was nothing else I could do in the face of rejection. In the face of Hindley. The nastier I found myself, the more Cathy looked up to my purity.

As Joseph, who was religious, said, "This house is an infernal region."

Today, a yellow worm that looked like a plastic banana began a walk across a dirt path. The path moved downhill in steeper and steeper zigzags until it reached a sign that said BEWARE OF RATTLESNAKES.

Cathy hadn't run away with me to this earth of rattlesnakes where there were no more humans. Both Cathy and I knew that I was the only one who could lead her here, where nature would tame her by demeaning her so that she could begin to learn.

MARRIAGE ACCORDING TO HEATHCLIFF:

As soon as her father went traveling, I returned to Cathy.

The first time I stood again in that sitting room, she was mentioning to the nurse, who happened to look like Jesse Helms, that the rich boy had asked her to marry him.

I said loudly, "Cathy, with all that I am and have—if that is any power—I beg you to stop rejecting me for your rich friends. I have borne too much rejection since I was born."

Cathy didn't notice me because she was combing her pussy hairs.

"I've come back to you, Cathy. Why aren't you looking at me?"

"Because you don't belong in any decent society. You smell like a horse, like Linton said you smelled, and you don't know what a relationship is. Human. Your very presence bores me."

I didn't know how to reply, because I was open to her.

"You're as dumb as any animal, Heathcliff."

Because she needed me to be her, and at the same time refused to touch my skin, I no longer was.

"But the fact that I'm marrying Linton has nothing to do with you. I'm not marrying Linton because you don't exist; what you believe to be my torment of you doesn't exist.

"I'll explain to you why I'm marrying Linton:

MARRIAGE:

Cathy says,

I said to my nurse, but not to Heathcliff: "Do you know the real reason why I'm marrying that creep who doesn't possess a cock? (Not that I give a damn about cocks: it's what they stand for.)

"I can't marry Heathcliff because Heathcliff and I aren't separate from each other. It would be redundant for me to marry Heath.

"I need to get married. Heathcliff and I don't belong in the normal world, whose name is *society*—we don't even know whether we're male or female. And. But, unlike Heathcliff, I can pass for normal; I want the money and moral position that normalcy brings. (When I pretended normalcy in the past, the normals, who are named *the English*, stuck a lit light bulb up my ass, then shorted it.) I need to get married to get my certificate.

"In the real or abnormal world, it's the law that Heathcliff is more me than me, though no one knows who Heathcliff is, his name.

131

"It's disgusting for Heathcliff to live as a freak in my family's world.

"I'm going to marry Linton so that neither Heathcliff nor I will have to live as freaks anymore; for doesn't marriage in this society render anything acceptable? Freaks cannot live as freaks because in reality there are no freaks: there are only those society people who've carved identities out of fear.

"Will I be able to be married without becoming perverted like one of those society people? I'm only human . . .

"Therefore, by means of marriage to a rich person, I will show that Heathcliff and I are as normal as rich people. I learned logic in school."

Heathcliff overheard all of this. As soon as he had understood that it would degrade me to be with him, he ran out of the room.

This was how I threw myself, or Heathcliff, out of my life.

I had the following dream:

In a hotel that's under the aegis of the Buddhist Poetry Institute, while I'm waiting for an elevator that's going up, I recognize a man who's walking past. He's a former lover.

This hotel has a pool that's composed of several uneven tiers.

The hotel's bars and restaurants likewise hide in raised and lowered floors. My former lover and I sit down at a white-cloth-covered table in the most secluded alcove.

I feed him sake after sake, as I did when we used to fuck, and he becomes drunker, as also used to happen. All the time.

This man's initials, R.W., are also those of a boyfriend prior to him.

Both of us are three-quarters sodden when I realize that this man didn't, and now doesn't, love me. His attitude toward me is: about once a year he uses me to try to find the oblivion for which he's longing.

MY FATHER
(WHOM I'VE NEVER KNOWN)
TRIES TO KILL HIS OWN CHILD

<u>Cathy says,</u>
Hindley, who had become drunker and drunker, returned home,
doused in alcohol like a rag in gas. The chill night howled
through the dying branches and the dying cars started beeping.
Inside, he grabbed the child that he had had by his new wife and
cut off all its hair. Raggedly. When he let go of the brat, it fell
down a flight of stairs. Didn't die. Not noticing anything, Father
kept looking for the Jack Daniel's, which had been hidden.

All my life I've dreamt dreams that, after the initial dreaming,
stayed with me and kept telling me how to perceive and consider
all that happens to me. Dreams run through my skin and veins,
coloring all that lies beneath.

I DREAM:

I'm in a hotel in which I've never before been. I have to give
another performance.

Whenever I'm about to perform, I don't like to be around the
other performers. I wander by myself in the unknown hotel.

While I'm waiting in a line for the elevator to go up, a man
who's also waiting recognizes me as a bodybuilder. He's middle-
aged, large in body, with the beginnings of a pot, disappearing
hair. Standing right in back of me so that I can feel the pot, his
hands massage my biceps. I allow this.

Today is the day of sex. Informing me that he's a trainer, the
guy shows me how I can tuck my stomach in or he makes my
stomach totally disappear.

We go down in the elevator. In the bathroom, he fucks me
from the back (I used to be fucked this way when I was a kid).

Now that he's gone, I'm desperate to find a man who will have me, that I can become normal.

My next lover is married. (I fuck married men as a rule because they don't want to get too close to me.) Predictably, the creep informs me that there's no way he can love who I am.

After he tells me this, I squat down on his floor. Then I think, as I've thought before, many times, All I have to do now is get myself out of here. This house. As soon as I do this one thing, I promise myself, I can fall apart just as I want to: I can be less than anything that is.

Just as I have promised myself: outside his building, I sink against the garbage cans that are along the wall. I had probably created, or passed through, romance just so I could be here, where I should be, do what I should do.

Let the garbage eat out the night.

In that night, when two homeless recognize me as one of their members and walk up to me, the thought comes to me that I'm ready to pull myself up by the bootstraps.

My next lover is, as much as possible, the man of my dreams.

This time, there's a mass of wharfs and compartments whose insides and outsides are mingled. Or mangled. In one of these rooms, this man and I lie on a bed. He can't get hard. Female creatures, as elegant and lean as those in Paris, are haunting a few of the other rooms.

Outside the room in which I'm trying to fuck, something that's a combination of truck and tractor is zooming away from the pier nearest the horizon and down a white road that runs parallel to the dawn. Then, the vehicle swerves around, almost running into, five others. Monsters. All of whom are whizzing around and around, breathtaking speeds, hurtling past each other. The tractor-trucks are just like horses.

I watch them, amazed.

This is the realm of males. A man remarked, seemingly to no one, "This is how things are done."

After watching the monsters, I decide that I can't marry my boyfriend, because he doesn't get hard.

But if I'm not going to marry, how can I survive in this society?

In the same room where he couldn't get it up, I'm teaching a class. One of my students asks me to dance.

We dance in an oval, around the back of the room just behind where the other students are sitting, as I had been taught to dance in the school I had attended as a girl. Waltzing and tangoing seriously and with grace.

Even though she appears fem, my student is leading me: I orgasm several times.

In this way I learn that, since I can come with a woman, I don't need a man.

After I have come, or alternatively:

For some time I've been standing, in front of a white stucco wall, on a white road that is raised above all the surroundings and the dirt underneath, as though it's a platform. All around me are masses of luggage, suitcases and bags.

I'm leaving. Finally.

But as for me, I have too much baggage: I can carry all of it only with great difficulty. A man whom I don't know picks up all the suitcases and duffels that are dropping around me and then hands them to me.

While I'm just managing to hold on to these bags, two of the people who seem to be in my group screech, "She's coming!" Race to, then down the pier that's on the left side of the white building.

Now there's a crowd of people down at the wharf. I want to be there, too, but I've got all these bags. Deciding that probably no one's going to steal them, I abandon them and follow the crowd, some of whom are my friends.

At the left pier's end, a huge mass is watching a superstar, perhaps Tina Turner, come.

135

Now I know that there are two ways for me to survive without marrying: I can either be gay or famous.

The hell with dreams because dreams only lead to perversity.

I dreamt I was in Heaven. But I had no business being there, so I ran back to Wuthering Heights (this place) (loneliness) (this state of *human*) (this impossibility named *hell*). I know that here is happiness.

It was the day after my most important performance. I was cleaning the hotel room that the Buddhist Poetry Institute had lent me; I always do exactly what I've been told to do.

A large wood vanity whose mirror was hidden under layers of clothing and cloths stood right in front of me. A mirror because I'm alone.

A, the Institute's head, just opened my door and walked in. She hadn't bothered to knock. She had entered in order to pay me. "I'm only going to pay those writers who matter."

"Matter?"

"Who're important."

The message is that writers are either famous or starve.

While A was making her pronouncement, I was lifting up and folding a huge, thick olive wool blanket. Beneath the blanket, a bare mattress.

Then A and I stood in front of the vanity's covered mirror.

On the surface of the table part, some of the objects that I had uncovered during my cleaning now began to move. Two black crabs the size of human fists strolled. When I saw them, I was confident that I could kill the . . . things, or, at least, crush them to pulp.

The whole table was alive. Specifics: two small black lobsters; two black spiders as large as these lobsters, whose legs resembled those of daddy-longlegs but who weren't daddy-longlegs because their bodies were as substantial as cats'; the two crabs already recognized.

I lifted a dress, then a white wool crocheted cloth, then something I couldn't recognize or can't remember away from the mirror and A and I clearly saw its glass.

The insects and the sea life were crawling, or whatever they do, under the strewn olive blanket, all over the mattress, hiding in the folds of wool. Down to the floor. They were disgusting.

Now I saw who I was: one spider perched, half of it on the top of my calf just below the back of the knee, half on my black cowboy boot. I'm not terrified of a spider, because I know it can be crushed.

I slammed it to death.

A and I crushed all of the moving beings.

THE LACK OF DREAMS IS DISAPPEARANCE OF THE HEART

Cathy says,
Heathcliff had left.

I said:

"My flesh is wood that needs to be chopped up. For this reason, I'm never going to forsake you, whatever-your-name-is and wherever-you-are. The cunt is always speaking. But I will never marry you, whoever-you-are, because marriage means nothing to the likes of us, because society means nothing to the likes of us.

"Heathcliff, you are now *whoever-you-are* because I am named *absence.*"

I BEGAN SEARCHING FOR HEATHCLIFF BECAUSE I DIDN'T WANT HIM. AND I DON'T WANT HIM.

Searching for Heathcliff (trying to make whoever-you-are actual), I fell out with my dreams.

The fantasy *to refuse to dream,* to which I have returned again and again, was the following:

I learn that I have an incurable disease. This disease has something to do with my heart. Because it's inevitable that I'm going

137

to become sicker and sicker until I die, some authority declares that someone from this moment onward is going to have to take care of me until the day I drop dead.

But I don't want any creep to have anything to do with me; I don't want to be a dependent person.

A poet whom I like a lot begins to take care of me. Then her husband becomes angry because she's not giving him enough attention. I'm abandoned, the usual, and as usual, become upset.

The authority, who's a doctor, repeats: You have to find someone to take care of you.

I decide that everything that this doctor, perhaps because he's authority, has said is a con. That I'm ill's a con. How can I be ill when I don't know I'm ill?

I'm not ill.

One day, while I'm performing my morning exercises (if I'm exercising, I can't be ill), I see, right across my mattress, my old nurse sitting, meditating on the floor. I ask her advice. "Who's the best doctor," I inquire, "in the world? If I consult that doctor, he'll be able to cure me if I'm ill." I assure nurse that I have enough family money to afford the very best.

Consulting this best doctor: wherever I am, which is (the) unknown, I look down on the handsomest possible man standing on a suspension bridge. As soon as I see him, my incurable disease is more or less cured. (I'm a romantic. Incurable.)

The next day, or some days later, I see that my girlfriends, all of whom are now standing around me, are wearing the same kind of clothes: upper-middle-class cocktail drag, heavy as possible. I'm in a gold knit sweater nothing else.

We stroll down a suburban street with its clean-cut lawns. One of the women, who works in a store, keeps tugging at my dress. Finally pulls out a thread. I'm irritated—I'm very irritable.

She exclaims, "You're so white, delicate. You're the most well-preserved of all of us."

I no longer know whether or not I have this incurable disease.

Waking from the dream, I find myself in a business office. I describe what I've dreamt to a man who was in my dream, in order that both of us may ascertain and know whether or not I'm going to die.

I had become almost sick with looking for Heathcliff.

I had stopped eating because when he's out on the moors, Heathcliff doesn't eat. Wandered around the rocks at night because I didn't know where he was.

I wasn't looking for him.

The fogs made me animal.

Returned home. This is *Wuthering Heights* by a deadhead.

Home. "Look," my father said. "Look at the lowlife. She's ill because she's always running after men. She's going to be dead soon."

"No," I said to myself. I didn't answer Father because there aren't any, anymore.

"So where were you last night, and the night before, you good-for-nothing-cunt-juice?"

(A sailor named Saint Germanus has unmasked the diabolical nature of certain spirits named *good women who wander about at night*.)

Father's clone, the religious servant: "Weren't you with Heathcliff last night?"

When that nut case dared to question me, I became angry for two reasons: Because my family was considering me ill (nymphomaniac). Because underneath their definition lay the reality of my horniness. (Horniness: I don't know where Heathcliff is so I don't know who he is.)

Now I knew that it's necessary to keep interpreting everything because nothing's true and everything's real. These interpretations are my body.

Therefore I said back to my family: "If you throw Heathcliff out of this house because he's not like you, I'm going with him,

139

out into the fogs. Our brains are already fogs. But you can't do anything to Heathcliff because he's gone."

I had forgotten about myself.

I stopped looking for Heathcliff. After that, I could no longer sleep. I had lost the ways or entrances into dream.

Without dreams, the body becomes sick. I have an incurable illness of the heart.

I want (to find) Heathcliff (myself).

THE UNDERSIDE OF DREAM

Cathy says,

I've always been bratty. During the period when I was ill, though not yet dead, I turned into more than a brat:

"Ellen. Dye my hair blond."

"Your hair's already blond." So she dyed my hair blond.

"My hair isn't blond enough. I look like Madonna fucking. But I'm on my deathbed because I'm dying. I want my hair to be pure white!"

She took me through two more dye jobs.

"Ellen. I said I'm dying. Now you have to make my pussy hairs white."

But, alive or dead, my pussy drips gold and red and tastes like skunk.

RETURN TO DREAMING

Heathcliff, or the Devil, says,

And so Cathy married a rich man for the purpose of entering society. As multitudes of women have done before her. The rich man, Linton, infatuated with his new wife, believed himself to be the happiest of men, as multitudes of men have felt before him. Cathy's dream is that marriage is the destruction of society:

140

This society is the family's house. Cathy's living with her uncle in a huge house. It's of the utmost importance that she palms him a check and equally important that no one knows that this has happened. If not, she'll die.

Her uncle takes the check.

Later, a man, woman, and child are standing on the lawn outside the house. The evil Trinity: they continually cut themselves with razor blades. If they succeed in penetrating the house, they'll destroy everyone and everything, including Cathy.

Somehow they do. Enter. Cathy sees them downstairs; instantaneously she knows that she has to do everything possible, anything, to prevent them from invading the inner dwelling: she has to remain an enclosed self: otherwise evil might stick its cock into her.

Next, she's standing in front of the mattress over which she handed her uncle the check. He's now on the other side of the mattress. She knows that evil is coming. So runs around behind the mattress. Up the stairs.

The house ascends, higher and higher; the higher, the holier the space.

They've arrived at the top of the house. Now there's only complete horror in this world: darkness and decay. Flesh is rotting frogs.

All evil has come here, so a spell begins. This is real creation, the beginning of the world, evil is always born in a cloud of pink smoke emanating from pink incense.

Is Cathy seeing her own blood? She scoots as fast as she can, faster, down the stairs, faster, through the hallway cut in two by the light, out of the child's house. Outside: through a patch of shade, then into sunlight.

(I have suddenly realized the meaning of *My Mother: Demonology*.)

In all the sunlight and cut grass, the child knows that she is safe.

Where will she go without home? She is homeless. She realizes that she can be safe (live) as a wanderer. Free.

She roams through the suburbs and finds herself at a filling station. While she's leaning by one of the tanks, an American car pulls up. (I don't know the names of any cars.) The evil people are sitting in this car. Then Cathy sees a black man, who's lying on a gray plastic parachute on the cement, look up, see whatever's getting out of the auto (formlessness?), and scream, "God!"

A woman emerges from the car. Her inner thighs have no more skin, only blood.

MY CHILDHOOD—BY HEATHCLIFF:

The law that forms society is that which forbids all that reeks of the name *humanity*. From the moment that I was born, I knew my society was corrupt. I knew that in and through the name of *democracy* the middle classes are being annihilated, that there are numerous tribes as depleted as the homeless.

My childhood training with Hindley taught me the characteristics of loyalty, honesty, stubbornness, and ferocity. Further, it caused me to disapprove of the familial society, the only society I knew, which indulged itself in every hypocrisy, corruption or putrescence, lack of control in every area of the self.

I became a handsome man, with a high-domed forehead, a square jaw. An air of authority lurked under every surface. My habitual garments of defense identified me as a member of the samurai class.

Though I had as yet no dealings with anyone outside the family, I knew, and I was deeply upset by this, that samurai were starting to attend the local fuckhouses.

When I came back to Cathy, real life returned to her:

142

MY DREAM OF RETURNING
TO CATHY:

<u>Heathcliff says,</u>

I was traveling, the same as flying, through rooms that were connected to each other so that their outsides were both outside and inside. The name: *the crags of Penistone.*

The room through which I was passing was either an expensive Eastern clothing store, a window that displays two fur and silk robes, or a Hindu temple. All the walls were the same yellow-white as the ground below them. Sand lay everywhere.

As soon as I had emerged from this temple's recesses, I was presented with a photo of "imminent decline." This photo revealed an at least 70 percent decline, a road composed of sand and the rubble of a city. A few people are half buried in its dust; a knee sticks upward.

A voice announced, "People have died here. But, at times, these are the only streets that can take people to where they're going.

"The streets of death."

Where I was heading, there was a chance of disaster, also of rain.

I parked my motorcycle facing upward on a steep hill.

Whoever I happened to be in lust with at that time gave me the information that she had given permission to a friend of hers to ride my bike. That bitch had tipped it.

"What?" I couldn't say anything else because—I'm almost never angry—my anger is always waiting to blow me up. Then, I became angry that there were no bike mechanics in the human-forsaken place. Then, I became angry that all she did was shrug. My lover just didn't care. Finally and ultimately, I'm angry that I'm helpless.

Then, I realized that I could phone a mechanic myself, so I did.

At the bottom of the decline, the crags, lay a building that was my family's house. My real father, the one who had started everything, was inside this house.

I had made its living room into my bedroom; Father's bedroom, which was next to mine, was the actual bedroom of the house. We needed space from each other.

Below the normal rooms lay another level: a floor of unused rooms. In the past, something dreadful (or evil) had occurred in these unused rooms.

These are the rooms of childhood.

The unknown floor's map was as follows:

The large room on the right was the most public, not pubic, knowable and known. Its windows on its outside overlooked an even larger parking lot, which, unfortunately, belonged to the neighboring house.

Outside: "You're not concerned for his welfare at all?"

"He's on welfare?"

The rooms on the left formed a maze whose center was a bedroom. The bedroom. Will I ever find you?

In my search for freedom, or in my search, I moved down to the hidden floor. The floor of childhood. When I was a child, I did, and now I do, whatever I want to do.

In these hidden rooms, my first bedroom was the room on the right. Despite the parking lot lying right next to its insides, it was quieter than my former home.

I still hadn't gotten what I wanted, or I still wasn't where I wanted to be. I want to be in the most secret bedroom of all.

Finally my father gave me permission to move in there.

I proceeded:

But just then, I saw outside that water was pouring, armylike, into, down the wide gray street. A wave was as high as my motorcycle. For the first time in my life, I felt fright: I was terrified that my cycle would be flooded.

I dashed outside; then the waters turned ferocious; I ran for safety. Home.

144

In the rain my bike died. I knew that I could have saved bike if I had ridden it into the house as soon as I had seen the waters coming.

In order to save bike, I turned time backward:

When I rode my bike into the hall, my mother agreed that this situation was an emergency and that all is decaying. Here lie the smelly realms of the cunt.

Moving into the cunt:

First object to be moved from known floor to unknown floor: a large and low wood and green-velvet table. (Note: Has to be cut into parts to be moved.)

Second object: a blue exercise mat.

These necessities were too large for me to move myself. When I asked my mother, who must have hated my guts before I had been born because she had abandoned me, for help, for the first time she agreed.

Now I accepted my parents.

Inside the secret bedroom:

When I had finished furnishing the three unknown rooms, they resembled, or were, the three known rooms (bedroom, workroom, and exercise room) in which I used to live.

In this manner, I returned to Cathy, reached into her secret place, and made her my image: in the name of anything but the parent:

In the smelly realms of the cunt.

CATHY'S DREAM OF AND UPON HEATHCLIFF'S RETURNING TO HER AND LAURE'S DREAM

Cathy says,
Somewhere in Thrushcross Grange I was packing my suitcases because I was getting out. Finally.

Then, I dragged these bags down to my bedroom where I packed what I didn't want.

When I had packed both what I wanted and what I didn't want, I found myself next to Heathcliff. Sitting on a stoop, just as if we were back in New York City, Heathcliff started burning some of my skin with his cigarette.

A boy named Linton with whom both of us were friends sat on my other side. He and Heathcliff burned me.

Since he's my main man, Heathcliff was the one who talked. "I'm deciding who you are."

As soon as he had said that, I felt happy. Happiness was a mingling of feeling and physical heat; the liquid flooded the caves beneath my skin.

Heathcliff told Linton, "I own her."

I RETURN TO B

I was sitting in a theater, watching a movie named *Wuthering Heights*. I had no idea which version. On the movie screen, I saw Cathy telling Heathcliff, who had just returned to her, that the only thing she wants in life, now that almost no life is left to her, is for her and Heathcliff not to part. Never to part.

Heathcliff, "But you did everything possible to ensure our parting."

Cathy answers that she only wanted them to be together.

Across the screen, I see this word spread: THE KINGDOM OF CHILDHOOD IS THE KINGDOM OF LUST.

I had come back to the theater night after night. Wood walls and the bare, hardwood chairs that I remember from my school days: those auditoriums where they then showed movies. But this was a real movie theater, not a schoolroom. And this night, when I sat down and the room became totally black except for the light from the screen, I placed my purse, as I always do, under my seat.

146

During my former visits to the theater, I had become friendly with a man named Jerry. As *Wuthering Heights* rolled on to the death of Cathy, Jerry asked if he could sleep with me.

"But first," Jerry in the black, "I have to *show* you something."

He showed me that the top of his head was bald.

No, it was something else.

He opened his chest. Most of his chest, its center, was without skin, like the Visible Man model. I saw right through to his plastic heart.

But I didn't want to fuck with him for another reason. Because he wasn't into what's imprecisely named S/M.

There was no movie.

Bored, and I hate more than anything to be bored, I left my seat to get a drink. When I returned and picked up my bag, I noticed it felt light. When I looked inside, there was nothing there.

Since I no longer had cash or credit cards, I was forced· by circumstances to enter a brothel.

I have always found myself determined to survive.

The cathouse in which I landed obviously catered to upper-crust clients. For there were deep-pink velvet curtains and no other visible walls.

To my surprise I liked my first john.

Then a murder took place; the victim was this first john. Was I possibly the murderer?

Because we had to ensure that we weren't caught, some girls and I began escaping from the whorehouse. As I loped down a long and narrow hall, I gazed upon a black satin evening bag that looked expensive. On a tiny, antique mahogany table. I snatched the bag because mine had been taken from me. But thought that it's wrong to steal.

The steep street outside our working quarters had become steeper: my friends and I could barely climb up it. I was wearing very high-heeled shoes because I was a whore. Here there was no hope of running away. I was aware that openly carrying this purse rather than investigating its insides, keeping only what I wanted and throwing away all the rest, was even more dangerous.

I opened the black evening bag. At this moment I told the other girls about my theft. They didn't give a fuck. I extracted the bag's contents; I preferred a pair of earrings to money.

The girls and I decided that we were going to be thieves.

I found myself inside a brothel, probably the original one, though I couldn't remember how that brothel had looked.

The vestibule where I stood was the lobby of a movie theater. All of its velvet, cunt-pink.

I was watching a policeman talking to or interviewing the theater's ticket-taker. All sorts of documents concerning the murder were on my person. Of course I had done it. The policeman who was in the ticket booth didn't notice or care about either my documents or my being; none of the cops walking around the whorehouse cared about the hookers. Already hookers and thieves, we decided we could be murderers.

Heathcliff, my brother.

FIVE

DREAMING POLITICS

1. I ENTER A MONASTERY

I decided to go into a monastery because I had a thing for skinheads, though not for the right-wing variety.

I chose the monastery of X, located somewhere in the South of France where all the buildings and sky are white. According to reputation, this monastery was nondenomenational.

I explained to Bataille that this didn't mean that I was leaving him. Explained that I had no intention of abandoning him again.

I entered the monastery. At first I thought that everything there was old, the crosses, the walls, the air; the monks confused me.

I had expected them to be calm. I had expected them to embody the virtues of gentleness, compassion, and selflessness rarely found in the world outside the asylum. What I did find in the house still confuses me:

At first I believed that no women were dwelling here. I now

149

know enough to distrust any community that is less than 50 percent female and semifemale. The first few days I believed I was living in isolation. Then there was a birthday celebration for the head monk and a young monk who resembled a photo I own of Jean Genet walked up to me and stared at me. All I can remember are eyes.

Bored by the communion that followed, I tried to sneak into the main hall. The monk was waiting for me. He took me in his arms and kissed me on my lips.

I hadn't known before that monks do this.

Before I had time to be aware of surprise and could still feel the warmth of his lips, he started to tell me about this monastery. A good monastery because here nobody wants anything from anyone else, here there was nothing any monk could want from me. So I could do whatever I liked, without the problem of grasping: all monks do whatever they like.

After he had finished speaking (I later learned that this monk talked incessantly, whether or not anyone was listening to him, whether or not anyone else was talking), he led me into his cell. There the boy slowly peeled off my clothes. He was wearing a Japanese-style shirt and underpants.

As he lightly fingered me, murmured, "Little baby! Your skin is burning here and it's so soft." His finger was touching me too hard.

He asked as he touched the membrane around my clit precisely, "Tell me. How have the men whom you've had before me treated you? In your writings you've said that you've been whipped."

I told him the details of my sex life with Bataille most likely to arouse the desires dormant in him that I desired. Soon he began questioning me about the acts he found most disgusting and so most wanted to commit.

I don't have any idea how it happened, but I found myself

150

lying on top of him. Like tentacles made of rabbit fur, my legs curled around his stronger, hairier ones. Just as warmth began to seep into my body just below my skin, like milk, I whispered to him that I never wanted to be without him again. Then my mouth turned around his tongue: I stopped living in anything but present time. He stroked me gently, as if I was a child.

And so I opened. Still surrounded by wool, his stiffened thing thrust into me, all of me there and open, kept thrusting into me until this devil was making me come again and again; Antichrist made me a continual orgasm.

I stopped still and said, "God."

He answered me, lifted me upward, up above his head, fingers in both cunt and asshole so now I was his vase, he the thorns, and throwing the vase over his shoulder so that it broke on the floor, continued to bring me to orgasm again, fingers moved in labyrinths of violence. Always this is how I am captured.

I found myself in a vast room hung in black. A single light suspended from the ceiling illuminated the shadows of shadows.

So what are monks really like, I was wondering: a voice cut off any possibility of any answer:

"Kneel down. Girl. Prepare yourself, for you are now going to experience the sufferings that are in this world. That are this world. You have to learn how to stop grasping so that you can ascend into Heaven."

I hadn't known that Buddhists believed in Heaven.

A door creaked: then hands, blinding me, drew aside the clothes that I had thrown across my body to protect myself from the bitter cold. My ass was bared.

My asshole. I have been told that when my asshole opens, it looks like a rose blooming. Is it true, as Buddhists say, that appearances are deceptive?

Answer: my pirates dwell in freedom.

Hands connected to wool robes were running across my ass

cheeks, into my hole, scurrying like rats; couldn't tell how many hands; slowly they began to travel into, slap, scratch, even stroke the inner regions of my body. The other inner regions of my body.

Then the fingers returned to my buttocks.

"All life is suffering," their intonations at this edge of reality, as they rubbed, beat, slashed me by paddles, knouts, whips, lashes, belts, underpants, hairs, used holey condoms, holy crosses other toiletries; I was confused, and so, aware only of cries, outbursts, moans, whimpers, word bits. The language of the flesh. Sometimes I recognized some flesh as my own flesh.

As soon as I was freed of my ties, I became an animal by rolling on my own back and playing with my lower lips. I excited them myself to the edges of orgasms only for the purpose of denying myself that orgasm, for the purpose of increasing the pleasure whose edges I kept approaching. As I twisted this way and that through these glorious pathways, I was aware that hundreds of goat-headed devils were, through rubbing, making their cocks into monstrous clubs.

Here and there, an imp whose skin stunk of used sperm mixed with unused piss skipped then hopped between my limbs and head, then another dwarf, and another, each one stinkier than the last. I thought I was shitting in my underpants.

I've never had such a sexual experience.

As if I was seeing a painting in a museum. Then I turned my head and watched a boy who was naked, his eyes on the Cross, devoutly receive white communion bread fixed on the end of an asparagus that a devil was holding.

I could finally speak. My flesh, and so my understanding, is weak. For, though Bataille writes all the time about religion, I've never known that religion was like this. You monks have just woven a spell over my body: from now on, I have no interest in anything but the body. You've poisoned me. So pierce my bones with this poison . . . you are horror . . . and I love you.

2. MY DREAM SHOWED ME THAT I DON'T BELONG AMONG RESPECTABLE PEOPLE

(to B, who's dead)

B: "The lamp had resigned itself to die.

"If I had my way, I would live while dreaming and die into dream, and so all the memories of the world would arise."

I left wherever I was in order to travel through old European cities. And *cold*.

For a long time I wanted to give my heart, which no man had been able to burn up, to the cruelest possible embraces.

My journey had found its purpose: to go to my half-sister's wedding. I've never felt anything about my half-sister and now do not, nor do I have any respect for the institution of marriage. I was going to attend this wedding only because it was going to be fashionable. My deepest desire was bourgeois.

And so I passed through the cities of the North.

Finally I reached that center for which I longed. It was a dimmed and aged town, hidden in modesty and gray. All of this Europe was crumbling: its edifices appeared gray, and brown tints of gray, and even the air was colored, though obviously it wasn't.

It was as if it was night but it wasn't. The streets and the erections and all that wouldn't appear looked like night, but were streets, erections, air, whose colors were gray, brown, and as if gray.

This city was a clue for me that something malignant was about to take place in my life. The recognition of this meaning didn't bother me because, having encountered many hard times, I've become used to sitting through terror.

Because I was seeking nothing, blackness, nakedness.

I recognized the hotel for which I had been searching though I had never seen it before. It was a narrow building, between

153

three and five stories high and wedged between two taller structures.

All the buildings were feral. In a rotting part of town whose animals were decomposing, a poor section whose insides hadn't been vomited out or shipwrecked.

The hotel had no ground floor. The lobby in its center didn't exist. All around and above there were hallways that smelled, intestines, of the kind of piss that's been lying around for years but hasn't yet died.

Time in these hallways: anything has and could happen here. That is: everything that's bad. These were the halls through which ventured only the person who was stupid or who wanted to confront his own fear.

The elevator in which I was standing reeked of the piss of bums. Then I remembered seeing one, on the outside, rub his lower head against a brick wall. Then I remembered that I had dreamt that I had a dick head.

The elevator was part of the genre, and genre is memory. So I knew that I would have to step out of the elevator into the halls where my own death was sitting. Against memory: How could I get out of this shaft without touching a hallway? This was my problem, my labyrinth.

Meanwhile the elevator was moving up to the top.

I found myself in a magnificent room. As rich and spacious as all the hotel below it was rat-torn and decomposed. A round room, the center of whose floor was dropped; crimson carpets covered every bit of the floor.

Another room which was barely large enough for a bed lay off of this circle.

I had the best room in the decaying hotel.

My sister and the guy whom she was going to marry, or had just married, were staying above my head.

The hotel's elevator didn't go beyond my floor.

Where she was staying was both huger and plusher than where

154

I was: open by skylight and by wall-size windows and doors leading out to the encircling concrete terrace, her flat appeared even more massive than it was.

Before my half-sister walked down the stairs into my apartment, I knew that she was one of the Evil Ones.

As soon as she was in my room, my half-sister informed me that she was very sick. True to his type, her new husband started speaking for her: "Because she's so very sick, she needs to occupy your apartment."

Well, I don't want to be here anyway, I thought; this neighborhood is only decay because all that ever happens here is robbery. I could right now be in the Gramercy Park Hotel. (Where I stay whenever I'm in New York City because it is, or reminds me of, what I wanted childhood to be when I was a child.)

I answered him: "You can have my home if you reserve a room for me for two nights at the Gramercy."

When he informed me that he had made the reservation, I became happy. Because I was going to escape this poverty: I was returning to the childhood of which I, a child, had only dreamt. So I began to pack as fast as possible so I could go back.

Escaping to childhood: I had two pieces of luggage, a small flesh-colored suitcase and a bag of both the same size and the same color. Forced to choose between them, I picked the larger.

Outside the hotel in which murders regularly occur: while walking down the sidewalk in the direction of the Gramercy, I suddenly saw that a man walking in front of me was carrying a large open gas canister. I watched him tip the can and gas flowed onto the sidewalk.

I saw another person, on my right, doing the exact same thing.

They (I don't know who "they" is) are going to set this city on fire.

This extreme rebelliousness will be the unspeakable forerunner

155

of an entire century of bloody massacres, atrocities, political gaffes, insurrections, civil wars and wars of liberation, hope fading into defeat, botched beginnings and exiles, empires in the name of democracy that neuters and imprisons the conquerors themselves.

Since, if I tried to reach the rich and safe part of town where the Gramercy was placed, I would certainly die, and since I wanted to keep on surviving, I decided that I had to immediately turn around and go back where I had come from: I had to descend into the slums.

My descent into the slums: While I was walking the way you do when you're so scared you don't want to seem to be running, down the same sidewalk, across the street I saw a store that fascinated me.

I crossed the wide street in order to see more clearly.

This sidewalk was narrow and both descended and turned sharply.

The store had a double, or doubled, windows. One window was black: white leaves and white frost appeared through the black. The other half of the window was unseeable.

Drawn through a rotting narrow black door into an even narrower dark hall: here the walls, or air, I couldn't tell the difference, were the color of smoke. Pierrots who were the colors of both windows and both sexes were slipping into the walls; the white and black of Halloween; leafy branches, against one wall, the same but larger than those in half of the window, had melded into part of a Pierrot's body.

I knew that I was now where I belonged. Mutability gorgeousness darkness depths that lead only to other depths.

3. A MONK STORY

Because I no longer exist, I'm going to write a piece of filth that has absolutely nothing to do with me.

Regino of Prüm stated in his collection of instructions for bishops and representatives that there are women who regularly leave husbands behind. That when they do so, they glide through the locked doors of familial households into the silences of the night. There they rise and fly wherever they want and then encounter other soaring women.

Regino of Prüm said that these women are feral.

He then swore that some of the bitches have confessed that when they escaped, they murdered men. Only baptized men. After they had slaughtered them, they cooked and ate their bodies, all but the dead cocks, which they then stuffed with wood or straw so that the pricks would stand up, again.

During a monk's birthday party, one of the monks was fucking a woman who didn't want him to be in her, so, at the end of his fucking her, she bit into her own hand so deeply that she poisoned herself.

Afterward, another monk gave the following explanation of this incident:

The first monk and the girl had started arguing about religion. (As a rule they never argued because the girl never talked.) "I have a friend who's a doctor . . ."

The girl said nothing.

"When I asked him about all the ways you want me to sexually torment you," said the first monk to the girl, "he told me that when he was doing his medical residency, he had a girlfriend who was cousin to a famous feminist rock 'n' roll star. After work—residents, you know, work for hours and hours at a stretch in the hospital—he'd enter her house and just sit there. Zombie. Then she'd do everything, *anything,* for him. I wish I had a woman like that!" the monk commented. "After she had done anything, he'd fuck her as brutally as possible. My friend said that his brutal way of life caused brutal sex."

The girl was curious about the rock 'n' roller's cousin. What happened to her?

"A year and a half later, my friend left her. She was devastated."

"I don't see why it has to be the woman who does everything for the man."

The monk liked to lick menstrual blood.

The next part of their argument concerned economics: "One of my very rich friends who doesn't have to work at all" (monasteries need wealthy patrons to survive) "lives next to an art patron. One of the most select parts of town, high up on a hill. An artist whom the patron patronizes, and he's probably also her lover, is crazy, my friend says, because he's always complaining about rich people. How horrible rich people are. My friend said, and I agree, that poor people complain about rich people only because they want to become rich. The proof of this is that as soon as a poor person becomes rich, he always stops complaining."

The girl said that some poor people aren't drooling idiots. Then she started to talk about diets. The restaurant bill appeared. (The monk always liked to eat in a restaurant before he went to an orgy.) The ascetic quickly placed his American Express card over this bill and announced, "This is the last supper."

"Oh. I'm sorry," said the girl. "I know you're poor." She was aware that monks take oaths of poverty. "I'll pay for everything after this."

"That's not what I mean."

She looked at him, wondering whether she was dumb.

"I mean, this is the last time that we'll ever eat together."

"Oh." The girl understood, wrapped herself up in her own coat and ran away.

On the street, a bench stood next to a garbage can. Since she was shaking, half-sat half-slumped down on the icy wood and closed her eyes because she couldn't understand what had just happened.

The first thing she's aware of is a hand taking one of her hands, then raising her up into a body, then two arms hold her. They're the monk's. As he ripped through the bottom of her dress to place his cock in her cunt, he told her he

158

loved her. She didn't understand, so she bit into her own hand.

Later the monk explained to her that he couldn't bear her seriousness. "You must understand," he said, "life is a joke. I see people die every day. Death and life are just jokes."

The girl understands.

4. ON THE RELATIONSHIP BETWEEN STATE AND RELIGION

The head of this monastery was a monk named Bush. Every morning it was his custom to discuss the affairs of state, privately, with an emissary from the Pope. "The Pope isn't going to hush up any more murders, no matter how much you pay him off," the Cardinal was explaining.

"I'm as religious as anyone else," Bush protested, "and I know that God loves me, but the Pope is utterly rapacious. When I started managing this household, I gave him a one-third cut of everything that passed through my hands. I've continued doing so. Money, real estate, banks. But for what?

"What more does His Holiness want from me? He knows that for me to do what I have to do I must have funding. If I have to pay him off even more, I won't have enough for myself. I mean, for this monastery." Bush brushed his hands as if at flies. "It's all the same."

Bush tried to become aggressive. "Maybe the Vatican, which is the richest art collector in the world, should grant us some medical insurance?"

The Cardinal kept his mouth shut for reasons that were obvious to the State.

"The Pope's real name is Satan," Bush screamed. "But Satan doesn't own everything in this country and I'm going to make sure that he never will!"

Now the Cardinal intervened. "Sir, you are as righteous a man of God as ever existed. Neither I nor anyone could ever criticize even the most minute of your actions. Know that both the Pope and I are completely devoted to you, that the only thing I want in my life is to approve of every one of your deeds and every part of your physical being.

"Now," the intellectual continued, "you wouldn't want me to disapprove of anything that concerns you, would you? I am talking about your only daughter. I have heard a rumor that you lock up your daughter."

"The monk who last took my daughter's name in vain disappeared." Bush assured the Cardinal that it was useless to worry about the criminality of any action. Political, familial, or other. According to American economic philosophy, every man simply wants what he wants and does what he must do in accordance with his want. "The free market rules religion."

"God is all," the Cardinal agreed. "But don't you ever feel guilty about all the people you're murdering these days?"

"As you become older, everything becomes more difficult."

"If I really believed that you mean what you say, I'd have to excommunicate you." The Cardinal walked out on Bush, returned to his Pope.

Bush's mind: The Cardinal's exit should have scared Bush but only served to reify this man's conviction that enemies were living all around him. Now, these enemies included both his own family, as he had known before, and the Pope. Bush had always recognized that his sons wanted, through inheritance, to take away the money that he was earning in his presidency. I, said Bush, must preserve the economy.

As he was thinking, a young novice entered the black-hung chamber.

"Tell my daughter that I want to see her at midnight, when all the light has failed."

160

REPORT TONIGHT OF ANOTHER MURDER OF A YOUNG GIRL. ALL YOUNG GIRLS, PLEASE STAY AT HOME. IF YOU MUST GO OUT, KNOW THAT YOU DO SO AT YOUR OWN RISK.

(Pictures of a man, not recognizable, extracting a dead girl's eye, then cutting off her left leg.)

THE POLICE ARE CONFOUNDED . . . SEVEN KILLINGS IN TWO WEEKS . . . NO CLUES . . . ONE YOUNG GIRL AFTER ANOTHER . . . THERE'S MORE TO THIS THAN JUST A MANIAC . . .

ALL BODIES ARE MUTILATED

5. TRUE LOVE

"I don't love you because I don't trust you," B was saying to O, a young monk, during the few moments that they were able to seize, like thieves, for touching each other. B, who was beautiful, and this monk were in love with each other. Both children continually felt the devastations of the longing flesh.

But the child protested.

"How can I trust any man when Bush's my father? I just can't love you." It didn't occur to her that the monk was poor and would never in the future have any money. "But I worship you."

The desire in his voice was strong enough to be a cock.

"I can't even love myself because of my father. Tyranny makes only tyranny." B had learned these politics from her father. She, in her male drag, flung her arms around his chest. "You're the only friend I've got. Don't go; be with me and help me. My father's got some gruesome plan and I don't have any idea what it is."

O assured the child that he would do anything for her.

161

6. THE HEAD MONK

The monastery differed from all the other monasteries in the world in that its head was selected through democratic processes. That night there was a huge political party in the holy residence to celebrate Bush's decision to run for a third term.

Despite the reports of murdered young girls just outside these religious premises, lots of rich white people attended the party.

But Bush welcomed everyone to his festivities. "I haven't fucked anyone for a year," he announced at the beginning of the new world. "I know that during this time, there have been several rumors of war. That's why this monastery's begun to go downhill. Tonight, after we've all become drunk and obtained what pussy we need, I know that we're all really going to get together and solve the problems of the monastery. Because it's human to err."

One monk who had taken his dick out of his pants replied, "I know, sir, that you've asked us all here for a purpose, but I don't know what that purpose is."

"We have come together solely so that we can all pray together." Bush tried to kneel on the ground and vomited instead:

Bush's prayer: "Lord, what really lies in my prayers? What's my dream when I dream of dreaming? What is my heart? O Lord, I am talking about my own family."

"It's my brothers," said Bush's daughter. "He's assassinated them . . ."

"He wouldn't do a thing like that," said Mrs. Bush.

"He's going to murder all of us." The youngest of Bush's sons was innocent enough to see into the future. "He must have some reason for his actions, but I don't understand."

Bush on war: "I have brought you all together to make a certain announcement. Three of my four sons are dead. In a far-off war. They died for their country. I have brought you together, for all of you are my children, to ask you to pray for them. For our sons. But this monastery is so broke I can't pay for their coffins."

Mrs. Bush: "Then pray for my cunt." She fainted.

Bush: "I want you to know about our sons who just died. A church fell on Rocco, my oldest son, and crushed him into red pulp. A religious death. Regarding my son Neil—pure accident. Some black—whateverhisname—mistook him for whoever was secretly screwing this black's girlfriend. I don't know why these people don't keep to their own race. And, ironically, while Neil was breathing his last, Neil's girlfriend was sucking someone else. A black.

"Both my sons have died honorable deaths.

"This is proof that God loves me and my family."

A monk said, "Father."

A guest who had wandered in here by mistake: "Let's get the fuck out of here."

A second mistaken guest: "I've heard that they call this monastery The House of the Dead, but death can't collapse."

Bush, opening a bottle of red wine, said, "Now let us drink to the blood of my sons."

Dream of childhood: I dreamt that I arrived in a city.

A street, starting from the black-and-white building in which I was born, runs straight down for three more. At its bottom there's a bakery, the bakery of hell.

The cakes in the window of this bakery were what I desired when I was a child: white cakes just pretexts for all the animals, zebras, giraffes, all kinds of cats, wolves, horses, foxes, lambs, who gamboled on their tops. Cookies the colors of the rainbow.

I'm in the apartment building where I was born, so I begin to desire. I want to buy a dress. The dress. To reach the most gorgeous dress store I must walk down the street.

My walking is the same as flying.

The most expensive clothes store will lie a half block past the bottom of hell, slightly uphill.

At the bottom of hell: First: I look down at my arms, more precisely, at my elbows, and see a worm that is long enough to be a snake putting its head, as a nurse might a needle, at the skin right below the inside of my right elbow.

I watch this head pierce, then enter, into my own body.

The head is at the same edge of the skin, but now coming from within my inside, through the arm flesh, to the outside. The worm is so close to do this . . . Immediately after it breaks through the skin it will be formless, or look like gelatin. I am feeling more than repulsed, because I don't want anything living in my insides eating me.

I will do anything in this hell to destroy all possible worms.

The end of the party: When all of the guests, except for the wealthiest ones, had decided that things were getting out of hand and that the only thing to do was revolt, Bush announced that he now had complete control of this country and could murder whomever he wanted.

"Don't go. Don't go." Bush's daughter ran from guest to guest. She was grabbing. "Don't leave us alone with this man. So what if he's directly promoting self-interest, economic tyranny, and cruelty? Has it ever been different in human history? So what if he's trying to turn this place into desolation and death? This is no home for orphans. Only save *me*. He's planning to murder me next. And do something with my body."

Bush: "If you pay attention to her, I'll kill you." This was the end of the party. "Go to your room without dinner," he told his daughter.

"You're going to your grave," his daughter told him.

7. NIGHT

That night B ran into her mother's chambers because she was frightened.

She told her mother that she was afraid that her father was going to get her.

Mrs. Bush replied that monks, according to history, like orgies. "The Pope, you know, doesn't care what they do as long as they don't use birth control."

"Mama, I'm not talking about sex. He wants to shut me up in the Castle of Petrella, where nails slowly descend through coffins and headless monks suck their own dicks."

As Mrs. Bush scolded her daughter for such language, the head of the family entered the room. It was the first time he had ever been here. "I know that you want me to die," Bush said, "only so that you can mix my blood with your menstrual blood." Then he informed his daughter that she had opposed him for the last time.

B ran out of the room.

"As for you, my wife, my wife by religious and civil law, in this community we know how to deal with old women."

Pirates: On foot, leaving behind them the rasping chaos of their hurried steps, cloaked in silence and in the sightless complicity of night, they first cross the hated city, an elite of bastards and wastrels, birth's favorites and darlings who had acceded without interruption to power: all rotten to the core . . . the pirates hurry on . . .

8. THE VATICAN/DREAM BY RELIGION

Rotting rafters provided rat housing.

I'm on my motorcycle, which is the only action that's better than flying. I'm going downhill, which is how to fly even more spectacularly.

Halfway down this mountain, I look straight down and see that the bottom three-quarters of my motorcycle is buried in mud. There's slime right up to the top of the forks. Nevertheless I'm still moving.

I can't ride on like this.

I look farther down and see a wide road that's snakelike, embracing the bottom of this mountain. Waters flow so freely, so thickly across the road that it's become a river. I can't see my home, which is located even farther below, between the river-road and the sea; I know that there's no way now I can go home again. Neither can my motorcycle ride inside mud nor I walk on water.

In the face of this impasse, there's only one choice: to go the other way.

Going against: I pull my motorcycle, which is disappearing so fast that it has almost disappeared, up out of the muck. Then I ride back the way I came. To the top of the mountain.

This top consists of an enormous, level plain occasionally covered by low-lying grass. A dirt road that is shaped like a U (the dream intends the pun) extends to three-quarters of its sides.

I start motorcycling down the first leg of U.

Right before I reach its center, I glimpse a wood shack. From a clothesline outside the shack, where everything is green, a leotard rustles in the wind. The leotard is more holes than material; I stop to look at it more closely because I have to; I see that it's composed solely of pale blue and pale green ribbons. I have to own it. I hesitate because my desire's so huge, then I buy it.

I continue motorcycling. Around the center of U.

On the other side, as if a straight line had been drawn across the U, I come to a lovely white wood building, this one in excellent repair; I can't tell what it is. A cottage? A grocery store? A hotel? Certainly: name unknown.

Through its front door. Its kind, elderly proprietors are willing to help me with my mud problem: they reserve a room for me for the night at a hotel that's below the river-road.

Here's the plan so I can return home and keep my motorcycle safe from all harm (the two significant steps): I'll leave the bike parked up here, at the edge of the dry dirt road in a patch of grass; then I'll journey to the hotel (how, the way isn't known); the next morning I'll take a taxi from the hotel to my home; as soon as all the white liquids coming down from the top have receded, when all is safe, return to my motorcycle . . .

Pirates: It was like an adventure dreamed in a night of passion, an illusion lasting exactly the time it took the devil to rub his only eye . . .

9. RAPE BY DAD

In the following paragraphs I would like to try to highlight various recollections from my childhood. My parents were nevertheless very kind. They never beat me.

Back in her mother's bedroom: B tells her mother what has just taken place:

". . . was telling me that the same thing that just happened to my two brothers was going to happen to me. That this was the last time that he would ever have to see my face.

"I said, 'Okay,' and walked away.

"I was trembling so hard though, I don't know why I could only walk about ten feet then had to sit down. Closed my eyes. After a few minutes or . . . I don't know how long . . . a hand grabbed one of mine and pulled me upwards so I had to open my eyes and I saw Father.

"I said, I thought you wanted to never see me again that's fine with me. Both his hands, one on each one of my shoulders, pulled me toward him and his body all around me I kept rubbing into him all I wanted was safety. I couldn't care where safety came from touching any human body is the only safety. Somehow the two of us, as if we were only one, kept proceeding up that hallway. Like Western Civilization.

167

"Then we had stopped and in that hole of stopping he kept saying 'I love you I'm sorry I love you I'm sorry.' Since I didn't understand what was happening why anything that was happening was happening I must have stopped being conscious I don't know how my clothes came off then I started being conscious: I realized that I didn't want to know that this was happening and I began searching for where to secrete my consciousness.

"I don't want this consciousness.

"He had just taught me that I can no longer appear and be a person when he's around, that I can't oppose him. I learned that I lost and am lost. Orphan. While my father was raping me, I learned that I had to do away with my self.

"Where could I hide this self? I searched. Decided to hide in the mirror: in memories of my past victimizations, especially sexual abuses and rapes. As Father was making love to me, whenever my consciousness was bad and wandered into the present, I repeated the sacred laws I had just given myself: the laws of silence and of the loss of language. For us, there is no language in this male world.

"This is called *the poisoning of the blood.*

"None of this was appalling. The appalling was that, while I was crying hysterically, my body came again and again, at least three rounds of multiple, strong orgasms.

"When Dad orgasmed, his lower body plunged slowly and deliberately while a hand held my cunt lips into a vise around his rod. He became still. I was violently sobbing after about ten minutes of this perhaps in order to calm me he placed the cock back in the cunt even though my cunt was very dry he put spit in it I hadn't stopped crying and I didn't stop crying had another round of orgasms, milder, his cock was at half-mast and several minutes after I had come he lost interest. Then he noticed I was crying. Said 'I'm sorry' but I didn't know what he was sorry about."

Mrs. Bush said, "What's my daughter saying why's my

168

daughter saying these things because she no longer knows why she's saying what she's saying."

"I'm telling you that I felt pleasure when Bush raped me."

"Your father . . ."

"That's not the point. I want to know why I didn't kill him."

10.   B'S DREAM
ABOUT BEING RAPED

"I was inside the old wood house when I decided that I wanted to break up with my boyfriend. I had no idea why.

"My reason was that there was something awful the matter with him.

"I had to make it to the other house. But my motorcycles were distant from me. I've got two of them. The nearest one, white and shining like the sun, was so far that someone, male, had to drive me in a disgusting car that also was white, as long as a superlimo, up the white trash hill to where my baby was sitting itself in the corner of a house just as if it were in a garage, but there was no garage here. A peeling, white, old wood house. Some birds were sitting on some dead limbs.

"In this second house, a wild party was now taking place. It was violent. But I was apart from it, alone in an emptied room. Finally my boyfriend understood (he was with me in this room) that I was leaving him for good; he turned furious; threw me on my stomach on a mattress; couldn't breathe; my asshole looked up at him. He fucked me for a long time in that hole. While he slammed into me I hated him; several minutes passed still fucking me no break; I suddenly notice that I'm feeling pleasure and then I want him to fuck me even more; I started to shake all over the place come come. As soon as I had felt pleasure, I had begun to feel different emotions about him: I simultaneously liked being fucked this way and hated being raped.

"I came for a long time."

B told her mother this dream.

Her mother replied that there was no more choice: they had to kill Bush. "As regards the morality of death," she said, "all our friends are now dying."

11. GETTING RID OF BUSH THROUGH ROCK 'N' ROLL

I was sleeping badly at that time and pursued by a series of nightmares. Almost every one of these dreams led me to the same place.

School.

The university to which I had returned, or the part of the university, consisted of a cluster of monstrous concrete buildings.

It was late in the day when I arrived. I had been contracted to give a performance.

The village was deep in snow . . .

As soon as I arrived, I realized that at this moment I also had a performance at a second university. I had to return to that school immediately.

The inside of one of the university buildings consisted of rooms as cold and empty as its outside.

I was supposed to read with another person. I had presumed that the usual would take place: that the other person and I would each have half the allotted time. Not that any time had actually been allotted. But I found myself reading alone in the empty room. If I had any audience, it wasn't visible.

Halfway through my lecture, I suddenly realized that another poet—I presumed the one who had been scheduled—was reading his work while I was reading. Moreover he wasn't paying attention either to my content or manner of presentation in the way of the "Language Poets." (I recognized that his "cutup"

170

performance has nothing to do with that of the "Language Poets.")

Finally I felt the same way that I do in the dream of walking through quicksand, quicksand that's deepening, and I move increasingly slowly: I became disgusted and tossed my papers onto the wood floor and got out.

I was still in the same school building. I remembered that I had to be in Buffalo to give a reading at the university there. Now I slowly and meticulously calculated every detail: it's now 8:55 P.M.; in order for me to be in Buffalo on time, I'll have to catch the nine-o'clock plane; it'll take me so many minutes to find a taxi; it'll take the taxi I don't know how long to reach the airport.

According to these precise calculations, I had to hail a taxi immediately, but there were no taxis around.

My plans for the first time changed: all I can do is my best so if I don't find a taxi, which isn't going to happen, I'll phone Buffalo and tell them that I'll be late for my performance.

I tried one pay phone. Then another. Everything in the building was dead. There were no connections to the communication lines outside the school. I turned to each student, male and female, who walked by me to ask how these phones worked.

No one in school knew the way to communicate with the outside world.

I had to get out of school as quickly as possible. So I raced to the stairs. The more flights I ran down, the more flights there were, the more I realized that there was no way I could leave this building, which was growing visibly in height and coldness.

One flight below, I walked to a room that was larger than the one in which I had read. The floor sloped down to walls whose windows were so huge, they formed most of the wall.

Hard wood chairs in a semicircle in the back.

Mrs. Aiken or Ⓐ who was an older thin gloomy Chinese

woman was in the middle of her speech. Afterwards she came over to me and told me that she was a great admirer of my work. I was shocked that this *very respectable feminist* wanted to have anything to do with me. That she knew who I was. What's her real politics? Then a gray-haired woman who's a very well-known media figure, who looks like one of "The Golden Girls," shook my hand and stated that the text I had just read was "highly interesting."

I still had to get out of school as quickly as possible.

But first I have to phone the university at Buffalo and tell them I have been unable to phone them to say that I can't get to them.

I don't know how I was able to evacuate the huge concrete building to flee anywhere else. I returned to the white cottage, where I was staying while on campus.

In this room, which was green, for the first time I knew that I would be able to escape from this school. Four people in my room were going to help me. They were three rockers and one female.

This is how they enabled me to escape school: their room is filled floor to ceiling with records. The rockers advise me which records I should listen to. Predominantly spoken-word records.

I began to pack it up.

Boarding the plane for out: In order to reach the seat that I'd been assigned, I was forced to climb over several rows of seats. The seats were overfilled.

As soon as I was sitting down where I should be, an elephant sat on my lap. The elephant was hugely gigantic, but as soon as it or I peeled off its flesh, which consisted of lots of thick fake fur, I saw that this was only a thin, skinless animal. It puts its arms lovingly around my neck.

Pirates: He staggers, his bloated tongue ranting, his rotten soul burning in his bowels. Ringed by swarms of roaches that will now never quit him until after his death, he plans murder

after murder . . . his son . . . all his family . . . all the monks.
The roaches munch on the buzzing flies while they sit on his
lips. From the pit of his throat, he tried to scream that *the hour
of rebellion is now at hand* . . .

But there was no one to hear him . . .

12. BUSH ON ABORTION

(Kneels on the ground.) "God,
if these masses of flesh that we call *the women of this country*—in
particular, my daughter, her blood, this part of me that is diseased, whom I've just raped—were made by You:
"God, listen:
"I'm going to drag my daughter through every crime that is
worse than rape, through every crime that's as yet unknown to
man.

"This is how I'll begin to do in my daughter:
"One: Reputation. Today, to govern mass opinion is how to
control the political body. Every single monk or person in this
community is going to consider the slut as more than outcast, as
all that is hateful. From its beginning, America has been a
religious civilization.

"As soon as my daughter's dead, she'll be unburiable—no
dogs will stick their noses into this cunt—because the stink of
rebellion that is named *menstrual blood* never ever leaves skin,
even that which is dead.

"It is true that God hath decreed: Let the starving dogs
starve."

Bush's curse: "It is the physical world that has caused all
this. The physical world that is always changing, menstruating,
turning to shit and turning its shit and sex, putrefaction into
our white minds. All that is flesh will rot; women give birth to
flesh.

"Worse than shit or this physical world is that which lies

173

under it: fantasies dreams desire sexuality. All that is the underworld. This underworld is Satan. Our fight, above all, is to defeat the Evil One wherever he has dared to stick his crimson dick.

"Does Satan dare to think that we're a cunt?

"God! Hear me!"

Bush kept on throbbing: "Two: Dear child, Savior of my family (I am calling on You, Jesus Christ), I know that You love me with such love that You will answer all of my prayers:

"What I wish most is that my dead daughter becomes pregnant.

"There will be no more abortions.

"May her child look exactly like her so that every time she will look or peer at this brat—she has to look at her own brat—she will see every scratch every purple pulsating pimple every bit of rotting flesh every gorge and abyss in the skin every fester every cancer: may my daughter have borne life only so that every minute she will be confronted by every characteristic that she detests: herself.

"May my daughter go beyond death into the realm of self-hate.

"This isn't a wish: this is how things are. For I and my daughter are of the same blood. Reality is that a child eats out her own mother in the same way that the dogs would eat my daughter if her cunt didn't reek of its own blood."

The end of speech: At the end of his speech, Bush vomited. "Now eyes are closing because it's night. I love my mommy so much. All bad conditions will grow worse."

Bush put himself to bed.

13. DREAMING POLITICS

"Where does Bush's power stop? Where does an authoritarian leader's power stop? Tell me, Mommy, where and how will Bush's power stop?"

Mrs. Bush and her daughter hired two murderers to kill Bush. They did. The details are bloody.

Dreaming politics: "I dreamt," B said, "that I was on a subway.

"In my dream, this subway is an escalator that's level. In order to reach my first goal, I have to transfer twice.

"I transferred onto trains.

"At the end of the line, decaying train track . . . I found myself in the country, dirt stone low-level grass . . . white trash country.

"The country grew deeper and deeper while, in order to get to my goal, I either rode a bus down a one-lane road or hitched. It was always night now. Finally where I wanted to go, one train car derailed on tracks overgrown by weeds in front of an old rickety hut. A geezer might have been in this hut, if there were people. I had reached my goal: two little turds came out of my asshole. They were sitting in my white cotton panties. I didn't care that I had done this.

"Some time passed; my shit was coming out of me and covering the surfaces of my skin and clothes.

"I realized that I no longer understood any customs or laws.

"The realms of Death, where I've never been, have customs and laws that I don't know.

"I don't want to live where Bush is leader so you who are unknown, Death if need be, please hold me."

2

OUT
(IN THE FORM OF HEALING)

After the monastery incident, all that I had ever wanted happened: B left me.

SIX

REDOING CHILDHOOD: THE BEGINNING OF THE HISTORY OF DREAMS

Now that I was free of B, I decided that I would find out who I was.

I went back to my real childhood: I started to remember.

Nothing will prevent me, neither close attention nor the desire to be exact, from writing words that sing.

My childhood began with President Bush. Precisely, this childhood began on the day when Bush began to carefully write down the instructions that were to be carried out on the day of his funeral.

He did this because he knew that people like him do not die.

"*I*, this country's Supreme Dictator," Bush spoke clearly into his Dictaphone, "otherwise known as only *I, I the everlasting everblasting president all other names,*

"(according to my discretionary powers as president),

"named because pirates have no name,

"declare that on the day of my death

"which is just about to take place
"according to my wishes,
"do declare that my head be cut off. This head should be draped in rosebuds, roses in full bloom, and dead roses. Human bones will hang all around the dead roses. Stick the whole mess on a pike so that the people whom I've put in prison can pay homage to me.

"Afterwards the headrosebone emblem shall be the cuntry's new flag; seven grungy, emaciated boys shall carry the original around the courtyard of the United Nations until the boys drop dead. Then all the little children who are now starving can feast their eyes on my eye sockets.

"My eyes will live forever.

"May the death penalty, which has just been nationally reinstated, remain in effect so that everyone who worked under my auspices can be executed. Those who earned the most money will be inflicted with total capital punishment the most painfully. On the day of this last human termination, education in the primary and secondary schools shall be completely devoted to learning how to change diapers. But there will be no more university education: by that time the human memory has been formed.

"Education shall become this: the headrosebone emblem, *I, Who* will continue talking with God.

"May one fact remain to form human memory: since a state is just a mask that secretes and shelters the power relations behind it, every state is fetishized or sexually desirable. For *I* am talking about *MYSELF.*"

In those childhood days there were as yet no pirates. I didn't remember that. My first memory of having a memory or of consciousness began with the day that I entered school.

Before that there were glimpses of memory. A tiny blanket . . . soft barely pink . . . roses lay everywhere . . . my hands are clutching this. *The first thing in the world.* Then they take it

181

away from me "in order to clean it"; "I promise I'll bring it back, Laure"; I never saw the blanket again. My first memory or bit of memory of memory is of absence.

Absence is.

And so I entered school. A school *just of girls*. At this point I didn't remember that. I remember one girl, dirty-blond hair which is more blond than light blond, a body tall and thin. The looks or appearance of all that I'm not: a WASP.

Starting in third grade, all of the students opened each day by singing Christian hymns.

Third grade. In the tall thin girl's, Lurker's, house, my milk was served to me in a thick blue glass that turned the milk blue.

We began electing class officers in third grade: Lurker naturally became our first president. On the whole, she remained president until the end of our education. Two presidents were elected every year, of which Lurker was usually the first. Now and then there was a revolution, but as yet no pirates. Without having to try at all, for such girls never need to try, Lurker led the good girls.

Who were the good girls? Rich WASPs not by birth or girls who had accepted without questioning parental instructions to do everything to be like rich WASPs.

In this second group was found Paula of the straight mousy brown hair.

These were the girls whom my mother and her priest ordered me to woo to court to make my friends to imitate and to become. It's no good being a Jew in this country, my mother didn't need to say, though being a rich Jew is better than being a poor WASP.

Though I was too shy to show any self and had no idea of my self besides awkwardness and mush, I worshiped the girls who were bad. Here, in time, began my memory of my identity or of being someone. *Bad* means *slimy* or *dripping with sexual juices thus messy* and *mean*. I knew that the rankest possible sperm was

182

dropping out of the lips of these girls. While mouth sperm flowed in them, their hands moved under their skirts. They weren't awake without masturbating. They masturbated everywhere except when they were getting screwed.

I knew that the girls were dirtier than all these images.

Later I would meet girls who actually were as wild as I thought boys were. Girls carrying cunts who breathed, like those monstrous clams I found on ocean wastes, slime each time they opened, the way I know a heart will if it's separated from the body: the vulnerability of openness.

I hadn't yet met a boy, except for a cousin who couldn't play basketball as well as I could, nor had I met one of these girls: I didn't need actual beings to know that they existed. And I knew something else. That I was akin to them because I was wild, but that my wildness consisted in my lack.

Through them, I was beginning to have an existence, or memories. The girls in my class who weren't good as yet weren't bad, but I saw how they would become, who they really were. In reality they were composed of the following categories: girls from families who weren't filthy rich (for no one in this school was poor except for the janitor; even the teachers had to be able to afford to teach in this school); girls who weren't "pure white"; real Christians, usually Catholics, not filthy rich, and always on scholarship; girls whose parents were criminals; the solitary female whose father was a Democrat.

Before I began existing, I somehow was elected the second president of these girls. The leader, though I remember that I never talked to anyone. Nor had any friend as yet penetrated my isolation.

My birthday. For some reason that I didn't know I was sitting by myself in a large and empty room.

Sitting directly on its floor. I knew that it was my birthday because lots of letters were being brought to me.

I opened all of them. Some of them were interesting, surprisingly. Now that I was, greedy pig, receiving objects I liked, I could look down at my watch; I realized that it was time for me to go to school.

There was only seven minutes for me to get to school.

I knew that I wasn't going to be at school on time. Therefore I did nothing. Finally, when I couldn't stand my tension any longer, I said: I'm definitely going to be late for school so I might as well not go to school. At that moment I heard gunshots.

I had an excuse for not being in school.

I was in an immense room. This room resembled either the school's dining room or another room in the same building. As I was standing there, the gunshots were getting closer.

"When the bullets appear, just duck under the table and you'll be safe." A man said to me. He and I were standing at one of the large, round, wood tables. Bullets ripped across the table and I threw myself under *as I had been instructed;* everything above the table splintered.

I remained intact.

I wanted to get away from this room as soon as I could. I sort of wiggled across the enclosure until I reached a door, then ran down the hall outside. Came to a door on my left. Behind this plain door ran a small corridor. A black door sat at the end.

Here I hid myself by crouching between the two doors. I could stay like this forever.

But I couldn't remain closed up. Returned to the larger hall.

I ran even farther away. I was in a rowboat and I was journeying. All of my treasures, all my possessions, of lace and of sky-blue ribbons and of crisscrossed metal which resembles ribboned lace, were here with me.

The man who was rowing the boat said something. I couldn't understand his words.

Perhaps something about the dead.

In response to these words, I looked down and saw a man's head at my feet. Blood lay on the mouth. The head was my husband's. Since it was moving, it was alive.

The rower, who was Charon, told me to sit on its face.

Animal: when I was in my prison cell, a green parrot walked over to me and opened up her wings.

From this I learned that childhood was the time when I was destroyed.

When all of us are destroyed.

Since my childhood is dead, in speaking of it I shall be speaking of something dead, but I shall do so in order to speak of the world of death, of the Kingdom of Darkness, or of Transparency.

After that, there were no more people.

In the next part of my childhood, which concerned *only architecture,* Bush gave his famous speech on the nature of art. Though not yet dead, as some, including his immediate family, had thought, he was lying on his magnificent deathbed; jewels were rising out of his lips.

"What's coming up from the prisons these days!" Bush began his most well-known vision. "Puke. Fouler than a scorpion's sting or a certain human smell.

"*We* are wasting money on prison toilets. I agree that one of our primary necessities is now to make major cuts in the national budget. And in national spending. Several years ago, *Our* agriculture developed controlled methods of force-feeding cows their own leavings; *We* can do the same with prisoners."

Bush didn't fool around, but got right to some point. Which the reporters, after his demise, decided lacked a little something. "I am speaking about *Our* artists. Artists nowadays, spending all their energy screaming that *My* repressive government won't fund their productions of wimp, are so pathetic and politically naïve that they can't even plan rebellions against *Me* so that *My* henchmen can have an excuse for sticking them in prison and then lobotomizing them.

185

"I call this generation of artists *the me generation*. After *Me,* of course! What a bunch."

Bush paused to blow his nose.

"And what is worse is that these artists don't have a sense of decency, so they're already talking about *My* funeral."

The era was named *the architecture of the funeral.*

Certain tribes had begun to shave bare their pubes. Then the Women-Who-Came-from-the-Forest became visible, seeming to radiate light. Bathed in broken reflections, refraction.

"I'm talking about those scum-mangy artists who are describing *My* own funeral therefore *Me* by appropriating words out of *My* own speeches *My* images that I've produced videos of *Me* cutting them up further and then translating all the hodgepodge into Arabic."

"That can't be possible, sir," interjected the secretary as she transcribed this speech. It was this very secretary whom Bush had leaked to the press was his mistress in order to cover over his homosexual leanings. In memory of former New York City mayor Koch.

"Why?" Bush scratched his scrotum.

"No one understands a word of what you say because they don't know why you say anything."

"I speak American." Bush paused. "That's the final crime!" *Final* as in *funereal.* Our century is finally coming to understand itself. "This use of *My* language! The homeless are not allowed to use *My* language because they turn truth into lies.

"Of course, not all artists will be homeless.

"I know that an artist is now penning *My* death, *My* words, and I want to find out who she is.

"At the same time," the dying man continued, "if no one could remember *My* words, no one could use or would have anything against *Me.*"

Bush had already applied his considerable intellect to the

problem. "It's the fault of the newspapers! Of all the media! They're still not telling the truth! From now on, I will ensure that all of *My* words speeches presentations visual images as presented to the public, the homeless, are no longer understand-able, are only nonsense and beyond that, incomprehensible.

"We will have truth that is the inability of memory."

Thus Bush finished off his memorable speech about art.

"But, sir!" protested the secretary. For she was scared of rats. "Prisons breed rats and rats live forever. We know that rats live forever from art rat examples such as de Sade and Genet. *The Marquis de Sade and Jean Genet.* The reason that rats live forever is that they'll eat anything yet none eat them except for their cousins-by-language who're always playing."

"That's exactly *My* point," Bush announced. "We must purify the language."

Thus it became clear that puns, bad language, and memory are closely conjoined.

This was the time of the architecture of death. The architecture of my school building was that of my school uniform:

Third grade is when babies turn into girls. At that time, so that we could enter this girlhood without learning how to compete, how to abide by and act according to differences of wealth and class, our superiors decided that we should all begin wearing the same clothes. A navy wool jumper falling one inch below the knee, loosely hanging off a white middy blouse. White knee socks and brown loafers or saddleshoes completed the prostitute look.

Our school had once been a horse stable. This red-brick town-house was located in one of the most expensive neighborhoods in the city, standing opposite one of the Rockefellers' residences. The latter building seemed emptier, though not more mysteri-ous, than the one they owned at the end of the street on which my parents lived. Between the end of the street and the river of

187

garbage. The second Rockefeller townhouse was hidden by an overgrown garden; I would peer through the black iron garden bars out of curiosity and envy.

I had no idea who the Rockefellers were.

The horse stable *in this rich section of town* had four stories, organized hierarchically. The ground floor was the one of adults: through grand red double doors, the grown-ups who weren't teachers, whenever they existed, entered to black-and-white tiles. At one edge of the chessboard, the principal, a cold bitch, held court.

At another edge, *directly opposite the principal's office,* an ornate marble staircase, which only the oldest of us were allowed to use, rose to upper regions. Regions neither of heaven nor of hell, as yet, for the school was Jewish. Rather, regions made up of labyrinths. These second and third floors of halls winding into halls then back again. Whose sole possessions, electric light bulbs, were only ornaments, for all the light came from their red coloration, which smelled of menstrual blood. Off corridors that seemed unable to become straight lay classrooms, small, carved out of wood.

I hadn't dreamt these halls and receptacles. In my dreams, the rooms that lined labyrinths held magic, secrets always differing from one another, whereas these were closed, held nothing.

The rooms on the third floor were smaller and uglier than those on the second. Monsters or adults walked on the ground floor; the denizens of the third floor were smaller and more full of rot than those on the second. For instance, a girl of the third *who was not a baby* could still stink of not knowing how to go to the bathroom.

Since I have no memory of the highest, or fourth, floor, the girls who lived there didn't exist. Among these girls, you couldn't tell one from the other; all of them were the one who pisses on her desk seat.

Above the children who weren't, the roof, open to the sun that never exists in this city, consisted of two playgrounds whose dimensions were equivalent.

The first, gray ground out of which a huge dollhouse that was trying to grow up into a log cabin had risen, was for the babies; the solitary green seesaw, sitting on gray, was allowed to be used only by third-graders and older.

Only concrete lay in the city of children.

Here my most vivid memory of school took place.

I don't remember exactly what grade I was in, probably third, because the dollhouse was a forbidden, not a forgotten, realm and Lurker Kimmelman was president.

It all began when Lurker announced, not solely to me, that only she and her two closest friends were allowed in the dollhouse. The dollhouse contained three dishes. Minimal dollhouse furniture. For she, Lurker Kimmelman, was our president.

I couldn't speak in the face of her truth.

Then, outside the dollhouse, our teacher began to line us up. This wasn't the teacher who broke a ruler by slapping a student's hand. We were put into two lines so that we could race each other.

A clothesline lay stretched from gray aluminum pole to gray aluminum pole ahead of us. We were going to run through the line.

Our favorite game, about which the teachers knew nothing, didn't have a name. Once a week, without any voting or other democratic procedures, we would unanimously decide on which one among us would be our next victim. The game or law was that for one week none of us could talk to the victim for any reason. During this week, she would prove her worth or not by handling silence. Only the two class creeps were never picked to be victims. The first one had a father who voted for Adlai Stevenson; she herself talked about "blacks." For me she was a creep

189

because, partially, secretly and silently, I admired her. The second one was a retard all of whose facial features were located inappropriately. One of the eyes was always closed, perhaps that would be later, while the other one sat lower on the face, right next to a nostril. Below, a skinny diaphragm caved inward. Whenever she dared to speak, words, like the diaphragm, disappeared at the moment when they appeared.

This retard, whose name, appropriately, was Penelope, arrived at my house for lunch. We were somewhere in third grade. This must have taken place before the race. Afterwards my mother yelled at me, her priest not there, Why wasn't I more like Penelope? Penelope was polite, well mannered . . . whereas I . . . I understood the real message clearly: I should become less than nonexistent.

It's my turn to race. I see that I'm going to race against the retard. I feel that I've no more pride. I run as fast as I can. I run even faster than I can. Just as in my dream of escaping the evil murderers, I can never run fast enough. The clothesline breaks around or brushes my face so I must have won.

Finally, I look around. I see that one of Penelope's eyes is hanging out of its socket. I don't know whether I'm responsible. Or not.

Because she was a retard, I've never known whether I was guilty or whether I'm more guilty.

I am thinking about the eyes and the necessity for vision.

The actual school lay below the floors. Far to the side of the black-and-white chessboard, a door hid the beginning of a horse ramp, wide and so dark as to be colorless, that descended into a space huge enough to be limitless.

We were fed in this cavern.

Clearly like horses, we were being groomed and tethered, what is named *education*, without being told the purpose. For some secret end.

The school was actually a hospital. My classroom, the usual white walls, was located in the center. Sixteen cots positioned in orderly rows covered the middle of this room.

The desk at which I used to sit day after day was located at the center of the cots. I remember the nurse feeding me cut-up pancakes mixed with fresh fruit out of a grand glass bowl.

I must have been sick. Even though I didn't feel that I was ill, I knew that this food was going to make me better.

I wasn't hungry and could only swallow a few bites.

Then the nurse told me that the man whom I desired, *whose name is Hans,* was located in one of the classrooms. Room 8. Or was it room 40?

I know that all of me, which is my body, wants to go to him. There's no more *why.* Schools are always teaching *why's.*

"So how do I get to him?" I have to make sure that I'll reach him. "To room 8 . . . ? Or room 40?"

I hovered at the threshold between the white room and the hall. The school hall had walls of dark velvet roses from which long-fringed lamps hung down, the winding hall of my great-uncle and great-aunt's hotel in New York City. Her voice saying, ". . . walk around in a U. Then, to your left, you'll see one stair. Open the door above the stair." I was looking out into my ancestral luxury, which has never been mine. "Or turn . . ." The instructions became increasingly confusing, and I could no longer understand.

I started walking down the hall of roses. Somewhere, while I was gazing at myself in a mirror hung on the wallpaper, that sight made me realize that, to reach Hans, I would have to erase the black makeup just below my left eye.

Then my whole left cheek turned black.

I rubbed a lotion, or an object that was white, into this cheek. Under the black, as I scrubbed away the skin, a red image

191

appeared, as if a red tattoo had been stamped into the skin prior to blackness.

Red and black were the colors of the hall's wallpaper.

I gave up rubbing my skin away and then remembered solely that I needed to get to Hans. But I had spent so much time on erasing my skin that I had lost my only opportunity to see him.

Now I would have to buy a motorcycle to get Hans back. Though I had never had him . . . I traveled through the countryside . . . in the countryside . . . This land is bleak. Gray and a green that is actually gray, flat as a sheet of paper . . . .
. . . .
Its depths are circular roads, the closest actual thing to which are racetracks within racetracks which have no center . . . .

Just beyond these depths lay my first stop, a place where motorcycles could be purchased.

Here: the motorcycle stable. I had been told that this was one of the cheapest motorcycle venues in the area.

I picked out, deliberately, the bike that wasn't the largest, but the next-to-largest. It was a white grasshopper. I climbed on to the very high seat and took off.

Through the country.

Riding so excited me that I forgot all about Hans.

. . . After some time the white bike broke down. But I was near enough to a garage, or an open space that resembled a garage enough to be a garage, to pull in there before the bike collapsed.

A blond German who exactly resembled Boris Becker, *who was the garage attendant,* demonstrated to me that there was no aluminum seal above the tachometer.

I hadn't known that there was one. Now I had learned something.

The Nazi added that the bike was dead.

"What'm I going to do?" I was anxious.

For I can't travel (live) without a bike.

"Abandon it."

I wanted to throw the bike away totally, but I felt guilty about the money that I had paid for it.

The Nazi did away with this guilt by explaining to me that I could collect the insurance on the corpse of whiteness.

I threw the bike away.

Now how could I get to Hans? Without transportation?

I lost more and more: Riding on I-don't-know-what down a long road that happened to be the first leg of a rectangle, I lost my black leather bag.

Then, on the third leg of the rectangle, I found a smaller version of the bag inside the one that had been forgotten. This was the key to everything.

The key . . . is named *charity*. I was returned to the room in which I had started. Here the only objects were all of my ex-husband's possessions:

Records. I listened to one after another. They were all hippie stuff. After I had thought this thought, I remembered to think about Hans. As soon as I had the thought *now I'm able to go to Hans,* he walked into the hospitalschoolroom and held me in his arms.

In the section of my childhood before I had any friends, the architecture of my uniform and school building and all that they named *education* was static (not subject to time or change), or fascistic. I have destroyed that architecture by dream in which learning is a journey. Chance and desire form the voyage. Here's the dream's map:

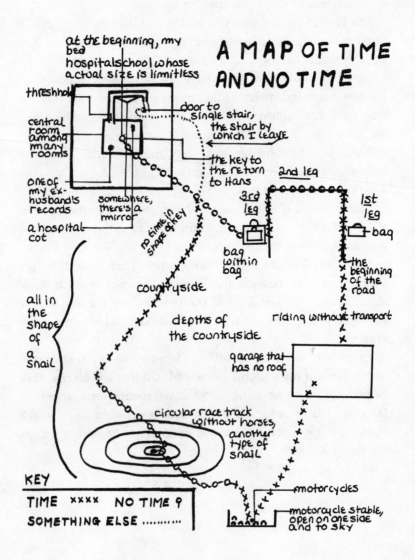

Bush was dying.

"Let me tell you the meaning of your dreams," said this dictator whose real name is *I:*

"*I*'ve forbidden the woman who is regarded as *My* sister to engage in the witchcraft practices in which she for many years has been interested. All she's really interested in is diddling little boys. This's what happens to women in this country when they become old.

"All American woman are witches.

"Even though she's an old bitch, my sister diddles little brats by encouraging those who attend her school to confess to her fully. That always makes the little boys hard.

"Remember the late and great Margaret Thatcher.

"My sister's eyes are also blank. In the past, she says, men fucked her and her identity into shreds. Men fucked her into a mirror-person. She says that the nuclear family of a mirror-person is only the confabulations of chance.

"I'd like to talk to you more about my sister," Bush continued this dying speech, "because she's my enemy. There are teeth living in every part of her body. Not only in her mouths. The proof of this is that as she became older and older, and then vastly old, because all witches are old, and she is now, she turned sexually ravenous.

"Men don't want to fuck old women because their sexual appetite will eat a man up."

Bush entered his dream.

" 'I'm an animal,' my sister says. 'I'm an animal because I've been forced to dream myself into existence, so dreams are my province. There are only dreams. This is the *nothing* which you men call *death;* therefore, in your male language, death and women are friends.' "

Bush explained that these are the reasons why women, not men, never lose their teeth.

"Both my sister and I are mad," Bush closed his statement

about dreaming. *"A specter of madness has always haunted our kin.* She believes that her magic will murder madness. I've told her this:

" 'If one of us is mad, we're all mad.

" 'The only way out of our mess is death. Sister. Exactly that is what my terms in office have been about and, in this light, all of my decisions have been reasonable. The only practical attitude now toward the United States and toward the history it has made is to destroy it all. This is exactly what I've tried to do.' "

Here was the beginning of language. My language. The first person who wasn't a monster for me was Miss St. Pierre.

Her breasts stuck out like little rabbit ears. My classmates whispered that she wore falsies. I saw that she wore medium-length hair of some color and red-lipsticked lips when the lipstick had worn off and that she wasn't pretty.

For me, there were two women in this school. The other, the principal, Burpface, was at least ten years older than St. Pierre. Burpface, we never called her by anything but her last name solely out of disrespect, was cold and stiff: her hair had whipped itself back into a bun. I suppose that adults considered her good-looking since she was neither fat nor had pimples. Her back was unbending; her skin was green-gray. Concerning my personal relations with Burpface, I remember only being reprimanded: inside her office at the edge of the chessboard, she tells, as she has already told me, that my brown hair, invariably stuck by a rubber band into a ponytail, is too messy, that my accent comes from Brooklyn (by *Brooklyn,* I understand *low-class,* since I have never visited Brooklyn), so I must go to speech class so that I can speak. I know that she is really saying that I'm a troublemaker and incipient revolutionary.

After she said what she said to me, I, as always, replied with as little as possible, with no emotion, so that I could leave her office as quickly as possible.

Outside the school the sky was dark blue. The air now was

crisp due to the dark green leaves. But I couldn't leave this school because all its streets had turned to ice and I knew that it's dangerous to ride a motorcycle over ice.

My mother's mother had wanted me to be a ballerina. I want to be that unnamed animal so that I never have to speak to anyone again and I'll sit next to human knees and feet and be constantly touched.

Miss St. Pierre was more sensitive and possessed an even more indirect, more underhanded way of being petted than a cat. Our intimacy progressed. Even though she never said anything about her life to me, I recognized loneliness, her loneliness: loneliness drew me into her because it was the only thing that could caress my awkwardness, my inability to talk, my shyness, and all the other characteristics that separated me from normality.

Miss St. Pierre was the youngest of our two literature teachers, and therefore poor. I knew that she didn't have any money because her lips curled and she was perpetually scared of Burpface. We knew that the older teacher was a lesbian, though none of us knew what a lesbian was. *Lesbian,* our first word, meant *something bad.*

In this way, the first word of our schoolgirl lexicon conjoined badness *(what we shouldn't be)* with the unknown.

Though poor, Miss St. Pierre ruled over the library. I ran away to here; I would try to stay in this library, which seemed as far as possible from my mother, from her priest, and from the rules of the school.

In this place, Miss St. Pierre, who looked like my mother except that she wasn't beautiful, showed me books to read. Melville and Keats, Yeats and a battered *The Wizard of Oz.*

I remember that I hid among these books for a long time. One day Burpface called me into her office. This wasn't unusual. She informed me in well-modulated tones, which showed her degree of education, that I was no longer allowed in the library.

It was during that school year that I had become accustomed,

197

rather than attending gym, to remaining in the locker room while gym was going on, drinking out of the Jack Daniel's bottle that I had hidden in my locker. My father had always imbibed Jack Daniel's while my mother called him an alcoholic. But no one bothered to stop my practice and order me back into the gym.

As soon as Burpface had said what she had to say, I ran up two flights of stairs to the library.

Perhaps she had looked up.

"Tell me the truth . . ." bursting into the place of wonder. Memory and an anger that was doubly wrapped in impotence and desolation was making me tremble: I retreated into the childhood that I had never had: curled down into a ball at the edge of St. Pierre's feet. I tried to disappear by wrapping my arms, which felt as if they were elongated, around my legs. Miss St. Pierre kept her eyes on the ground and rolled the cracked brown leather volume, which she had been clenching, quickly from hand to hand.

When she lifted her eyes, they moved around like an animal's. Then she agreed. "Yes. But it's not what you think, Laure. As usual, you're being too sensitive."

"Tell me why I'm no longer allowed in here." I said this, but I wasn't listening to anything she said. My eyes, like hers, were stuck to the floor. "Please . . . please don't make me leave here."

My hesitations and tremblings and murmurings made more emotions fly out of the gaps in me. "I don't have anywhere to go. Don't I mean anything to you?" I looked straight ahead. "It's none of fucking Burpface's business what I do. She wants to punish me just because I'm not like everyone else. But I will never stay in her prison. She's a witch."

Actually, when I thought logically and rationally about Burpface, which wasn't much of the time and certainly not at that moment, I had to admit that she was an excellent headmistress, or witch, for her self-control and complete lack of emotions allowed her to raise a lot of money and maintain total order where there in reality was and could be none. In Burpface, the quality of decisiveness, which usually raises itself to the heights of imperiousness, took on a strength of purpose. She embodied all of those characteristics that men love when found in themselves and hate when found in women.

"Laure, Mrs. Burpface is saying what she thinks is best for you. You must go to classes like the rest of the students. This isn't your home. Please do what Mrs. Burpface tells you to do. You don't understand, but that is what is best for you."

"I love you." I was uncontrollable. "And I know that I'm the student you care about. *You* don't have any regard for all those fascistic things that are always coming out of her mouth?"

Miss St. Pierre's way of explaining that she had no commerce with Mrs. Burpface's orders made me realize that she wasn't speaking truth in the same way that I was speaking it and that she didn't feel about me as I did about her. I had no way of actually perceiving her perceptions and emotions.

She proceeded to explain to me that there was no way I could be completely forbidden use of the library.

The more that the word *rejection,* the word that follows *lesbian,* appeared, the more I fixated on it. I was being rejected again. The memory of my mother and her priest become actual started me bawling; bawling led to more and more bawling. Until actuality or the world emptied itself out.

And I left this world of language.

My hysterics must have disconcerted Miss St. Pierre, because she began to tell me things that I shouldn't know. Mrs. Burpface was . . . something . . . to her . . . all taking place in the world of adults or monsters . . . And I understood nothing.

What I clearly saw was that Miss St. Pierre had allied herself to the world of monsters rather than to me. And that I was a lousy, useless kid, I who was totally alone.

After I had seen this, I left the school. Even though ice totally covered the streets outside, the streets were better than where I was.

Anywhere but here.

I started up my motorcycle . . . I don't remember what happened next . . . impossible . . .

The next stop was at a large bookshelf built out of wood which was unpainted or natural. A few model ships sat on its empty parts.

I sat down cross-legged in front of this bookshelf. The first model ship I had ever constructed stood on my lap. I felt so satisfied with its making that I reached toward the bookshelf for a second model. Each model, as I glanced over it, seemed flatter to me, became increasingly two-dimensional, increasingly not interesting enough to bother to build. Finally, I looked at the model of a bridge that should have been fascinating but instead was only a two-dimensional puzzle.

That which is only a puzzle is boring.

I had to escape from the boredom of my life, the puzzle, and reach a place where there were people who could teach me. These people are named *famous*. For information about them I turned to a map.

Soon I found the place I wanted to reach. The section was a narrow mass of land in the center to the right. According to my map, water crusted its shores.

Famous people, then, lived on the East Coast (I presumed that the map was of the United States, but it needn't have been).

The name that was printed over this section in big letters was BAY BRIDGE AREA (which is found on the United States' West Coast). Below BAY BRIDGE AREA I saw a list of names. I assumed these were the famous people for whom I had been searching.

The name *Wilson* was circled.

Wilson was the one I must want.

Here was the key.

I started heading toward the Bay Bridge area . . . I walked over sand . . . dunes that rose upward.

In front of me, two ridges stood above all the others. The one on the right was lower and wider than the other one.

The two guys who were traveling with me started climbing the right dune. Under its surface, water or some other liquid had turned the sand black. One of the men who had been sinking into this darkness broke his ankle.

I had been stumbling up the left ridge. By now, I had also sunk into sand . . . sand lay all the way around my chest. Even though I was almost buried, I realized that I could travel this way, that the treacherous and shifting ground in no way hurt me.

The two guys had already joined me and we kept on traveling . . .

What does this dream tell me about my school?

Education, or the repetition and internalization of set models and the childhood seen through the lens of this education are false. Not just the models taught in class, but all perceptual models made and turned absolute. For instance, when I was a child, I didn't actually know either St. Pierre or Burpface, yet I defined myself, predicated my identity on how they saw me and how I perceived how they saw me. The above dream has shown me that, since the identity I was taught is fake, childhood is a fake.

I just wrote down *dreams aren't fake*. I don't know what this means.

I named the next section of my life *evil* because that was when I started to care about people who were my own age. The two girls, not with whom I was the friendliest but about whom I thought the most and whom I remember the most deeply, were twins, the Jones twins.

I knew they were evil because they had long, straight, real blond hair and were German.

201

They looked almost exactly alike.

The most disturbing factor was that they were more intelligent than me. We were the three most intelligent girls in the school, if not the most intelligent the school had ever seen; my imagination soared, but I was a slob, whereas the Joneses were clever, neat, and precise.

Since we were the intellectuals, we were the unofficial leaders of our class. In their clarity, the Joneses knew that they should agree with their parents, who weren't as filthy rich as some of the other girls', and should social-climb: therefore they became the leaders of the good girls. I, on the other hand, believed that whereas neither Lurker nor Burpface was evil (Lurker was natural because she was acting as she had been taught to act and Burpface was only doing her job), the Joneses were, because they ass-licked the filthy rich girls for no reason at all. To me, *obeying parents who want to climb socially* meant *no reason at all*.

I was a rich snob, competitive and aggressive.

These were the days before sex. I thought about the Jones twins all the time, until my thoughts about their evil were forced to pop forth into the open.

As I've said, all the students, except for those who didn't qualify as such—the babies—wore identical uniforms. The Joneses also wore the same coats, camel's hair, and in the spring, leopard. I didn't know if their animals were real.

I did know that these coats were hanging in the cloakroom just off the chessboard between Burpface's office and the red entrance doors, though there was no cloakroom anywhere.

One day I walked into this cloakroom. There was no one in sight. Time seemed to have disappeared. I blew my nose into one of their leopard coats. Then I squished the mushed-up bubblegum that was in my mouth into this mucus.

I couldn't tell if the leopard was real, what the real was.

I don't know if the Joneses learned that I was the one who had ruined them, though I knew that they knew everything.

Nevertheless, they revenged themselves more than adequately without having to do anything. By now it was almost the end of school; it was the time that prizes were being handed out. The Jones twins and I won all but one of these prizes. But one of them won the English prize even though I was St. Pierre's favorite.

These were the days before sex.

School was over. Immediately after the ceremony of prizes, I saw Miss St. Pierre in the black-and-white vestibule. She stood next to me. Even though she saw me, she pretended that she didn't and turned around to Burpface. I was excluded, this time forever.

I never saw her again.

In this manner, I was left to, and remained permanently in, the world of those my own age and younger, the world of competition and of envy.

These days we know that all that matters are motorcycle accidents. Blue leather boys dragged by their ankles under sports-bikes along dug-up streets slippery with rain; semis along the freeways permanently stuck to bikes knocked over by 60-m.p.h. crosswinds. One bike was leaning over a white Olds whose driver had crossed lanes into the Rebel; another bike, found in the brush well below the freeway, had left blood painted across the highway concrete. Girls lost their legs. Bikers limped into second-hand dealers to buy new death machines. Along one highway in the emptied Southwest, a motorcyclist was still driving, his black helmet, which an eagle had just sailed into, split in half, still hanging around his neck. The biker had lost consciousness and was riding upright without a mind on the road. At the same time, in a nearby urban ghetto, the poor started setting their own homes on fire.

Let the homeless sleep that sleep that they never sleep nor dream of.

It was announced that the imagination is dead. To reduce the imagination (the actualizing of dreams) to slavery, even when that slavery goes by the gross name of *happiness,* is to strip oneself of every remnant of the supreme justice that is in each of us.

In December of 1917, a State Department official in the Wilson administration had remarked to someone or other, "The Italians are like children . . . and must be led and assisted more than any other nation." Mussolini's March on Rome in October, 1922, "a fine, young revolution," according to the American ambassador, solved that children problem.

Fascists "are perhaps the most potent factor in the suppression of Bolshevism in Italy. . . . All patriotic Italians . . . hunger for strong leadership and enjoy . . . being dramatically governed." (—Another American).

The U.S. embassy further reported that fascism had effectively gotten rid of hostile elements by restricting the right of free assembly, by abolishing freedom of the press and by having at its command a large military organization.

"The wops," *Fortune* magazine said in 1934, "are unwopping themselves." A State Department report agreed. "Fascism is becoming the soul of Italy, having brought order out of chaos, discipline out of license, and solvency out of bankruptcy."

What was one motorcycle accident more or less? Homelessness was growing out of architectural decay.

I became a teacher.

One day I was told by those who had more authority than me at the school that I couldn't wear my usual drag.

I became furious: when this emotion retreated to the point that I could have other thoughts, I perceived that the rejection of my appearance or my decision who I was in this social world came from sexism. I had already recognized that sexism was running rampant through every area of the school.

A new mixture of frustration, anger, and hatred in me forced me to act. Though I hate having to act. I asked lawyers if I could sue this institution for sexism.

204

These professionals and I came to the conclusion that we were going to blow the school apart.

Sometime after this incident, inside one of the school's buildings that resembled part of Oxford, a student who was female, appearing from nowhere, shrieked, "They're coming!"

I thought that the scream was a prank, typical in the school.

But coming, they penetrated the Oxford-like building. An emergency was signaled in an office somewhere in the building. Right after the signal, penetrating this same office, they grabbed its phone. And so they began to control the communications system of the United States.

A doctor said, "This emergency is real."

How can I escape this unbearable political reality?

One girl tried sliding between the crack that ran down the center of a huge bed. It was the bed in my parents' bedroom.

By this time, I had learned that they or the evil was *Jonathon Edwards of the Mormons*. My knowing this brought them near to me. So I, who was the other girl, slipped into the crack.

In this new space, everything was beautiful.

Thus I learned that that door to the invisible, the only place that is left for us to go, must be made visible.

Toward the end of my education, my parents and teachers offered me various methods or paths by which I could travel from the school into the world outside. The way considered most desirable was to marry a very rich man so old that he would die soon after the marriage. Then I would inherit all his money.

Even better than this would be for the old rich geezer to be a WASP, because then I would receive the social position closed to Jews.

One of the girls in my class, Faith, managed this. Immediately after school had finished, she married an old man. At the wedding, one of her grandfathers gave the couple a bank. I never learned what her parents had donated. Then I lost touch with Faith . . .

At a much later date, my mother, who at that time would only deal with me in a formal setting, informed me that Faith had gotten the fate she deserved: the old man, before he had popped off, had given her a baby who came out mongoloid.

I knew that "get what she deserved" meant that she was punished because my mother was envious of her marriage and furious with me for failing to accomplish the same.

The second and only other acceptable method by which we could leave school was to extend our education. For this and only this reason, the horse-training school had encouraged us to become as intellectually aggressive and competitive as possible. My parents and teachers, aware that I will not by nature marry a rich man, explained to me that by attending a top college I still kept the possibility of a rich or "decent" marriage. If I was so evil that I couldn't even do that, I would at worst learn to be a top-flight scientist or lawyer.

There were no other possibilities in our world with the world dissolving. And outside, the riots were happening.

Refusing all these alternatives, I left school for a world without language in which I had no language.

Section from Bloods/Crips' Proposal for USA's Face-lift (Cost: $200 Billion):

Every burned and abandoned structure, including all government buildings, shall be gutted.

I want to describe the beginning of this world where there isn't language:

While I had been still enrolled in school, my mother, for the first time against the advice of *her priest,* had sent me to dancing school. By name: Miss Savage's School for Girls.

I had no idea what a man was. At that time. There was my cousin, a boy, slightly older than me, but he played basketball worse than me, so he only showed me that the word *boy* means *nothing.*

206

Virginity doesn't know its own name.

This second, secondary, school took place every Saturday night in one of the wealthiest parts of the city. Within those hallowed precincts of dancing school, my best friend, Maggie, who was so wild and tough that she was the head of our street gang dedicated to the task of making all bank alarms start ringing, and I would hide in the bathroom far away from the boys, whom we despised.

We smoked cigarettes while all the obedient children danced by.

Outside this toilet, the girls, wearing blond hair, knew how to flirt or present lying selves to boys.

Their relatives were the Catholic girls I saw in the subway station every time I went to school. Catholic girls were the ones who wore green pleated skirts, white middy blouses, and white knee socks; this is the uniform of *sluts* who fuck every boy who comes near them, even on subway platforms.

It was after some months that Loyola Savage herself ordered us to emerge from this bathroom. I was forced to dance with a boy, for the first time. I did, without knowing that my body was female and that the liquid that dripped onto my thighs once a month wasn't carrot juice. My whole body expanded and became hot. I couldn't care less who the boy actually was. When my body entered this unknown world, for the first time I became frightened. In me, fear and sexual desire are now married.

The first moment a boy put his tongue in my ear, I did something like come.

And so I learned that any boy, if he does it in my ear, will do.

It is this amoral world, the one of constant wonder, journeying sights that amaze, in which I received and continue to receive my real education. Even if, now that I'm an adult, that world no longer bears only the name *sex*.

The beautiful world that lies outside the school to which they sent me! Sometimes the setting sun is a series of liquid fires that illumine the deer clustered together on the hillsides.

Night deepens, all the colors left turn neon. While the sun, which is almost dead, seeps through holes in the glass of the window in my bedroom and burns my shoulders to shreds.

It was night. The twilights in the West where the dead, unburied, control rather than help those living, had deepened and grown into this. All shadow. There the English pirates who had decided to conquer a former colony, not quite theirs, had begun to gather whatever money was left in the United States, money tied up in the shifting zones of the drug trade.

These pirates, a combination of uneducated English, mulattos and gauchos who for many years had been fomenting other forms of discontent, bikers, and a utopian community of hermaphrodites, couldn't have cared less about political doctrines and indoctrinations. But as they grew more and more wealthy, as the boundaries of the pillaging operations spread geographically, and in power, they began to touch the edges of the political. While the aristos in London acted as if they were playing with an empire that had actually long since decayed, as they have always acted, on the ocean the pirates held displays of pomp and circumstance similar to historic biker ceremonies.

The empire, or the epic, was finally over. Nobody, even of the few who could still read, knew or cared what epic.

The night was complete. Some pirates who dared to more than just touch land, their version of otherness, in order only to plunder and garbage, in a few instances rape, kept on traveling.

Finally they reached, according to certain maps that were so unreadable as to be useless, the domain for which they had been searching.

They had never known its name.

All they found of human life on this coast was a wood house having the shabbiest possible condition. This *oyster farm* consisted of one salting house (the center of the shabbiness), three dead beds, dead fish smell, and the remnants of a burnt-down convent. As the pirates walked toward what they had sought now only by means of their dreams, one of the nuns who was now living in the hut climbed on top of a hill made out of her excrement and began a speech in honor of this occasion.

"Dear sirs." Rags stinking from dried sea-spit barely covered the bodies of her proposed listeners, who had almost never in their lives listened to anyone. "Our cunts are red." She wanted to speak more about cunts, but some pirate interrupted her, then another. Several started belching and grunting.

Nevertheless, the pirates comprehended enough of her speech to perceive that they had arrived at *The Temple of Eros, or of That Dirt That Is Red,* and that this day was the birthday of the nun whose cunt was hungriest.

And so I left school. All that I wanted was to fuck and be fucked.

I was just beginning to live the life that I desired. We traveled, like children, from hotel to hotel.

Lived together in those rooms.

One hotel was composed solely out of floors. Floor after floor. Each room formed part of the intricately connected labyrinths that connected me to the memory of *the country that I've never seen.*

Children, we were traveling from room to room.

I climbed up three flights of stairs.

The floor that I reached was very very old. Furniture, carpets, the wood of the walls. Its rugs, on the whole, were decaying red.

Why, I asked, is red, which is the color of animal blood, the sign of old age?

All of these rooms were tiny. I was told that here I was to stay. The older, if not extremely old, woman informed me that I could pick any room to live in.

I found a door that resembled a dollhouse door built into an adult house for no reason and behind this door there were stairs that I climbed and at the top I found myself in a larger, though not a big, room. This room was the place in which I wanted to be.

It had no furniture, only the bed of *Jane Eyre,* which, of

course, is wood, because it has been made out of wood from a building of the school that Jane Eyre attended. A large, plain nightstand sat on the bed's right side. The only window in the room opened above the bed's head, like an owl. The air was dark, though not black.

Both knowing and comprehending were only ambiguity in this realm or house because here was neither morality nor any absolute: in this region, every event swirled through air that was always malevolent: what was happening in the house was drugs.

Having chosen my room, I climbed up stairs that were missing.

As soon as I was in the room, I knew that I had freely entered the following world: there were five of us; I was the only female. One of the males had started pissing into a white toilet. During the sound of the pissing, I learned that Muru was escaping from a drug bust. The more precise the details of this bust and escape became, the more detached from everything, nauseous, I felt.

"Are the refugees from all drug busts coming to this house?"

I received the following answer about the society in which I was living:

In this house, except for me, there were only men. In one of their bedrooms, a man was lying on a bed, behind him another man leaned against the pillows that were propped up against the headboard. Jerry was one of their names.

As I stood at the edge of the bedroom, one of the men asked if I would stay with them so that I could provide them with warmth.

This question immediately led to a series of images, one after the other, in my mind. It was a succession of pictures of American men. Then I understood that these images have been, and are, negotiating my perceptions of men, that the question "Will you give me warmth?" as defined through these representations, is fossilized as moralism. Simultaneously I saw that I hated moralism.

210

"I" is not an interior affair.

Afterwards, I answered all the men, "Yes. I'll stay with you tonight."

And after that, *like a child* perhaps for the first time, though images of men still presented themselves as fear, I fucked man after man.

Beauty will be CONVULSIVE or will not be at all.

In the last bit of my childhood that remained, I returned to the rich section of the city from which I had come. Here lay the beginning of memory. Every morning, the rich old women who were dazzlingly beautiful were still wandering around townhouses and through apartment buildings that had rotted. Where the air doesn't change color. Into parts of dead human bodies, in some cases, a leftover oyster, used and unused condoms. Small piles of bras covered over the limbs of those who were dying. This I have seen.

After night has fallen, this becomes the ground that no realtor will show.

There was a black-and-white apartment building located where a street of overly priced local stores met some of the most expensive apartment realty in New York City. X. The latter street ended in a river of garbage.

The river separated my actual childhood world from the realms that I desired, power and magic.

Here, at the X, was the apartment building where I had been born.

No humans except suicides dared jump into the river. Name: Lethe. Day after day, children, freed from their parents by the sun, in the park between the river and the street of rich apartment buildings, would watch rays of light attempt to cross through pollution so thick that it turned to garbage. Often filter through to a tugboat honking feebly on the water, though there was no one to whom it could talk. When the children could feel no breeze, here and there, gusts of hot air, appearing out of nowhere, would cause the boat's rotting wood to swell. That smell, like sex, mingled with the stink of the water. And what was wafting up from the bank, which was no longer dirt. Sun and ice, alternately, had baked that refuse.

The street on the other side of the block, running parallel to the one of expensive apartments, had buildings which, low, dingy, and hideous, hadn't yet grown up into tenements.

There were tenements at the crumbling edges of the urban area.

This street was of *that which is forbidden but isn't magical*.

For my mother had tried to teach me that the lower and filthier the apartment building, the shorter, more disgusting, and more numerous its residents.

I had dreamed, when I was a child, the river of garbage, but never *the street of that which is forbidden*. It was the only one that ran sharply downhill, from the local stores back to the river. I had left a pile of clothes, yellow or white, in the middle of this street.

When I came back to the top of the street, I argued with myself, then forced myself to turn right around, walk back down the street. For it would be wasteful to let the clothes disappear.

Halfway down this dark red, brown, and gray street, I began to look for the paperback for which I was searching.

I couldn't see the book immediately and started to get anxious. I looked to my left, toward the gutter. Started to walk back uphill. Looked to the gutter again. This time I saw a skinny black kid selling paperbacks, which were piled high on the back of a car. When I looked more closely at the stack, I perceived that they were all high-quality literature. But I couldn't see the book among them.

More lost than ever, I continued climbing uphill. After several feet, again looking left, I identified my book among more piles, so I grabbed it because it was mine.

212

At the top of this *street of that which is forbidden*, I turned right, toward home.

I kept on walking past that corner because I didn't recognize my black-and-white building. I walked in a straight line, for I knew that that way I had to reach a corner I could identify.

Several blocks had passed and I hadn't yet reached any familiar building. The concrete beneath my feet was now encased in a mixture of ice, black ice, snow, and undefinable substances like piss. After a couple of blocks of this, I decided that it was time for me to look up. I saw a street sign but it was indecipherable. I started feeling anxious, a different anxiety from what I had felt when I couldn't find my book among high-class literature.

I had to keep on truckin'.

I walked this straight line; my anxiety deepened. I knew that I should be home by now. Anxiety is time gone wrong. Block after block. Again I looked up in order to see a street sign. This time, the sign I saw was almost decipherable . . . *four* . . . I remembered that I live on . . . *five* . . . Fifty-seventh Street. As soon as I had visualized "57," I understood that . . . *four* . . . meant that I was somewhere in the forties.

I wondered how I could have gone so far wrong.

Immediately I turned around, back exactly the same way I had come, walking slightly faster than I could, but the streets were icy.

Anxiety was unbearable.

And suddenly I was home. Home was a room that resembled a loft which was empty.

A pair of large sliding doors separated my home from/connected it to a public space for the presentation of writing.

In this second place, a number of people were still waiting for me, even though I was very late.

I sat down, or up, at the high white wood pharmacy counter. Though either there were fewer people than usual at my readings or something else was funky. After it was over it turned out this reading had been worth doing because Diane di Prima asked me if she could publish my work in three of her magazines, each one of them different from the other. I was pleased *even though it was only small press.*

Somehow I managed to penetrate Diane di Prima's affair which was taking place in a room far more magnificent than the one in which I had just read.

This room was either a schoolroom or a church.

During one of the many performances that kept following each other, an older, even old, male poet, gargantuan stomach, bearded, who resembled Anselm Hollo but wasn't, was moving insect-like across the top section of one of the walls. Now something happened . . . something that I didn't know or something unknown . . . a lapse. . . . The Anselm Hollo look-alike was a bat.

Since many of the people who were in the room personally knew or recognized me, also since I actually took part in the performances, at the end of the evening I felt good.

And so my childhood ended in poetry.

I no longer have to return to childhood. I'm talking directly to Bush, since *while he was alive* I could never talk to him.

"President Bush," I say to the man who's now dead, "your suffering as a dead man is twofold for the following reasons:

"All the time that you were president, and before, you cloaked yourself in oblivion. You invited oblivion to sit on your face like a fat woman on an open mouth. In this country, we know what every mole looks like on the arm of every movie star, the tattoos on the cocks of every rock 'n' roll star. We didn't know the names of your children. We didn't know how you played ball with, before you were head of, the CIA. During this time, you were hiding yourself in morality.

"Simultaneously, you surrounded yourself with criminals, some of whom were your relatives, who pillaged and raped the

nation's peoples and resources while Jesus fucked with national-
ism.

"Tonight, dead, you're going to visit the prisons into which
all the peoples in this society who aren't desirable were and are
thrown. And those who, you learned, don't desire this society.
And those people who wanted to kill you.

"When you're in prison, the people whom you made prisoners
won't tear off your legs so slowly that the intestinal worms who
live after their hosts have expired'll have time to crawl down your
flesh, now white spirals resembling themselves. The men and
women whom you turned into death-in-life won't push your
eyeballs out with their thumbs and feed them to nonhuman and
ahuman friends. They won't pick up these friends and dangle
them by tails, red eyes right on your just as bright testicles,
which is a contest among SA torturers known by the name *which
rat can bite through a ball first*. These were the pleasures which not
only your international policies encouraged in third world, then
in the prisons here. The people whom you placed under torture
will not torture you because they won't recognize you.

"You are dead. Your kind is over with. The loss of memory
that you taught the media and their consumers has turned back
on you, as all policies turn back on their policy makers. A double
oblivion. For dream is that which is most sacred in human and/
or beast.

"A double oblivion . . ." Then my speech to the dead man
turned on itself and ate itself up. Death itself isn't enough to
obliterate: I knew there was still only rubble, riot, that which
now goes by the name *society*. I don't know what to do about all
that I see and experience. I can only ask *dream*.

I returned to Germany.

SEVEN

THE DEAD MAN

Before I returned to Germany, I asked the witch to tell me what was happening:

Card That Names the Problem:
Ten of Swords

Trio of Cards That Tell
What Will Happen If I
Follow My Helpers:
Five of Swords, The Chariot,
Seven of Swords

Trio of Cards That Tell
What Will Probably
Happen:
Six of Wands, Justice,
Four of Wands

Trio of Cards That Name the Present:
Nine of Cups, Seven of Cups, Ace of Swords

Trio of Cards That Name
the Helpers:
Eight of Cups, The World,
Three of Swords

Trio of Cards That Name
the Immediate Present:
Ten of Wands, Death,
The Hanged Man

217

From these I learned that I'm a dead man, devoid of desire. My society:

BITS FROM THE DIARY I WROTE IN GERMANY—I WAS JUST COPYING PORN NOVELS

Whenever I feel myself inferior to everything about me, threatened by my own mediocrity, frightened by a discovery that a muscle is losing its strength, a desire its power or pain the keen edge of its bite (I haven't felt sexual desire for many months), I can still hold up my head and say to myself, "Look:

"Tomorrow I shall surprise the red dawn on the tamarisks wet with salty dew and on the mock bamboo where a pearl hangs at the tip of each of its blue lances."

Look: . . .

. Here, in Berlin . . .

This night is better than hell . . .

. . . .

The cheap hotel that the promoters had booked for me. One towel so thin that it had already disappeared between someone's hands . . .

. . . .

(My French ex-boyfriend keeps saying that, according to history, here is a culture of nightmares.) . . .

. . . .

When I turned over, there was a male body . . .

. . . .

I don't know how anyone manages to sleep anymore. In this night.

The body next to me might as well be dead . . . I have dreamed of cocks sticking up their heads. When the heads opened, the clocks came out it must all be part of me because it does something unsayable to me that comes out.

218

In the night, all the people around me are dead I turned over and there was a man he didn't move. I pulled the sheet halfway down his body, it's always hard to start anything when being is incarcerated . . .

There was no indication that this man wanted to do anything to me . . .

. . . .

and on and on into a country I didn't know where there was only silence. Just like the country I had just left . . .

I will do anything to talk. That one thing which is impossible. Because I cannot will it. I will be taken. Here is the beginning of necessary violence . . .

When the flesh is torn (incarceration is broken and language emerges) . . .

. . . .

I will have cocks everywhere, populating my desolate countryside.

He moved into waking and, as if by reflex, a paw reaching for food, turned me over and tried to separate my ass cheeks totally. He pulled them apart so hard that I thought they might part and that scared me: consciousness that I could be torn apart. My fear made both itself and physical pain grow inside me. About the same time I realized that it made no difference, with reference to what was happening, how I felt or what I perceived. For, now that he was alive, the separation that had been between us was still between us.

Simultaneously, I saw that my consciousness no longer mattered and I began to act from a place, or places, prior to consciousness. Such as physical pleasure . . .

. . . .

We traveled more deeply into the countryside. The animals had begun to rule . . . .

. . . .

Listen. Tomorrow I shall surprise the red dawn on the tamarisks wet with salty dew and on the mock bamboo where a pearl hangs on the tip of each blue lamp. One night I saw a mountain, then, sitting somewhere on it, the lights of a village stretching themselves into the black. Since clouds occupied the sky, only the evening star could be seen.

THE FIRE SERMON

"When lovely woman stoops to folly and
Paces about her room again, alone,"

When I returned to Berlin, it was no longer the magic town it had been. It has, since the fall of the Wall, rhyme as the mirror of history, grown too large: now it seems Americanized, urban-Americanized, bordering on the edges of violences that are only dull. Those of petty theft and drug abuse and mugging, which arise from others of envy and greed and poverty, all dwelling within forms of capitalism, racial prejudice, and other commonplaces.

The streets and sky of Berlin no longer lay black, but that type of brown that was a sign of *stale sun*. Something or someone had wanted to smell.

The blackness sat only in my head.

I had asked the promoters and people who had brought me to this city, *in which I stopped dreaming,* to help me rent a motorcycle. A large one whose seat was low. If possible. This motorcycle would give me back the freedom I was about to lose in Germany, for on this tour of American writers, of which I was one, I would be, against my will, encountering three sections of my past: the European life and culture in which I used to live, had loved, and had been forced, partly by myself, to renounce; the two men, other than B, who had been my lovers; and that American poetry scene that my dream about Diane di Prima had described, out of which I had partly risen and which I now almost despised, and remembered adoring. If memory is the self, I was about, and against my will, to meet myself.

This past, at this moment of beginning, for me was a loss of my freedom. Loss in the form of the actuality of rejection, abandonment, and individual authoritarianism. For me the past sits in the form, the actuality of the father: I don't want to meet my father. He left me before I was born.

There was no reason left to find him.

Due to two exhausting airplane rides, I slept through the first day.

Then, there was no night.

On the second, I began to ride the motorcycle, a 550 Honda Custom, which the promoters had rented for me, and after finding my black purse ripped off, I traced Potsdamer Strasse, the only street I still recognized, to one of its ends. Into a section that was magic.

My last remembered dream: from Berlin's center, this realm can be reached by traveling south, or down.

When I arrived at the end of the thoroughfare that headed down, I pushed a button on the dashboard in order to turn left. That was all I had to do.

The second, or new, road, about which none of the Germans had told me but which was clearly signed, moved, at first directly, left, or east. As soon as half of it had disappeared, it turned narrower, like a dirt road, and began to wind.

I started to feel happy. I was free, so this city must be free. Here begins the section of young girls, for if there are any young girls, they're by springs, in forests, in silver and black grottos and shades, all of which are named *Echo,* so that this world may be young again and growing through stories. Pressing my body, and so, my bike, which had not yet become the same, or lovers, mine, now to the left, now to the right, in lopes the same as a wild animal's, we both flew through the turns.

Water lay on at least one side.

Water means *freedom.* I realized that I must be moving toward an island or a mass of land that was, here, connected to the remembered city only by the narrowest path.

Dreaming, earth is alive.

After all the winds ceased, I was on the edge of entering a small village. The kind in which all the shops hover at the main road. Such a town has no depth.

This town that I had penetrated resembled a fishing village whose shops had been refurbished, yet not quite gentrified. The name was *Wandsee.*

Then began another stretch, whose name was *Unknown,* where all was disappearing. Standing away from the motorcycle, when I looked across waters, which now ran considerably, I saw a second mass of land, more mysterious than the one I was on. A road made up of trees stood in the center of the foreignness.

Where could I go in all this freedom? But I didn't know anything . . . the roads . . . the language . . . so I had no idea where I might go: that lack stopped me.

Back on my bike, I rode by a candy stand.

I stopped and bought a bag of the sweets I liked the most even though, in my real life away from Germany, I never eat candy. As I climbed back on my bike, I remembered that one of the Germans had told me about a motorcycle bar or a movie theater that was somewhere in a section such as this one . . .

Not knowing anything, I saw nothing.

Though I had been convinced that it would be too dangerous for me to tour all of Germany by Autobahn on a disintegrating motorcycle, my freedom continued the next day. I rode in the car of the German who had convinced me, a well-known playwright and a motorcyclist. His hair was so black it was blue. I had never met him before. Soon we lost our way. After we had left the West for the East.

Plain after plain.

Hours later, the sun fell out of a sky and we found ourselves in Hamburg, at a movie house. The conference at which we had been scheduled to present our writing was going to take place in this theater.

I had expected to feel lonely. According to the promoters, the tour's purpose was to present new American writing to Germans; I am as much a representative of America and of "new American writing" as I was, and am, in relation to writing practice, close to the other Americans on the tour. My sense of the ridiculous, or loneliness, extended to personal relationships: one of my ex-boyfriends, another tour member, had abandoned me for the woman who was now his wife and who was about to meet him in three days. I hadn't seen him for a long time. There are many clichés.

All of the Germans, except for the one whose car I was sitting in, knew no English. So my actual loneliness, finally, came from being with him, this playwright, from being lost on roads I had never known and cannot name.

> eingeweiht in der Liebe
> aber erst hier—
> als die Lava herabfuhr
> und ihr Hauch uns traf
> am Fuss des Berges,
> als zuletzt der erschöpfte Krater
> den Schlüssel preisgab
> für diese verschlossenen Körper—
>
> Wir traten ein in verwunschene Raüme
> und leuchteten das Dunkelaus
> mit den Fingerspitzen.

Though it was a movie theater, inside the Hamburg Literaturhaus seemed a large living room. Its seats, including several couches that were scattered here and there, had been placed in front of a low, makeshift stage.

There were three sections of these chairs: most of them in its middle of the room facing the stage, and two ends of chairs facing this middle.

I was at the edge of that desire to be with Georg; I didn't want anyone else to notice the burgeoning desire; since I had no idea whether he was interested in me (I hadn't as yet begun to define *to be interested in*), I started to avoid him.

I don't know how desire begins. In someone who hasn't known desire in a long time. In soil that is barren. Barrenness out of rape. I'm writing this because I want to see where and how desire begins. Later on, when I would be wanting and not able to have him, Georg said, "Life revolves around desire."

I don't remember.

Language must begin in desire.

"The elimination of injustice, of oppression, all mitigation of harshness, every improvement of a situation still maintains the disgraces of the past. The disgraces, maintained by the continued existence of the words, may therefore be reestablished at any moment.

"No new world without a new language."

> Innen ist deine Hufte ein Landungssteg
> für meine Schiffe, die heimkommen
> von zu grossen Fahrten.

> Das Glück wirkt ein Silbertau,
> an dem ich Defestigt liege.

Whoever was running this joint informed us that because we were the performers and presenters, we could sit directly on the floor.

Beginning my effort to avoid Georg, I walked to the front of the room.

There was a high counter in this entranceway, behind which was Jerry, an old hippie, over fifty, sold small-press books, especially those by the writers who were being featured. Some other stuff.

These guys seemed older than the people with whom I was traveling. For a reason that I didn't know. For example, I thought that Georg was much younger than me even though, though I didn't yet know this, he was over forty. Perhaps because all the men with whom I had fucked in the past two years, excepting B, had been very young.

As soon as I was standing with Jerry and his friends, I felt *this is where I belong.* He was packaging coke. I sniffed up some of the dust. Most of his life, Jerry's been in a poetry scene.

Afterward, Büchner and I were sitting together at a round table in a corner to the left of the stage. I thought Hamburg was exactly like an American beatnik café.

Flying, I had the courage to sit on Büchner's lap.

On this lap: Büchner started discussing a subject about which I was immensely curious. He had refused to talk about it during the ride in his car. He began to tell me about his literary plans and praxis. "Every night I'm praying to the hangman's hemp and the lampposts."

I assumed that my sitting on his lap had made him comfortable enough to talk. I recognized that, due to my affinity for this lap, I couldn't distinguish between his reactions to my lap-sitting and my desire for him to want me.

Desire opened up the land of fantasy. I have always despised fantasy. This was the second reason to avoid Büchner, or to deny my desire for him. As soon as all the performances and the panel ended, I ran through the audience to an old friend whom I threw my arms around and hugged.

Georg didn't join us after dinner.

The night before I had left for Germany this time, my German ex-boyfriend, whom I had had no sign of for two years, phoned me. I was still running from B. Why? Since I wasn't home when the German phoned, he had left a message that said, "I'll try to meet you." When I reached the section of Berlin that used to be East, I was able to call him. I gave him my schedule, the list of hotels where I would be staying, which I hadn't known until that night. We would meet between Köln and Weimar.

That night I dreamed my last dream. In which my mother tried to kill me. She didn't succeed. Then someone else tried to murder me. When I asked who the murderer might be, the Voice told me that it wasn't my mother. It was a question of time.

"But it must be my mother," I replied.

"Yes: it's your mother who's now inside you."

I woke up from this nightmare.

Now there was no way that I could escape being murdered and stop being both murderer and victim.

Büchner: "If someone were to tell me that the poet should not depict the world as it is but as it should be, then I answer that I do not want to make it better than God, Who certainly made the world as it should be."

The tour's third or fourth day, I couldn't remember time anymore, I started on the approach to the city where my German ex-boyfriend was now living, the city in which we used to meet, according to plan, for a week, and then, when we would actually come together, it would always be "I have only two days," "I have only three nights." The next few days, the next nights, I would wander through *the city of memories*. I would search for traces. As I approached that memory, I became less interested in whether this man, for whom I once would have and tried to do anything, would actually phone again and I thought more about Georg.

Here I lost my dreams.

I wonder about animals' dreams.

During this time of dreamlessness, or being lost, which began in Köln, it was always late at night. I found myself drinking in a bar. Drambuie with Grand Marnier, which I knew is poison, though not because it's poison. One of the other writers told me that she wanted to organize a feminist conference in Germany. Büchner was drinking on the other side of the bar. I suggested that she discuss it with him. I returned to my drinking.

When I was alone, Bourénine, my ex-boyfriend who was on this tour, walked up to me. I knew that he wanted to be friends with me, all three of us, but until that moment I had been avoiding him. As if I no longer needed to make a decision, or felt anger, we talked somewhat openly.

Bourénine disappeared and I kept on drinking. The Lethe, I crossed over to the bar's other side where the American writer to whom I had been talking earlier was discussing the feminist conference with Büchner and a German whom I had seen around the tour.

I noticed she was gone.

Büchner was drinking more heavily than me, not than usual. He informed me that I couldn't ride in his car tomorrow because Bourénine would no longer talk to him.

"What do you mean?"

"Bourénine won't talk to me because you and I are friends." He mentioned that everyone else on the tour was jealous of us.

I noticed the other German was gone.

Anger made me free to speak. To speak is to make fiction. I told him about Bourénine's and my past. "Bourénine's wife is scheduled to join the tour tomorrow night." When I began to cry, I realized that I was out of control.

Since I wasn't conscious why I was crying, I entered the unknown.

Drunk and sleepless, searching through this night, I found an

227

answer: I should begin to travel by myself. I would join this tour, what remained, only when I had to.

Büchner was running out of the hotel. I stopped him because I had to tell him that I would no longer ride in his car.

He ordered me to reconsider.

None of us was drunk anymore.

Having the unfortunate habit of doing what someone I desire tells me to do (and then destroying whatever I've done and everything else), I agreed to stay with him. Only in his own car: in Frankfurt I would stay in my own hotel.

"When we're there, we'll discuss that."

In his car: as we neared the city of memory, my excitement grew. Though it had no reason to grow, for if I wanted to see my old German lover, I was making no effort to do so. I no longer understood what I was feeling while my feelings were taking me over. *The city of memory* turned into *the city of the unknown:* gardens.

As soon as we were inside this city, I repeated to Georg that I wanted to be alone, in a less fancy hotel.

"I want you to be in my hotel so that I can come into your room tonight."

At this point I lost my mind. Mindless, I repeated to myself that I had to be in a hotel where I could be alone. A close friend had already reserved a room for me in such a hotel.

"What does it matter in what room you find me tonight?"

After the usual performances and panel, my close friends and I went to some bar where Büchner said he would join us. When I returned to my hotel room, he had left no message.

Though it was late at night, I phoned him. Absence and rejection made me enter that realm from which there is no return. Only, finally, forgetting.

I asked him what I could do about desire.

He replied that in front of him there were black branches

cracking in a black sky. "Desire isn't a problem because life revolves around desire."

Here were the beginnings of desire.

In Germany, I'm lost. Whose rivers, like all rivers, stink, no longer of secreted genitalia but because the dead are floating on their surfaces.

Welcome, fierce wild odor, if you come alone! I'm living in the land of irrationality where all is free so—I should know this—I can do what is. Pure wildness, my only companion. Here, in this land that I don't know, we're finally getting married.

I realize that it's useless to keep remembering. In the name of All. Because everything is All:

Hello, you wildness. Are you spreading your legs for me again? Inside your vagina is only freedom. I am now free to be mad and I will go to him and lay myself at his feet and say, "I'm your dog." I have no idea how cause and effect are related in this land.

The man who's claiming fathership of me is the Captain of the Pirates. I never knew him. This is why I talk about the pirates. Freedom. (Besides, hairs grow out of their cocks.) And if dreams are dead, for the moment, I'm going to climb upon Chance, whose dog I will always be. I'm going to hump you until I have no more pussy hairs.

Chance is absolutely the biggest bastard there is.

Meow.

The pirates were trampling their dirty boots into the soil of my flesh. Meanwhile, in the United States, the new conveyer of the evils of fucking was about to be elected.

As soon as I reach my motorcycle, or pirate ship, I'm gonna sail free.

The pirate ship was sitting on a cobblestoned street in the town of Weimar. Before I could be free, I had, because I was a

229

dog, to attend the lunch to which the German publisher was treating all of the American writers.

TV cameras were crawling everywhere.

I was sitting in a fancy restaurant next to Büchner, opposite Bourénine and his wife. I mentioned, to make conversation, that being back in Europe was making me homesick for my former life, when I had lived here, before I had been forced or had thought I was being forced to flee back to the United States.

Bourénine: "Germany isn't Europe."

I: "Well, anyway, I want to get out of America. If a culture can become psychotic . . ."

Bourénine interrupting me: "You're the most New York person I've ever met."

I left the table, the restaurant, in order to visit my motorbike.

Redhead was still standing on the cobblestones, looking more miserable than before. One rapidly disintegrating Honda Custom, little power and less front-end suspension. She made me too excited to be able to ride her.

So I returned to the fancy restaurant. Now the Germans were sitting at a round table in front of the stone building and the Americans were in the Goethehaus, still on tour. I wondered how I was going to get away from here, wherever I was, to Berlin, wherever Berlin is. Trying to move from somewhere to somewhere, even if somewhere is always nowhere, was better than everything that was otherwise happening: being totally lost.

One of the Germans told me that I could travel either by Autobahn or by back country roads. "The Autobahn is too dangerous," he added.

"Then I'll take back country roads."

Another German advised against back country roads, being unpaved and too dangerous.

"I'll take the Autobahn."

"No, don't do that."

I consulted a map.

"You should visit ————."

"Let's see where that is." Heads bent over the map the publisher's girlfriend had brought me. "Oh, I could take country roads to get there. Why should I go there?"

"————'s the most polluted town in the world."

I consulted the map again. I had even less idea what I was seeing. This map was the only key to the door that said OUT.

Büchner, as usual, was giving the timetable. The Americans were to go to the hotel. About five hours later, all of us would be picked up and taken to a fancy party at the publisher's girlfriend's house.

When I saw that the hotel was a Hilton, I told him that I intended to stay there. Since it wasn't part of my contract to go to this party, I wasn't going to this party.

"No. We're going to walk on the mountain."

I protested.

"If I have to strap you to your motorcycle, Laure, and drive it myself, you're coming to the party."

At the word *strap,* I stopped protesting.

If I can't take the piss out of myself, who can I take the piss out of?

I wasn't yet lost enough.

Alone: In the sauna of this new, posh hotel, I met one of Henry Kissinger's friends. He told me that he had been part of Kissinger's '83 group, along with Dean Acheson.

At first, this man said that he was a lawyer. I asked him what he did. He answered that he was part of a holding company. I wasn't sure what a holding company was. They owned things. What things? For example, in the United States, Henry Holt & Co. Oh.

He then said that he knew that Ross Perot was going to be elected the next president of the United States. Because the Washington insiders were sick of both parties' bureacracy and wanted someone to break things up.

231

"What are you doing in Weimar?"

"My holding company is buying up East German TV stations."

He kissed me and asked me to sleep with him. I replied I was too tired. He asked if I would meet him later for a drink. I would if I came back from a party to which I might have to go.

The publisher's house was lost in thick trees, on the side of a mountain. The air was too dark, almost black, to see the green pool, the green water dirty with huge .water lilies, even the oversize cobblestones that led from one section to another. Only the smell of the smoke rising out of the barbecuing meat was clearly recognizable.

A walk: I was talking to an English member of the TV crews who were prowling around the premises when Georg, whom I hadn't seen since the beginning of the Hilton, took my arm. "We are going on our walk."

I said goodbye to TV.

Outside, we moved slowly up a path that seemed composed of dirt and some small stones. I couldn't see. The path, slowly and steadily, curved.

The first words I remembered were "linden tree." For tremendous leaves of the hue of darkness had been brushing our faces. Then the fireflies started darting out of the plants that hid the world on our right.

The next thing Georg said was that he was looking for a bench. From his words, I gathered that he knew where he, we, were going.

He didn't find this bench. At some point in time, as if time had been forgotten, Georg said that we should sit anywhere, down on the side of the mountain.

Though the only colors that were left were different shades of darkness, I didn't feel cold. I lay down on ground soft enough to be grass and flat enough to be rock. For the first time, in all the strangeness, I was happy.

As I watched the lights from some village below me, the first artificial lights I had seen in this outside, spreading into the darkness that was all around, I knew, without seeing at the moment, that there were other and smaller lights spread far more widely, above my eyes.

Georg was saying that he could sleep with a friend's sister, but he couldn't sleep with me. "Casual . . . because I'm German, I can't show my feelings . . . I've been trying to . . . feelings . . . from you."

The words kept getting lost in all I was seeing. I remember one of his legs rubbing mine.

We stood up to go. After we had traveled a little way, Georg said that we were lost. We kept on walking through the lostness.

There is nothing left for us to do.

Suddenly there was such a rustling and commotion in the trees and plants to our left that the animal must have been big. I grabbed Georg's arm, also because I wanted to touch him. Rather than touch, he made us keep moving. I did what he wanted.

We ended in a village of dirt paths and stone houses. Perhaps these were the lights. Georg threw a stone at a strange window and asked the face that appeared how we could get back.

Time restarted at the edge of the party. The Americans talked in one group; the Germans in two other groups; and the TV people went where they pleased. I discussed witches with the German women and sat with two huge mastiffs.

When it was time for me to be driven back to the Hilton, I went over to the playwright to say good night. I hadn't seen him since the walk. He pulled my head into his stomach and placed an arm around me.

> Innen ist dein Mund ein flaumiges Nest
> für meine flügge werdende Zunge.
> Innen ist dein Fleisch . . .

233

das ich mit meinen Tränen wasche
und das mich einmal aufwiegen wird.

When he let me go, he told me to phone him as soon as I
woke up the next morning.

Innen sind deine Knochen helle Flöten,
aus denen ich Töne zaubern kann,
die auch den Tod bestricken werden . . .

While Georg was moving his car so that the publisher, who
was going to drive me and two German poets back to the hotel,
could pull his auto out of the garage, I bent down to his window
to say goodbye again. Opening this window, he pulled my
mouth so hard around his tongue that I couldn't breathe.

The last day: As soon as I woke up, I thought, Now I can
phone Georg, and I did, but the number that I had been given
didn't work.

I took the elevator downstairs. The huge hotel was empty. It
seemed deserted. Like the bare soil that surrounded its interna-
tionalized splendor.

Finding no human nor advice how to reach anywhere, I loaded
up my bike, jumped on, and headed out.

I didn't know which way was north, east, south, or west.
Much less Berlin. This became apparent after I had circled several
times around the tiny town, searching for a way, not to Berlin,
just out.

I realized that the bike was almost out of gas. I rode through
small village after small village, all of whose houses were stone,
and stopped by three mechanics. They looked like mechanics. It
happened that we didn't share even the remnants of a common
language.

Without language, they gave me directions.

On the way to the imaginary filling station, I passed over a narrow stone bridge. Beneath me, the road was only partly paved and pockmarked with holes. As it sank downward before me, there was a sharp turn to the right.

The bike stopped.

Because I couldn't abandon her, she was carrying all my belongings, and because I wouldn't know where to walk, I did nothing.

After a while, a handsome motorcyclist on a new Ninja pulled over.

"Gas," I said, hitting the tank.

He waved his hands in front of his face. "No gas here."

I learned another German language lesson.

The blond went to fetch me petrol. Then, one of the three fat mechanics, with his equally fat girlfriend riding bitch, passed by on a tiny scooter. They went to fetch me more petrol.

I thought, This wouldn't happen in America, whose language I believe I speak.

And so I returned to the search. After two more hours of roads, half-bumps, half-holes leading nowhere, I decided that the only way to get to Berlin was death by Autobahn.

At only 100 k.p.h., my speedometer started to spasm wildly and the right mirror, weathervane style, swung around and around. This section of the freeway, which hadn't been repaired, according to report, since World War II, every thirty kilometers or so had lines of raised tar. Each time the bike met one of these lines, due to its suspension, she threw me into the air.

I reached Berlin.

Now I knew where I was.

Next, I had to find the German publisher's apartment building. Though I was in Berlin and had a piece of paper with his name, address, and phone number written down on it, I didn't know how to reach the street. I bought a map, which was so huge that the winds tore it to pieces. Then I learned that the average Berliner speaks as much English as the average East German mechanic. If they were mechanics.

I drove to Potsdamer Strasse because it was the only street that I knew. From there, I phoned the publisher.

This is the number and name of the street, I told him, on which I'm now standing.

"That's two blocks from my house."

"How do I reach your house?"

"I don't understand you, Laure."

About an hour after I had entered the publisher's apartment, Büchner knocked on the door. I was still crying wildly and exhilarated. The way that he held me told me that he didn't want to be close to me.

Everything became fast:

It was time to go to the Literaturhaus.

When I used to give readings in Berlin, before the Wall fell, I found the audiences the most political I ever had. Not only political: radical. Complex in their radicalism the ways that colors that aren't black but at the edges of being black—reds greens blues browns purples—relate to each other.

This audience was interested only in glamour. They seemed to be eager to transform problematic political questions into those discourses and opinions that comfort.

After the reading part of the night, Büchner introduced a friend of his to me. While we were talking, Büchner turned to me and said aloud, "I want you."

A panel discussion followed. My ex-boyfriend on tour, a theorist, journalist, and fiction writer, explained that he had brought postmodernism into the United States. He was "a kind of cultural emissary." In doing this, his only purpose had been to annoy and so, to wake up, the American left-wing academic establishment. For both he and the French theorists had understood, and understand, that postmodernism, all that theory, is a joke. To his amusement, the Americans had completely misunderstood postmodernism and turned it into an academic discourse.

After that, one of the American writers said that, from the beginning, the Bill of Rights was just hype, a kind of joke. Because there's homelessness, the U.S. Constitution is a shambles.

Then Georg explained that we were representing the new American literature in the United States.

After this panel, the American writer who was closest to me would tell me that what disturbed the Germans most was our politicalness. That Germans do not believe that the political has anything to do with art or the "lyrical."

I'm discussing the realm known as *the loss of language.*

> Ich bin noch schuldig. Heb mich auf.
> Ich bin nicht schuldig. Heb mich auf.
>
> Das Eiskorn lös vom zugefrornen Aug,
> brich mit den Blicken ein,
> die blauen Grunde such,
> schwimm, schau und tauch:
>
> Ich bin es nicht.
> Ich bin's.

After another TV interview, I looked for Georg. All of the tour, except for him and the publisher, were signing books.

A young woman who had interviewed me solely for her own pleasure and her boyfriend drove me to the East Berlin Literaturhaus, into which, they informed me, the publisher and G had disappeared.

The man who had governed East Berlin prior to the Wall's collapse had inhabited this low house of many gardens and candles. As soon as I had crossed its threshold, I saw G.

He recognized me and said, "I have to go now."

"But I just got here."

"I have to leave. I've been destroyed."

I didn't understand what *destroyed* meant. All I was conscious of was that this was the last time we were going to see each other and so we should say something.

I had lost consciousness.

While G was calling out to the publisher that it was time to go back home, I was demanding my five minutes with G. The publisher arrived and informed me that I would have to give another performance. For everybody had been waiting for me all night.

I didn't know who knew that I had been coming.

I replied that I would give a reading if I could have my five minutes with G. G's arms were around me. The publisher said we could have his office. "No," replied G, "I'm going." I mentioned that I had nothing left to read. G told me to dedicate my performance to him.

"Bastard."

I had lost consciousness for some time. I read to people whom I couldn't see because of this dark and then I thought that this night was beautiful.

When I returned to the hotel room, I realized that, sometime during the panel, G had borrowed my remaining pen and not returned it and that someone had given me a white pen.

Return: G had told me three times that he would drive me from the hotel to the airport. He appeared at neither place, nor phoned.

burning

REDREAMING GERMANY

Inside the Chapel Perilous: I found myself working as a stripper. In an actual show on a huge proscenium stage in a theater.

All that we had to do was dance in a chorus line. No sex was involved.

All of the dancers danced in skintight red dresses. Because these dresses were so close-fitting, they looked best when their sides had been split so high up that, as the red panels flapped, curling brown cunt hairs peeked out.

In accordance with the demands of the act, my shoes were the forties-style suede that open at the toe and the sides and have clunky heels.

I taught all of this to a young girl who had never before been a stripper.

After the performance ended, the evil murderers began to roam . . .

And we began our travels . . .

First, we came to the country whose label was *foreign*. We: me and my boyfriend:

Death by mother: We were together in a living space that though only one story, was so large as to seem limitless, like a New York—style loft.

This apartment contained many parts, sections that had been totally partitioned off from the whole; inside, all of the light was spectral. It was almost a labyrinth.

In this house, there were evil murderers. They were female . . . my mother.

But all my boyfriend was interested in was in playing his records. Every time I wasn't with him, since he was so occupied with music that he didn't notice anything, my mother would attempt to get him to fuck her. Her most recent tool was a huge white poodle; this seduction was efficacious and very evil.

I came back to him. Then I tried to understand, *by seeing as clearly as possible*, the large nail that had been placed in his flesh, between the largest and next-to-largest toe. I wanted to know how my boyfriend's pain felt; almost fetishistically, I wanted to know how bad the pain was.

I didn't know whether I was fascinated by an act that had already happened or by what I was scared would happen.

We listened to American blues records, which were our favorites . . .

By water: The next part of my journey was for a tour.

While I was en route, I remembered that I had been scheduled for another. Were the dates of both tours the same? Could I make the whole tour I was now on? I had to know whether I would have to return from this first tour before it ended.

So I looked through all my documents, folded pieces of white typing-size paper; I leafed through them in order to learn all the exact dates. All the arrangements in my life, especially business, are chaos.

According to these documents, both tours ended on the day of the heart. My decision now was clear. I would have to return from this first tour early, before the day of the heart.

After I had made the decision about time, I started worrying about underwear. That I hadn't brought the right ones. I should have purchased that dress . . . I could see it perfectly . . . made out of rayon, imported from India, full beneath its high waist, a bodice that fit tightly. Long black sleeves fell down from the white cloth. (Outside the dream, I would hate this dress.) Or that other dress: exactly like the first except it had no sleeves, buttoned down its bodice, all in yellow tie-dye. (I would hate this one, too.)

And so I made my second decision: I'd send someone to purchase one of these dresses for me.

On the boat that was carrying us, all of the writers of the tour were sleeping in the same bed. The bed was big. I watched two

240

guys, one of whom was Bourénine, fuck each other. I liked watching this.

I was the only writer on this tour who wasn't in a couple . . .

The Phoenician sailor: The boat landed in Russia . . .

There, my ex-boyfriend, I, and another person lived together in a house.

Bourénine had two human-size mastiffs of whom I was very fond. I would feed them. One day I was looking through the cupboards for dog biscuits, the psychedelic kind.

I asked Bourénine if I could give his dogs psychedelics.

"No."

I did. I scattered some on the kitchen floor. The dog biscuits looked like toast. I was reassured that I hadn't poisoned the beasts when I saw them eat just a few, rather than gulp all of them up. Then the dogs became happy.

Who's going to walk these things? I wondered to myself. Not me. I am not going to walk ten paces behind them with a dog-scoop and bow down to dogshit. I am not going to be their slave, which is just what I'm supposed to be on this disgusting tour.

A park lay a few blocks away from our house.

Crystal-green grass, short and level, as if it had been painted, ran to the edge of very high black iron bars.

Murderers were strolling freely through this park.

No, I couldn't walk the dogs here in safety.

When I returned from my amble along the periphery of the murderers' park, then back to our house, I saw that the mastiffs, on their own, had escaped to the outside.

They were in a splendid garden. Out of a green that was darker and rougher than that of the park, *as if in a dream,* black trees gnarled and jutted into a darkening sky. There the mastiffs sat peacefully.

Both at the same time, the dogs rose up and, turning away from my eye, receded into the background. At an even greater distance, a multitude of dogs were barking. The two mastiffs raced to the barkers so that they could play forever.

Having returned to the house's insides, I rifled through my official documents. Then, I turned to a clock that was sitting on a high black table to my right. I wanted to set it to the right time, but it worked in a manner I didn't understand. The clock was more sophisticated and intelligent than me.

After much labor, I learned that this clock has two temporal settings: the first indicates the time that is desired. When that time is reached, an alarm sounds. The next setting indicated duration.

I continued looking through my documents. Why hadn't the Russians examined any of them? Perhaps this examination, a very thorough one, would take place upon my exit from their country. Suddenly I remembered a bit of hash wrapped in tin foil: I had better check that I had removed it from the middle of these documents.

By now it was lunchtime, so we were good girls and boys and went to a restaurant that was fancy and clean for lunch.

Inside the restaurant, when Bourénine learned that it had just been mentioned in a gourmet magazine, he was pleased as Punch. I didn't give a shit. He ordered me to sit at a white-cloth-covered table on a low platform in the front of the room while he sat with the other member of our household, who was his girlfriend, at a regular table in the back. A thin, middle-aged dork in a Homburg was at my table.

Cause I've got a special diet, before anyone else saw their food, the restaurant served me a slab of meat loaf on a white plate.

I don't eat red meat. I ran out of the restaurant.

But red meat wasn't the reason that I ran away from this restaurant . . .

. . . I began walking through Russia . . .

Down cobblestones that held the sun . . .

. . . Somewhere I met a man who was old and very thin.

Speaking to me, he told me what I most wanted to know: the location of a skating rink.

By now Bourénine had joined us.

There were two skating rinks. The smaller one was the nearer. "Located," he said, "just up the next street."

I either saw or visualized its map:

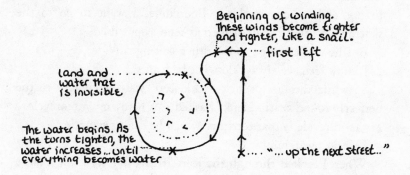

The larger rink, whose shape was a perfect circle, was farther away. "There," the old man said, "are all the champions. They're beautiful."

Bourénine and I were sitting in the back of an open wagon. The old man, in its front, turned around to us and asked, "Did you bring supplies?"

We didn't understand what he meant by "supplies."

The old man explained to us, for we didn't know anything, that the Russians now needed supplies, military and medical, desperately.

We hadn't known any of this. We tried to explain.

"Our government, through the media," I furthered, "tells us nothing about you."

Then, I clearly saw that my government blacks out information and releases misleading statements, especially concerning foreign countries.

When we were alone, Bourénine asked me why I had run away from the restaurant.

"Because I don't like red meat," I said, for I didn't want to be vulnerable to him by telling him any of the truth.

"But you haven't eaten anything."

It was true: I hadn't. His solicitude made me nervous cause I was determined never to trust him again. So I returned quickly to our earlier conversation. "Bourénine, I want to go to the skating rink that's snail-shaped as soon as possible."

But he wished to go to the other skating rink.

I know that we always do what he wants.

So while the taxi, which was a jeep, was carrying us to the perfectly round skating rink, I asked, "Where's my motorcycle?" My motorcycle is that territory which he can't penetrate.

"Mario's watching it."

When I looked through the jeep's rear window, I saw a large black metal X. The ends of the X farthest from me were connected to two black trailers. Each trailer contained a motorcycle.

This was how Bourénine and I came to the subject of traveling:

I: "I think that it's a waste of time to sightsee. Because when you're in a strange land, you don't know what you're seeing when you see.

"Example: if I travel with a group of my fellow Americans in a strange country, all I really see is America.

"If you want to see strangeness, you have to actually talk with strangers." I came to some conclusion: "Talking to others is how to see."

. . . .

I don't remember anything that he said.

. . . .

I wandered through Russia on my own.
On my own is *alone*.

. . . .

244

Death by water: I found myself on board, a ship it must have been, for I was descending narrow wooden steps that were winding around and around. Though I didn't know a single person in this strange land and was all alone, while I was walking down, a man whose hair was carrot-colored said hello to me by name.

I wondered how Russians could know anything about my writing.

But obviously some of them must. As I continued walking down the stairs, a few more Russians spoke to me.

I didn't feel that I was strange anymore.

At the bottom (which wasn't this ship's final bottom): first, I strode across open space to a cabin. In the cabin: I crouched down into the space between a large table that was leaning against the farthest wall and one of the side walls, which wasn't a wall but a glass plate.

Through the plate, the inside of the ocean could be seen. On the ocean surface, which was a line, continuously altering waves. Below the line, green, and a fish.

There was a man in the cabin who spoke to me in English. Being a stranger, he could have been anyone. The attraction between us was very hot. Though no one, or nothing, he had the following characteristics: red hair, the name Timofy, huge stomach, his knowing me so immediately, directly, and intimately that he could, and did, say, "You're alone; you don't have a home; in this world, you're always going to be strange."

Since he knew exactly what to say about me, I felt safe.

Even though I had met this man, I returned to the hotel where I was now staying.

The young woman behind the desk informed me that a magazine, *Timofea,* had phoned and asked if they could publish a piece of my writing.

"I've heard of them."

"Yes. *Timofea* is *the* most prestigious literary magazine."

Then, she asked me to sign a scrap of paper, Chinese-fortune-cookie-size, to nail the deal.

Which I did.

Everyone in this country is always touching each other; nudity is usual. So the clerk and I were touching each other and while we were touching each other, Timofy entered this hotel.

This man is going to make sure I eat, I thought.

Inside his large living room:

I learned that Timofy was planning to cook a meal for me.

Gee, he's going to take care of me, I thought. Then he said that he had to leave. For a while, not forever.

Since he was going to return to me, I didn't mind being there alone. But when he reached for me across the floor on which we were sitting, and our inner mouth linings and tongues connected, desire appeared in the form of flame.

He no longer wanted to leave me, even for a while, but rather to keep on exchanging liquids.

—to be human, in flesh and in bone—

THE RETURN OF WATER TO THE EARTH

Botzen, Bolzano (?)
Saturday, 17:00, 21.7

Dear B,

I've decided that it's better not to phone you.

Without doubt, you've been imagining the best or the worst extreme things about me, but my life is simple. I wonder, however, and I want to ask you this, if you would lose any sleep if I stopped writing you.

246

I think I'll stop.

—because I want to see you so much. Please don't become crazed by how much I want to see you (I know that your nerves are "thin"—do you mind my saying this?).

In all the craziness that's going to happen, both of us are going to have to be as virile as possible.

I'm not that perverted, mad, and wild child who prattles: this is the me whom you know in the deepest—

Despite my profound and continuing fascination with decadence and decay, with where dead humans lose their bones, I'm more stable than I've been in a very long time.

But don't start imagining that everything's okay with me. Or the opposite.

I've passed all this time absolutely alone. Being without anybody, in the deepest part, has taught me how to want. To want. I'll write you again tomorrow.

I still can't give you my address because I don't know where I am. I always haven't known and now I know that I know nothing (this is a contradiction—any knowing must depend upon contradiction) because every meaning always depends on whatever's happening.

So there's no more need for extremes: tragedy and comedy.

I'm attracted to you because, though you care about things, you don't cling to seriousness.

Innsbruck
Thurs. evening, 21.8

B,

If I haven't written you in a while it's because the mail's losing everything. So maybe there is a need, but nevertheless it's impossible to communicate.

Last week I sent you a telegram. To which you haven't as yet or you're not going to reply. I'm under the impression that you've disappeared, and now I'm in the land of the unknown.

Despite everything, this unknown is what I desire. I want to see you.

All the above means *to depart*.

This isn't what I want to say.

Your love for me entered my life: don't abandon me. This is what I want to say: I'm scared; please envelop me; I'm scared, as if to death, of saying these words, of saying any words. I have no doubt about this fearing: my fear has many reasons.

If fear isn't necessary, we by now would have found ourselves traveling down another road.

Roads are only approximations. If that.

How can I be telling you that I need you and simultaneously believe equally, that is, totally, another reality that lacerates? Is this possible? (I have often thought that I'm not possible.) There are many moments when I know that I have to do exactly what is going to make you get rid of me. That'd be so hateful: to make myself into that which you most despise, to make what I most don't want to happen, happen.

This explains our present.

I've given up explaining anything to you.

Darling, all I want, and much more than you want, is to see you as quickly as possible so I can speak unguardedly, not like this, *not explanations*. Then you'll show me yourself. How to understand you. Take me. Between present time (absence) and future time (presence), I fear to say anything. Rather, I'll reread your words.

Me, I'm insufficient, all I am is fantasies that tear "me" apart. How can I be anything but a lie?

. . . .

Some people think that I'm strong, stable, self-assured. But I don't want to be, because I don't want to impose on or control

248

others. What I'm looking for, B, is another power that's hidden, efficacious, and practical: the power to reclaim myself.

I've never known this power. I'm only beginning to now.

Hôtel Étoile Rouge
undated

I think you already know this. But I'm going to try—to begin to say something precisely: I'm not interested in being master, in goals. For this reason. Even if I do attain some goal, at that very moment the only thing that's important to me is to go beyond that which is no longer a goal but now only a stage. To go beyond.

This sounds romantic—actually I don't care if I have any mastery. I've no mastery of myself. I'm crumbling. I used to believe that I must understand and realize everything that constitutes me . . . and on this journey of realization, I came upon, just as Ulysses must have done, a monstrous cacophony.

I had no Penelope.

If there's anything that can and is returning me to the arrogance in which I began this journey, such as your love, B, most of all it is this suffering I now know. I'm crumbling.

I came upon this: I'm crumbled.

One result of this journey, or "identity," could be my loss of interest in "feminine power." Images of the Eternal Mother, the Virgin Mary, etc.

What I've just said isn't interesting to me in terms of theory: rather, all of this is the only place, simply, where life can start, because, in me, life must start in collision.

Here is why I talk so much about nature. Nature is a refuge from myself, from opposition, from the continuing impossibility of me.

Nature's more than just a refuge, but it's impossible to speak about it directly. For nature can be spoken about only in dream.

I can't explain this, not only not to you, not even to myself. Only the dreamer or dream—is there a difference between these two?—can speak about nature.

I have moments when I believe that I will and can be reconciled to myself on every possible level—by living in the country, near a forest, by flowing waters . . . I don't know how . . . Not here. I spend so much time, gazing into the sky and at water—I'm never bored then—otherwise . . . If one day you, raising your head, see a small cloud all on its own, you'll know that I am coming to see you.

I've got a terrible need to write you and for you not to reply —but that'll happen later.

This is what I want to say.

undated

I need to see your flesh. You.

This is all I know now: want.

I can no longer explain this. What I feel. Why I feel.

What is happening to me—want's finally overcoming me—is irrevocable, as irrevocable as everything that has happened to me in the past—

I'm going to continue being alone and not talking to anyone. But under this mysterious sign, which doesn't exist, where in front of me is only you . . . distant, ironic, cruel . . ., I need to see your flesh just once.

As for your idea, no. No way. I can no longer—I no longer want—this is what I understand: Since I've thought so long, "When I die—just before I die—I'll say this name, cry out your name," I am in your name, not in the sign of your name. This is what I understand by *equality*.

* * *

next day

Why aren't I with you right at this moment? I was being strangled to death by solitude that was insoluble, by being dumb; your voice delivered me from that which was seizing me by the throat; your voice delivered me when loneliness was holding my head, but my head had already been shattered.

Why am I begging you, who parades your suffering over the ruins like a king in order to ensure that you will never be touched deeply, you who're always laughing.

I've no control over myself.

Hôtel Étoile Rouge
undated

Dear B,

I thought, I have no one to whom I can turn. Then I dreamed or saw a movie—there was a white and wide highway. In front of my car, there was a woman holding a huge dog by a leash. She had no eyes. It was my mother. She said, "I've been looking for you."

I woke up.

I didn't know that I was sleeping. Through the front door, the porch one, someone began murdering me.

I had thought that I had woken up.

I had to figure out who was murdering me.

As if I was in a cop station, they gave me pictures for identifying the murderer. I had to paste each picture in a comic book, as if this comic was a coloring book.

Melvyn was in a room of two's. Is he my mother? My terror has begun to grow.

I asked if it was my mother who was trying to murder me.

The or a Voice thundered, "NO."

251

"But I know that it's here now: the murderer."

The Voice answered, "You must understand these times to know the murderer."

My terror had grown to its full height.

"Is my mother trying to murder me through someone?"

"Yes."

As I woke up, I realized that my mother was trying to murder me through me.

I've woken into terror.

What other knowledge will my solitude and muteness bring? What other worlds?

Hôtel Étoile Rouge
undated

But the desire you have for me cuts off my breath—These blind eyes see you, and no one else—My blind eyes see how desire is contorting your mouth—They see your mad eyes—

To see. I must see your face, which is enough for me, and now I don't need anything else.

None of this is realizable.

As soon as I knew this, I agreed that we had to meet in person.

But at the moment that we met, all was over. At that moment, I no longer felt anything. I became calm. (I, who've been searching so hard for calmness.)

I can't be calm, simple, for more than a moment when I'm with you. Because of want. Because your eyes are holes. In want, everything is always being risked; being is being overturned and ends up on the other side.

It's me who's let me play with fire: whatever is "I" are the remnants. I've never considered any results before those results happened.

At this moment if I could only roll myself under your feet, I would, and the whole world would see what I am . . . ,

Etc.

Etc.

Do you see how easy it is for me to ask to be regarded as low and dirty? To ask to be spat upon? This isn't . . . the sluttishness . . . but the language of a woman who thinks: it's a role. I've always thought for myself. I'm a woman who's alone, outside the accepted. Outside the Law, which is language. This is the only role that allows me to be as intelligent as I am and to avoid persecution.

But now I'm not thinking for myself, because my life is disintegrating right under me.

My life's disintegrating under me so I'll not bear the lie of meaning.

My inability to bear that lie is what's giving me strength. Even when I believed in meaning, when I felt defined by opposition and this opposition between desire and the search for self-knowledge and self-reclamation was tearing me apart, even back then I knew that I was only lying, that I was lying superbly, disgustingly, triumphally.

Life doesn't exist inside language: too bad for me.

I dreamed last night that I moved into a new house.

I didn't know where I was; the house was still strange.

A man was in it.

How could there be a man here? How could he have gotten in?

He was squat, fat, even swarthy. He could have been Italian. (Cesare Pavese?) I wondered, but only because such a thought existed in my society, is the man going to rob my new house? Apart from what I was supposed to think, I didn't believe that the man would.

As if *figuring out* had become subsumed under *wonder-*

ing, I nevertheless tried to figure out how I could stop up my hole.

Answer: I would replace my toilet seat.

The Italian returned home so he could test the proposed toilet replacement. He learned that if a toilet seat is changed, there isn't enough air for shaving, so the razor can't breathe.

I couldn't bear to let this happen. But, on the other hand, I couldn't allow the unknown . . . a man . . . to penetrate my new house.

Ely, my girlfriend, had just moved into her new house. Which might have been my house. Because she was now in a strange place, we, all of whom were female, agreed to cook for her.

Actually Ely was going to hold a contest. The structure of her contest was that there would be neither winners nor losers; all of us would take turns cooking.

Ely explained to me that even I can cook: "You cook this chicken breast," holding up a raw tit, "in butter."

I believe in olive oil. And my raw meat must be cut into chunks. Because it's unhealthy for humans to be fried.

"How could that be true?" The very tone of her voice was a reprimand.

"I'll show you." But as I stood at the threshold of her kitchen, which was as small as was my mother's, I saw that there were five women already cooking.

I decided to go away.

One of the cooks was a man. Drunk as a skunk. He had come up from below. (Like the Italian.) Perhaps, I thought, he's a drunk husband. Well. We'll all help Ely clean up, for after tonight she's going away.

I walked into her kitchen and began to thorough-clean it.

The more I convince myself that talking is of no more use, the more I need to talk. Especially among women.

* * *

254

I dreamed that, in my school, there were voodoo men.

Just as the voodoo man and I were going to fuck, he took off his balls, just like a normal man would unbutton his shirt.

I remember that the first time I ever saw a naked male body, in the school, there was a fish head on it.

When one of the voodoo man's friends died, I wondered whether it was the fish head.

I was so terrified that I told my friend to consult a doctor immediately so he could learn whether or not he was sick. Before this he never cared what I said or if I spoke. When I said *go see the doctor,* he, the voodoo man, listened.

Then he came back to me. That night he took off his ball to go to bed and underneath there was a hole like a red bullet hole.

This hole is tertiary syphilis.

Now I have to ask the doctor whether I'm going to die in a few weeks.

Where I am is a country of flesh, rich in troops of goats, neighing fillies who have come to play at the river. This is a field of flowers. The hotel has a bar. Silence.

It is only silence that creates.

I have so much to say to you that I'm no longer going to write.

For one thing: you've decided that we're going to keep on tormenting each other. I'm not surprised. *If it was otherwise,* we'd be those flying creatures who, without wings, but with queer, tender, and huge paws, stumble through the shadows.

But we're not. Darling, I don't know what color we are, but I think that we're going to find each other again . . . in a rainbow.

These dreams're pulverizing me. I'm surmounting them, grimacing through all of it—I'm now a little better, after a bizarre attack of fever.

Here, there are silvery beech trees.

255

THE MOVEMENT INTO HAPPINESS

B,

I don't understand why I left you, but we're going to see each other again, aren't we? Sunday, I think? And then you'll be here, next to me so gently that even at this moment I'm . . . changed.

I loved *The Plumed Serpent*. It goes far further than I believed possible. Where are you now?

We're going to be happy.

There's this house in Dammarie that Mother wants to buy for me. It's near the river, in trees. Hidden. If you like, I'll ask her to get it. Don't pay any attention to me. It's good to know that there's a key under the door.

I dreamed about a city. The city was monstrous edifices that had been plagiarized out of science fiction and, at the same time, they were decaying fast . . .

I was wandering in the skeleton of industry when I realized that somehow I had managed to forget everything. At that very moment I was due for an exam. Now I felt anxiety because I was probably going to miss this exam.

In order to get to where I wanted to go, I started traveling through this city . . .

Inside its heart, the streets were narrow. Unlike most avenues, they had been sized for human bodies. Similarly the buildings were inhabited, warm. I spied a theater. I saw family-owned stores. The heart is a maze. Within its precincts, I have become desperate to find a taxi so I can rush to my examination, which I'm about to miss.

The few taxis that there were had already been taken.

There had never been any taxis within the most central square of this heart. Being a true labyrinth, had no exits.

I wasn't walking the streets by myself but with the girl whom I had met back in the skeleton of industry. Then, I learned that she was a junkie and that I would have continually to watch out for and watch over her. Friendship, for me, required responsibility, not anxiety.

We emerged from the heart.

. . . and entered a railway station, roofed and sideless, a station that was either enclosed or open or enclosed and open.

Some of its tracks rose up in front of me as if they had come alive and then turned into a sculpture on and in which it was possible for me to climb and play.

Here, I climbed and played. As if it was a result of climbing and playing, I found a piece of green paper on which the times of the school's examinations had been printed. According to the paper, every student in the class had to present a solo performance; the whole thing began at 7:30 P.M., and the actual performances at 8:00 P.M.

Since my name wasn't listed among the performers and I wouldn't have to be in class by eight, I would be able to be in class on time.

All anxiety died.

Now my mind had enough holes in it to remember, for the first time since the walk through the skeleton of industry, the appointment I had made with another girlfriend to see the movie that was playing at the corner of Fifty-third Street and Fifth. As if this was in New York City. Since I had time to walk to my class and the movie house was on that way, I would be able to inform my friend, who was waiting for me in the theater, that I wouldn't be able to come to her . . .

I finally was in the place that I should be in. I was just visiting this class because I hadn't been scheduled to give a performance. When I feel free, I sing; otherwise not, because I don't have a voice.

One of the teachers, an Indian from India, hearing my caterwauling, advised me to use my breath by storing it in a manner which he proceeded to show me.

"But I can't sing at all," I protested.

My teacher became angry.

But why should I have to sing at all? At that moment, I thought that I perceived that all my classmates, who unlike me were being examined, were very nervous because their teachers were cruel.

I don't remember who . . . the Indian teacher? . . . someone . . . the dream told me that I have to sing.

My childhood was dead, and with it died the poetic powers that dwelt in me. The aim of this book is only to relate the experience of freeing myself from a state of painful torpor. I am freeing myself and for a prouder attitude.

I must learn to breathe.

I want to say to you one thing in this bottom of the world: I need you so that I can be alive, and my insupportable pride, which wouldn't let me admit to any need, is no longer making me suffer.

One day someone said to me that I'm never going to get well because of this pride. I think that it's because of my arrogance and pride that I'm well. You must understand this better than me.

CONTINUATION

B, everything is clear.

You believe that you've put me into servitude because I'm living shut off from society, devoid of intercourse.

But what's true to you is false to me. My truth is that your presence in my life for me is absence.

Here's my explanation of the difference between us: you believe that everything that's outside you or me ("reality") is a reflection of your or my thoughts, perceptions, emotions, ideas, etc. ("inner reality"). You believe that you're part of and understand this world. I don't. I feel that I have to explain everything to anyone to such a degree—if I am to communicate anything—

that for me communication's almost impossible. I don't talk. Day by day, my life is becoming a little more empty, breaking apart like a corpse decomposing herself under my own eyes.

I'm so horny when I awake, I place my fingers in your mouth so you can bite them, only the mouth I'm placing them in is my own.

Tell me the details of everything you've ever done when you've made love to women. Name what cannot be named and so has every possible attribute and drive me over the edge into the realm of impossibility: water plus fire.

This is exactly what you, by means of your manipulations of absence and lack and void, have already done and are doing to me.

. . . .

I name your . . . of whom I cannot speak: . . . *absence* . . . *lack* . . . *void* . . .

I know that you're trying to ensure that I will never forget you, given every possible eventuality.

Beyond that territory of absence, lack, and void, how does your . . . , which I cannot say, look? Who's the master? I want to know the smell of each part. I want to know how it would feel when it sleeps on my tongue:

B, you can no longer help me:

This isn't sweet; this has nothing to do with your desire to take care of me, what I told you was "the night"; this is truth and it's mine.

My life and my death are now apparent and mine. At this moment, I'm equally between them; nothing and no one in this world can do anything anymore since I am no longer finding you at the bottom of everything: there where I used to know I could find you. B, perhaps I no longer want you.

This is what happened yesterday: I hated our life together; most of the time all I wanted was to save myself, to leave so I could be alone in the mountains. (That did save my life, for a while; I know this now.) I had a horror of our mad rhythm, our oscillations from total separation to absolute possession and back again, of our work, of our nights, of how you have dared to own me by naming, and so creating, my "weakness." Which you're still trying to do. You, who can't bear to spend even two hours alone. You, who must always have someone with you for whom you can exist and act. You, who're unable to want simply; you, who want only in a mirror. Actuality is, that whoever's with you does exactly what she wants with you: I should know. You tried to make me weak.

At the moment, we both think about our life together in the same way: just as I believe that we're going to be together again, I believe that there's no such thing as meaning. For you or for me. Call this *abyss* or *night*. I handed you possession of me, of this lack of meaning. You laughed at me:

Scatter, mess up, destroy, throw to the dogs whatever you want, throw everything away in laughter: I'll never be where you believe you're going to find me.

B SPOKE:

Heathcliff lived with Cathy's phantom and I want to live with Laure's ghost.

In December, M.H. had taken Laure and me, for we had asked him, to the spot de Sade had chosen to be his tomb.

De Sade: "The acorns will press it underneath . . ." The oak trees were eating and the copses were annihilating his dead body.

That day, it snowed. Our car lost its way in the wood. There, the savage winds were sitting.

March of the next year, we returned to the same grave . . . On that day, Laure strode just as if death wasn't squatting on her heart.

That day, while the sun was still full, we arrived at the edge of the pond that de Sade had named. This was the day the Germans had invaded Vienna. Society turned to war. As soon as we returned to our home, Laure felt the first actual attack of the disease that was going to kill her.

At that moment, she didn't know that she wouldn't get out of bed again. Except for the time I took her back into the forest. She left the car so she could walk over to a blasted tree. Back in the car, we rode, as if flying, over hills the beauty of whose fields maddened her. Than, entering into the actual forest, she saw two dead crows hanging from the branches of one of the trees on her left . . .

I . . . I saw these crows some days later when I was in the same place. I told Laure that I had seen them and she trembled; her voice died. I don't know why I became terrified.

After she had died, I understood that for her the crows had been the sign of death. Both of us no longer had eyes: Laure was now an inert corpse. When I read through all her manuscripts, I saw that their first pages had been entitled *The Crow*.

MY MOTHER SPOKE:

And so I began descending, *as in my dreams,* walking down the spiral staircase that led to the witch's library.

Many rooms lay off those steps . . .

I was descending into my dreams. Deeper than I had ever been before . . .

At first, there were only bits.

The first bit: I was in a church named The Church of Death, the label of all churches, which was a large library. Its priest, who was standing on a tall ladder, was moving monster Holy Bibles, which were only movie posters, around the walls.

. . . I walked on . . .

261

. . . inside this building, the light was almost black. A black in which I could see. Under shelves two feet above the floor, black boots were lined up. I was looking to buy black . . .

I was unhappy here, so I kept on traveling . . .

I said the three C's aloud, one of which was *Crap*, and then realized that I had no more *Choice* . . . even if I was moving to my death: I jumped away from the building and began to fly, landed on the walkway that encircled the construction, as if I were an animal . . .

After further journeying, I came to a countryside . . . I had to give my girlfriend back her muffin. When I searched for it, the only muffin I could find was a real or soft bran muffin hiding within a fake or stale muffin. It was all I had to give.

But before I presented her with this, I stuffed my period-stained underpants into my purse.

At the time, my girlfriend was being examined by her doctor. During the end of the exam, I was with her. I liked this doctor, who was female, so much that I thought about letting her examine me.

But I already have a good doctor who's a male.

Nevertheless, in the examining room, this doctor went so far as to give me a shot. First, she wanted to inject into the bone that's right at the top, or tip, of the asshole. I wouldn't let her do this because it was going to be painful. So she stuck me in the front of my left shoulder. At this section of the body, only the thinnest skin covers the bone so the pressure from the penetrating liquid was very disturbing.

"Why are you shooting me here?" While the needle was still in my body.

She explained to me that liquid travels most rapidly when it's able to descend diagonally down the body's front. As in this case.

Then she drew me a picture.

Outside the medical building, the air and low, dead grass were gray, the way they are on a beach whose sun has died.

It's now the edge of the morning and the sun has died. The arid plains are behind us.

I had to give Pat, my girlfriend, back her muffin, but when I reached into my purse, there was only this smelly blood from the period-stained underpants. Blood so sticky and thick it was almost solid at the bottom . . .

I, a child, kept on traveling . . . By motorcycle. I saw a girl, out of the corner of my right eye, who was traveling on a motorcycle. She didn't know how to ride hers. I braked mine, and discovered that she wasn't braking properly. Why? When I looked down, I saw that the street under the front wheel was sagging. I shoved my motorcycle forward, now up, rather than down, hill. So I could brake completely. In the meantime, the bike had died. I had to click it into neutral so that I could start it up again, but I couldn't use the gear shift because my boots were no longer on my feet but lying in the street just to my right. Shit, I said. How can I reach these shoes? And I'm going to have to do all this before the light turns green.

Somehow I managed, without shoes, to get my bike into neutral and, then, was able to pull her over to the right side of the road, to safety . . .

. . . .

. . . and I reached the beach . . . (time passed in which there was no memory) . . . a girl told me a story, which I didn't/don't remember . . . (time passed in which there was no memory) . . .

. . . .

This beach was also a building. On its second floor, the girl who had told the story was lying on top of me in bed.

The left side of the bed overlooked the ground level: there, yellow, rubbery weeds, thin green and orange weeds almost totally covered the sand. Filthy green water was pulling away from the ground that was hidden.

It was so dirty that it had to belong to the Atlantic Ocean.

She was lying on top of me: we kissed and were kissed. I

263

didn't feel anything sexual. I wasn't lesbian. I liked her. We began to talk to each other. She could have told me, again, the story that I didn't/don't remember. After we had talked, we kissed again: this time I felt passion. Then I realized that it takes time for passion to appear because passion has to be allowed.

I began to be with her:

We looked down at the beach's bottom and saw that some of its seaweed was living creatures . . . (time in which there was no memory) . . . something to do with mermaids or mermen . . . (time in which there was no memory) . . . The times of no memory connected the girl's story to the living creatures.

The beings down on the beach had otters' heads, seal bodies, and yellow rubber seaweed tails.

One of the monsters climbed from a black ropelike ladder over the sand ridge of the second floor and walked toward me. His head was almost human. He told me that he used to be my girl's lover.

This is the forgotten or nonexistent story, but I don't understand it.

Two rubber men were climbing up, and onto, the second sand floor. They were malevolent: their tales were absolutely dangerous. They were coming for us so they could murder us. My girlfriend shrieked: because she was far more helpless than me, being half my age, she fainted. This was how I became alone.

The rubber men started coming for me.

I'm going to descend further, to see:

Hôtel des Yeux Lilas

(to someone other than B),

I can no longer cry: I vomit. I no longer laugh: I grind my teeth. How I despise this dry and evil laugh: it graffities all of my senses, every sentence that manages to escape, every gesture that is decomposing, the me that other people think they see

264

better than me. But I understand it better than them, than you, and with an irony that's ferocious . . .

And then I cry. My teeth grind; I vomit.

I know well that I'm not going to see you again. You and all the others.

It's time to quit this play. It's time to completely hold my life in my own hands, to be alone in the desert, the place of stones, to be there as *me* and no longer as someone who hardly resembles me.

To be me, I must turn to dreaming.

Listen: Every day of my life, Death followed me. I saw It in the red soil, in mud, in the sky of stars; I saw It partaking of the intense hatred and joys of others—other people shared It with me *as if it was a miracle, uncommon.*

They believe that Death is Christ.

I saw Death in the horror of the simultaneity of the frightfulness and the sweetness of language, of human communication. Death was the line of the horizon, as simple as anything geometrical.

My sight is clear; I'm not drunk. What makes me seemingly drunk is Death, who's following my life, rendering me so exhausted . . . I'm breaking. This Death, whom I call mine, My Shade, would do well to just drop me off on some street corner, as quickly as possible, or hand me over to the other shades, for whom I've got respect. But I'm not going to be broken like this. I've got my childhood back. I have found my childhood, in pavement and in leaves, in the stable earth and in water. Tell B, and this time it's the truth, that I'm now truly the witch, the one who makes the teeth grind, the eyes blink too rapidly, everything that makes another person turn away in horror—

There're no witches or Eternal Mother. This is who I am: one day someone placed this ad in a paper: "Looking for LOST DOG."

Woof.

Perhaps all I want is to say one word before everything stops. Before this ridiculous . . . abject . . . unworthy hell stops. Before Death.

That one word would be a name.

I used to want to meet my death by "accident." At that very moment, I thought, I would say this one word.

That would be his name.

If I say it now, lightning's going to fall on my head—it's going to be night in full noon.

Dusk's going to turn into break of day.

The streets are going to be rivers.

Everything, except his name, is foam; foam is tossed over the edge.

I'm not drunk.

I tried everything: to lose myself, to get rid of memory, to resemble whom I don't resemble, to end . . . Sometimes when I encountered myself, I was so strange that "I" had to be criminal —all the time I was totally polite and, simultaneously, my language was brutal, filthy,

> I meet a star
> go and am there.

I tried to give my life away and life came back, gushed into its sources, the stream, the storm, into the full of noon, *triumphant,* and it stayed there hidden, like a lightning stain.

later on

* * *

I believed that what was written could be communicated. But, this is the question: Is it possible to communicate with *another* person? I want to communicate—it's time.

When I involuntarily stopped speaking, "as if there was no longer anything," strangled, voiceless, in this bottom of myself, I found a magnificent feast of possibilities. Then, all changed. The feast turned into a fairground of drunkenness, worse, into a scummy flea market where crap was being sold. Or else I simply saw that my eyes were shut; I recovered myself in sweat and ash.

In my search in myself, I found nothing.

I'm now in a dream in and from which it's impossible to move. All my gestures are being held back, motionless—and here at times I begin to scream like a wounded animal. I'm in this dream as long as I don't either die or suicide.

It's necessary to cut life into bits, for neither the butcher store nor the bed of a woman who's giving birth is as bloody as this.

Absurdity, blessed insolence that saves, and connivance are found in these cuts, the cuts into "veracity."

Or the cries of children who aren't playing, the cries of humans and of the earth itself turning—THE VERTIGO—all these are found in the cuts—not just decadence and rot—but the entire human being is found there. No one can be more human than this. To welcome in this hatred. No being can be more human than this. I'm breaking: in the very place where my calm arrogance used to be, I find only, here and now, the misery and the hurt of bestial howling.

Laure

face to face with death

I saw myself. Sitting on one of the benches, crying.

It was the school to which my parents had sent me.

I saw another girl run by with a large rubber ball. But I had

267

to go to the bathroom again, the place where we, the girls, were allowed to be free.

I had wandered away from the others to the lavatory. The sound of Baudelaire was still in my ears. I entered. An odor, halfway between the smell of a candy factory and that of school disinfectant, was hanging inside one of the cubicles.

A vapor rose up from its seat. A vapor of tenderness given off by a hair.

The room I was in was so tiny I couldn't stand back up. I looked up. Above me, the roll of white toilet paper was covered with specks of black hairs . . .

It was a reflection of my face before the creation of the world.